D1534870

CELTIC REVIVALS

CELTIC REVIVALS
Essays in Modern Irish Literature
1880–1980

SEAMUS DEANE

faber and faber
LONDON · BOSTON

JEROME LIBRARY-BOWLING GREEN STATE UNIVERSITY

First published in 1985
by Faber and Faber Limited
3 Queen Square London WC1N 3AU

Set by Goodfellow & Egan Ltd, Cambridge
Printed in Great Britain by
Butler & Tanner Ltd, Frome, Somerset
All rights reserved

© Seamus Deane, 1985

British Library Cataloguing in Publication Data

Deane, Seamus
Celtic revivals.
1. English literature–Irish authors–History and criticism
2. Politics and literature–Ireland
I. Title
820.9'9415   PR8718

ISBN 0-571-13500-5

Library of Congress Cataloging in Publication Data

Deane, Seamus, 1940–
Celtic revivals.
1. English literature—Irish authors—History and criticism.
2. Politics and literature—Ireland. 3. Ireland in literature.
4. English literature—Celtic influences.   I. Title.
PR8718.D43   1985   820'.9'9415   85-5233
ISBN 0-571-13500-5

contents

CONTENTS

acknowledgements

Parts of the introduction appeared in *Two Decades of Irish Writing*, ed. D. Dunn (Cheadle, 1975); chapter 1, in modified form, and chapter 3 in *The Crane Bag Book of Irish Studies* (Dublin, 1982); chapter 2 in *Myth and Reality in Irish Literature*, ed. J. Ronsley (Ontario, 1977); parts of chapter 4 in *J. M. Synge: Centenary Papers*, ed. M. Harmon (Dublin, 1971) and in *Threshold* (Autumn 1978); chapter 5, in modified form, in *The Irish Press*; chapter 6 in *Encounter* (November 1972); chapter 7 in *James Joyce: New Perspectives*, ed. Colin McCabe (Brighton, 1982); parts of chapter 8 in *Sean O'Casey*, ed. T. Kilroy (Englewood Cliffs, NJ, 1975) and in *Threshold* (Spring 1973 and 1979); chapter 9 in *Irish University Review* (Spring 1984); parts of chapter 11 in the *London Review of Books* (25 June 1982); parts of chapters 12 and 14 in the *Sewanee Review* (1976).

introduction

Most of these essays appeared, in modified form, in various journals and collections over a number of years. Although they are all concerned, in one way or another, with issues raised in modern Irish literature, they are not offered as a comprehensive treatment. Their miscellaneous nature is not entirely countered by the presence within them of recurrent concerns. There are obvious omissions. George Moore, Patrick Kavanagh and Flann O'Brien are only briefly mentioned. A whole host of others, many of them contemporaries, do not appear. Their exclusion is not a silent judgement. But their inclusion would have meant a very different book, something closer to a history of modern Irish literature. That would be another day's work. Nevertheless, the authors I have chosen to write about are, clearly, among the most important to have appeared in Ireland over the past century. In them, the central strains and questions of the Irish experience have been absorbed and tested. What these are, and the quality of the writing which incorporates them, have been my chief interest.

The literature considered here derives from a culture which is neither wholly national nor colonial but a hybrid of both. For almost three hundred years, Ireland has experienced a series of serious social and political breakdowns. Constitutionally, the failures are legion. Among the most obvious are the Whig Revolution Settlement of 1688–90; the Irish Parliament of 1782–1800; the Act of Union, 1800–1922; Home Rule; and the Anglo-Irish Treaty of 1922, the effects of which still resonate in Northern Ireland. Along with that catalogue of political failure there is a long history of rebellions and of agrarian disturbance. The insurrectionary groups which plotted these – the United

Irishmen, the Fenians, the Irish Republican Brotherhood, the Citizens Army, the Irish Republican Army – represent the alternative, and more violent, tradition which culminated in the successes of the 1916–22 period – although these were also seriously flawed by failure. As a consequence of all this, the idea of society and the assumption of stability have never been securely lodged in Irish experience. History is an inescapable category, violence a recurrent phenomenon. The effect on literature could not but be profound.

Between the end of the Famine in 1848 and Sinn Fein's great electoral triumph in 1918, Ireland began the long process of its transformation from a British colony into a modern, independent state. The modern Irish literary movement was born during those years, although the precise date is inevitably uncertain. Perhaps it was the publication day of the last part of Standish O'Grady's *History of Ireland* (1878–80); perhaps the year 1893, when the Gaelic League was founded, when J. T. Grein's Independent Theatre in London produced George Moore's *Strike at Arlingford* and Yeats's *Land of Heart's Desire*; the same year which saw the publication of Douglas Hyde's *Love Songs of Connacht* and the delivery of Stopford Brooke's inaugural lecture to the Irish Literary Society in London on 'The Need and Use of Getting Irish Literature into the English Tongue'.

It could, of course, be argued that the foundations for this new hybrid literature had been laid a century before by Edmund Burke and there is no doubt that his contribution is in some need of reappraisal. I have tried to provide here the beginnings of one, although it must be said that it was the British Victorian rediscovery of Burke which gave his thought and influence a fresh impetus in the latter decades of nineteenth-century Ireland. It was in this period too that Ireland began to become more articulate about the central psychological aspect of the colonial problem – the contradiction of living politically as if it were one thing while culturally knowing itself to be another. Yet the United Kingdom of Great Britain and Ireland was a domineering political fact which, rather than blighting Irish self-consciousness, finally led to its emergence in a more radical and militant form than had ever previously existed. The Irish peasantry, who constituted the mass of the people, were politicized, both by economic pressure and by ideology. At approximately the same time, they were transmogrified both by literary men of genius and by propagandists. Riots, like those which marked the production in 1907 of

Synge's *The Playboy of the Western World*, showed both processes in a noisy collision which was itself an inevitable product of their silent collusion over the preceding decades.

The two Celtic Revivals, one beginning in the late eighteenth and one in the late nineteenth century (although there is a period of overlap between them), are part of the history of European Romanticism. In Ireland, these Revivals eventually took the form of a concentration on certain issues which had particular political resonance. For instance, language – always a crucial issue in a country which has had its own language destroyed by a combination of military and economic violence and another imposed by a coercive educational system. The linguistic virtuosity of Irish writers and the linguistic quaintness, to English ears, of the Irish mode of speech in English, are the product of a long political struggle – one still audible in the poetry of John Montague and of Seamus Heaney. Irish literature tends to dwell on the medium in which it is written because it is difficult not to be self-conscious about a language which has become simultaneously native and foreign.

Another issue was the land, or the landscape. Politically, the land question was dominant in late nineteenth-century Irish history. The Land League, formed by Michael Davitt to assert the rights of the tenantry against the landlords, and exploited with great skill by Parnell in his rise to power, was the most successful of all Irish insurrectionary organizations. In literature, this economic and political question was converted into a fascination with the regional landscape. Loyalty to that particular region, another characteristic of early Romanticism, when it was called 'local attachment', was both a literary and a political gesture in Ireland. The very naming of the land in both literature and politics – Cathleen ni Houlihan, Eireann, Eire, Saorstat Eireann, the Republic, the Six Counties, Ulster, Northern Ireland – is a symptom of that combination of political instability and regional loyalty which has defined modern Irish history.

This is particularly true when the fact of violence is taken into account. For all those names are associated with various forms of violence. The question is not the legitimacy either of the violence or of the name. It is a question of the impossibility of finding a name which is consonant with the notions of peace and stability. Further, the regional loyalty is subject to intensification in times of violence. Whether it is in the Yeatsian or Joycean versions of Ireland, or in the Northern poets' version of Ulster, it seems to be

13

true that the feeling for a region is at least in part governed by a species of political fidelity to it.

Language and landscape, so understood, can lead a protean existence in literature. In the early nineteenth century, Thomas Moore's poetry exploited the traditional *topos* of the ruin in a landscape to give it a specifically Irish political overtone and to breed out of this a specifically Irish form of nostalgia. The nostalgia was consistently directed towards a past so deeply buried that it was not recoverable except as sentiment. This fed into the Irish song tradition which, under the aegis of the Young Ireland movement, and in particular Thomas Davis and James Clarence Mangan, became a sentimental political tradition. The ballad has a noteworthy position in modern Irish politics because it popularized sentiments that otherwise might have remained safely preserved in literature. Although this was essentially a nineteenth-century phenomenon, it keeps a vestigial existence up to the present day. Its association with the Gaelic tradition is sustained by two factors. First, the melodies are very often based upon old Gaelic airs. Second, its iconography – harp, wolfhound, tower, old hag transformed into young queen, and so on – draws heavily on some traditional motifs of the Gaelic poetry translated in the nineteenth century by Sir Samuel Ferguson and others. The 'primitivism' of ancient Gaelic poetry was widely thought to be in itself a guarantee of authentic feeling with the corollary, felt since the 1760s, that English literature could well do with a new access of 'primitive' energy to restore to it a lost, pristine vigour. All these considerations help to explain why a poet like James Clarence Mangan has such importance in the Irish literary tradition, as Yeats and Joyce were keenly aware. They also help to reveal the latent Romantic sources of the literature of the Irish Revival, although the country's peculiar colonial position always ensured that the Irish wore their *Weltschmerz* with a difference.

Ultimately, Irish writers were obliged to find some way of dealing with history, a category which includes language, landscape, and the various ideologies of the recovered past which grew out of them. The essays in this volume are dominated by this theme. Although all the writers discussed are affected by politics, no one of them could be described with confidence as a political writer. At first sight this seems odd, given the self-consciously political conditions of twentieth-century Ireland. Part of the explanation is to be found, I believe, in the development of Irish nationalism. It is a moral passion more than it is a political ideology. It was and is so imbued with the sense of the past as a support for action in the present that it has never looked beyond that. This is particularly true after the end of the War of Independence in 1921. Once nationalism, although only partially triumphant, was faced with the future, it became little more than a species of accommodation to prevailing economic (predominantly British) forces. Its separation from socialism left it ideologically invertebrate.

This fact has had a bearing upon Irish literature. In the place of political ideology, we discover a whole series of ideologies of writing – those of Joyce, Beckett, Francis Stuart, Patrick Kavanagh and others – in which politics is regarded as a threat to artistic integrity: the heroics of the spirit which formerly were indulged for the sake of the Yeatsian 'Unity of Being' become a doctrinaire aesthetic of privacy, insulation, isolation and exile. Thus, in poetry, freedom is almost always realized as an interior freedom, with no political repercussions whatsoever.

The new puritanism of both parts of Ireland provided, with the theme of sexuality, an opportunity for the poet's adversary voice. It could be argued that puritanism was not a peculiar characteristic of the repressive aspects of the new states. It was itself part of the British Victorian colonial heritage. Yet somehow it began to be viewed as a defining characteristic of the new dispensation rather than as a colonial remainder from the old. The tradition of lyric poetry has made much of this theme. But, interestingly, when the same poets turned to longer, more 'epic' forms, in which the ambition was to apprehend the wholeness rather than the separate moments of a culture, they tended to produce lyric sequences rather than structurally satisfying narratives. Austin Clarke's *The Vengeance of Fionn*, Denis Devlin's *The Heavenly Foreigner*, Patrick Kavanagh's *The Great Hunger*, Thomas Kinsella's *Nightwalker* and John Montague's *The Rough Field* are among the best-known examples. A political sensibility has not yet arrived; but the desire to politicize the sensibility, or the fear of having it politicized, are the compensatory gestures.

Nevertheless, the demands made by a dramatically broken history on writers who are caught between identities, Irish and British, Irish and Anglo-Irish, Catholic and Protestant, are irresistible. The response of the Revival to history was heroic and astounding. Yeats, Synge, Joyce and O'Casey, in their different ways, were finally enabled by it. They produced work which was definitively Irish but which, at the same time, could not be

15

defined by that term. In that sense, they transcended without ignoring the insistent demands of their regional culture. Since then, and especially since Patrick Kavanagh deflected the Yeatsian influence by replacing the notion of the region, Ireland, with the notion of the parish, Monaghan, it has seemed that the pressures of history were becoming more amenable. But the transformations of the South, brought about in the sixties by the new economic policies of the Lemass governments, and the disintegration of the North, brought about unwittingly by the effects of Westminster educational policies and by the erosion of Unionist economic privilege in the aftermath of the Second World War, intensified the pressures once again.

We can look back now with some nostalgia at Patrick Kavanagh as the most characteristic writer in the relatively peaceful era of the forties and fifties. He is, in no derogatory sense, the Free State poet – the man who blended the traditional languages of regional loyalty and Catholicism with the adversary language of the artist in a body of work which, finally, expresses contentment at the spectacle of an ordinary but still miraculous world. That opportunity was seized, but the moment for it is now passed. History is, it seems, to blame – yet again. On the other hand, it also perhaps deserves some congratulation for having aggravated so many writers into action. At any rate, what follows is a series of reflections on the mutations of both Irish history and Irish writing and an acknowledgement that there is no escape from their mutual attraction.

1

ARNOLD, BURKE AND THE CELTS

The historian Arnaldo Momigliano began one of his lectures with these words:

> When I want to understand Italian history, I catch a train and go to Ravenna. There, between the tomb of Theodoric and that of Dante, in the reassuring neighbourhood of the best manuscript of Aristophanes and in the less reassuring one of the best portrait of the Empress Theodora, I can begin to feel what Italian history has really been. The presence of a foreign rule, the memory of an imperial and pagan past, and the overwhelming force of the Catholic tradition have been three determining features of Italian history for many centuries.[1]

The train an Irish historian would catch if he wanted to feel what Irish history was like would take him to the Boyne valley. There he would find the great passage graves of Knowth and Dowth, the hill of Tara where Patrick's Christianity had its bloodless victory over the political and religious centre of the pagan system and, of course, the site of the great battle of 1690 which inaugurated the triumph of the Protestant Ascendancy in Ireland and the last phase of the Catholic Gaelic civilization. Since the last century, considerable efforts have been made to construct from the pagan or early-Christian or early-Ascendancy past an image of excellence from which the present has sadly degenerated. The Ireland of Swift and Bishop Berkeley commemorated by Yeats, or the Ireland of Clonmacnoise evoked by Austin Clarke in *Pilgrimage* (1929), cannot easily be reconciled to one another. The trouble

[1] A. Momigliano, *Studies in Historiography* (London, 1966), p. 181.

17

about them both is that they disappeared so very long ago. Imaginative recovery of something so remote is rarely achieved without a powerful impetus from the contemporary moment. Even then, it is sure to contain strong tendentious elements. The Italians of the Risorgimento produced idyllic descriptions of 'Etruscan', pre-Roman Italy which tell us more of the state of nineteenth-century Italian politics than they do of the historical period they profess to restore. In modern times the Irish also have produced an idyllic version of Celtic Ireland which supposedly existed before Roman Catholic or British domination. Literature has consistently exercised a powerful influence in promoting this Celtic vision although, as with the Italians, it is hard to ignore the political polemic implicit in the nostalgia. The cultural response to the idea of the Irish as a Celtic people and the political response to the form the Irish problem took in the nineteenth century are closely intertwined. In the effort to understand this intimacy, it is inevitable that we should be confronted by the problematic term 'tradition'.

It is already a convention to say that Ireland has no continuity of cultural experience comparable to that of the nation states of France and England. It is equally conventional to make a virtue of discontinuity and to argue that fragmentation itself constitutes the only continuous experience we have. Conversely, it is claimed there is a continuous but subterranean Irish tradition, repressed by foreign domination and internal treachery. These are all popular versions of more specific and sophisticated attitudes which underlie much historical and literary discourse. The two most important connotations of the word, according to the *Oxford English Dictionary*, are 'continuity' and 'surrender or betrayal'. Law and Church history recognize this duality and so too do many local customs. For instance, when a man surrenders his farm to his newly-married son and moves with his wife into the 'west room' of the house, he is both surrendering his own position and maintaining continuity for the rest of the family. History and literature tend to invoke only the principle of continuity, hallowing the process and lending to it a retrospectively discovered pattern which often seems suspect. This is especially the case in Ireland where the principle of continuity can seldom be established. Even in relatively stable cultures such as the English, which pride themselves on the preservation of this principle, this is difficult. The Whig interpretation of eighteenth-century English history is a classic example of how it may be done. But in the nineteenth century, the prevailing English attitude towards Ireland gave assistance to the notion of continuity and coherence by emphasizing English internal harmony and respectability against the contrasting dissonances and disorderliness of Irish experience and of Irish people.[2] Bulwer-Lytton's wrath was aroused by the spectacle of early nineteenth-century Irish immigrants who roamed abroad at will, unrestricted by the Laws of Settlement to a single parish: 'they spread themselves over the whole country; and wherever they are settled at last, they establish a dread example of thriftless, riotous, unimprovable habits of pauperism.'[3] Although it can be pointed out that Bulwer-Lytton could not or would not see that these immigrants were the victims of conditions created by those laws for which they showed so little respect, the point remains – the idea of tradition as a mode of peaceful continuity always needs the help of contrast, polemic, ingenuity, to keep it fresh.

In Ireland, as in the Irish communities in England, hostility to the law was widespread. The Irish were therefore more inclined to think of tradition as continuity betrayed rather than continuity retained. The conviction that there had once been a traditional civilization which had been destroyed by foreign interference soon came to replace the memory of the actual past. Ireland had never been a political unit in the full sense of the term. But the desire to become that, awakened in the nineteenth century, created the belief that it had once been so, creating that powerful dialectic between a spurious Celtic Eden and an unattainable United Irish utopia which has dominated the national life for so long. If tradition, in the good sense, does not exist, it is necessary to invent it, even if it means building on the ruins of tradition understood in the bad sense as discontinuity and fracture. This the Irish did. The hypothesis of a tradition may be frail, the felt necessity for it is very real and powerful. Knowledge of the past affects it, but the demands of the present activate it. It is an enabling idea and of its nature involves a degree of idealization. The Ireland we live in is only a proximate version of the entity to which we refer in literary, historical or political discourse. The *idea* of Ireland permits us to observe and comment upon the *fact* of Ireland. The reverse is also true. As a result, there are no isolated facts; they all subserve the dominant idea.

[2] See P. Calvert, *On Revolution* ((Oxford, 1970), p. 166.
[3] E. Bulwer-Lytton, *England and the English*, 2 vols. (London, 1833), vol. 1, p. 217.

In the eighteenth century, the 'philosophic' historians, men such as Montesquieu and Voltaire, wrote the history of civilization as though it were a single entity. They dealt harshly or benevolently with the Middle Ages or with their own times in so far as these periods seemed to advance or retard the values embodied in the idea of civilization. Not until 1819 does the French word *civilisation* appear in the plural. By then, the idea of cultural particularity had replaced that of cultural homogeneity which underlay the great histories of the Enlightenment. Romanticism and historicism both looked kindly on regional cultures and the relation they bore to the genius of the peoples who had preserved them under foreign domination. Ireland was one of the beneficiaries of this change, although Germany and Italy are more startling examples of how remarkable a change it was. Now the new sense of continuity was derived from those sources which previously had been ignored – the ancient German tribes, the Etruscans and the Celts. Although the great eighteenth-century antiquarians – Bianchini, Spanheim and, above all, Wincklemann – had prepared the way, they contributed nothing to the essentially political idea, broadcast by the French Revolution, that there was a history beyond that of dynasties, political parties and master ideas. There was the history of peoples. For those cultures which had been suppressed by foreign influence this was an especially valuable concept. The people, their land and the language they spoke became the repositories of tradition. The dynasties and classes which had so carefully distinguished themselves from the people came to be seen as the representatives of that foreign and alien tradition (in the sense of betrayal and surrender) which had to be replaced. Antiquity and authenticity became interchangeable terms. Tradition took on its now customary romantic and picturesque guise and in the late eighteenth century the first Celtic revival, with its odd confusion of Teutonic, Celtic and 'old British' elements, achieved considerable success. From at least 1755–6, with the appearance of Paul Henri Mallet's *Introduction à l'Histoire du Danemarck* (translated by Percy in 1770 under the title *Northern Antiquities*) Norse, Scottish and Welsh landscapes were associated with wildness, loneliness and that farouche spontaneity which was regarded as the 'Origin of Poetry'. MacPherson's famous Ossian forgeries of 1760 popularized the Revival, while also damaging it in some ways. His spurious and bardic sentimentality presaged a greater wealth of bad literature in the Celtic vein than anyone then could have envisaged. In

England and Scotland, the Revival continued in the work of Hurd, Gray, Percy, Evan Evans and others. In Ireland, Charlotte Brooke's *Reliques of Irish Poetry* (1789) and Bunting's first volume of *The Ancient Music of Ireland* (1796) cleared the way for those two Celtic phenomena of the London drawing rooms, Lady Morgan and Thomas Moore, whose *Irish Melodies* appeared in 1808.

The Famine, the death of O'Connell and the extinction of the pathetic 1847 rebellion brought this first Irish Revival to a close. But before it was over, the second had already begun. The writings of Sir Samuel Ferguson, William Carleton and James Clarence Mangan, the essays of Davis and the popular balladry of *The Nation*, had laid the groundwork. With the appearance in 1878 of Standish O'Grady's *Bardic History of Ireland*, the improbable, second Celtic Revival got under way. It was only slightly less crepuscular than the first: an idea of tradition and continuity so vague as Ireland's needed all the dimness it could get. As the young Yeats was perhaps too keenly aware, twilight was the proper imaginative hour for those vanished Celtic civilizations. But there were two other features which made this second Revival different. First, continental scholarship, German, then French, had begun its mighty labours on behalf of the Celtic civilization and languages. A great tradition of philology was thus begun and Ireland was to make its own distinctive contribution here from O'Donovan to Bergin. Second, it was not only the sleeping Fianna that lay beneath the sod of that frighteningly silent land: the bodies of a million people who had starved to death also lay there. Scholarship and literature combined to revive the memory of a civilization in the generation that saw its destruction. The enforced intimacy between literature and politics was unique and tragic in Ireland. After the Famine, the romanticization of land and people lived alongside the need for a political settlement of the land problem. The vanished civilization of the Celts was, in this instance, no academic notion to a people who could still remember the disappearance of the Irish peasantry.

My interest here, however, is confined to one small aspect of the relationship between the two Celtic Revivals and, more narrowly again, with the word 'Celtic' as it came to be used in England rather than in Ireland, Germany or France. Briefly, my argument is this. Liberal Victorian intellectuals – Arnold, John Morley, Leslie and Fitzjames Stephen and Lord Acton – adopted a view of the Irish problem which owed a great deal to Edmund Burke.

21

Arnold is especially important because he went further than Burke would ever have dared – introducing the 'Celtic' idea as a differentiating fact between Ireland and England. He managed to give this word (previously kept within the preserve of literary historians and antiquarians) a political resonance which it has not yet entirely lost. Arnold thus established a link between Burke's view of Ireland – first formulated in the early (1760–5) and posthumously published *Tracts on the Popery Laws in Ireland* – and what we may call the Gladstonian view of Ireland, conceived in the run-up to the election of 1868. Using Burke as his guide in Irish affairs, Arnold managed to persuade himself and a considerable number of his readers that the dull and hard English could not, by virtue of their blighted middle-class nature, legislate effectively for the sanguine, vivacious and overly imaginative Irish. Although the argument for a separation between the two countries was implicit, Arnold refused it as vigorously as Burke would have done. Instead, he pleaded for a change in the English middle classes which would enable them to win over the Irish.

Since his death in 1797, one year before the great Irish rebellion that he feared, the greatest of all Irish political theorists, Burke, has been doomed to considerable neglect in his own country. Yeats condemned him in the eyes of Irish nationalists with loud, senatorial praise. Lecky saluted him but gave more prominence to others less deserving of it. Padraic Pearse mentioned him only to dismiss him. The notorious Quarterly Reviewer, John Wilson Croker, reduced Burke's thought to the mean proportions of his own intellect – a considerable feat. Not mythologized like Swift or sentimentalized like Goldsmith, Burke seems to have lost all standing as a commentator on Irish affairs. The English, however, took him to their hearts and used him as the most far-seeing and the most readable imperialist thinker. For Burke consistently thought of Ireland as a central part of the Empire and devoted considerable effort to keeping her within it. In 1773, he wrote a letter to Sir Charles Bingham, defending his opposition to a proposed tax on the property of Irish absentee landlords. His boss and patron, Lord Rockingham, was one of the most important of this parasitic class. Moreover, in his younger days Burke had advocated the imposition of such a tax. In these unfavourable circumstances, it is interesting to hear his defence:

Is not such an Irish tax as is now proposed a virtual

ARNOLD, BURKE AND THE CELTS

declaration that England is a foreign country, and a renunci-
ation on our part of the principle of common naturalisation
which runs through this whole empire?

Do you, or does any Irish gentleman, think it a mean
privilege that, the moment he sets foot upon this ground, he
is, to all intents and purposes, an Englishman?[4]

This is, from the nationalist or republican point of view, an
heretical sentiment. But it is a view of Ireland as part of the
Empire which is closer to the Commonwealth idea than to
anything we might find in Kipling. The same principle would
have applied, in Burke's opinion, to an inhabitant of the Thirteen
Colonies of America. And the misguided policies which were to
lead to the loss of the Colonies could lead to the loss of Ireland.
British support for the Protestant Ascendency was, in his view,
the crux of the problem. He was among the first to give currency
to the term, which appeared in 1792 in Irish political writing. In
the same year Burke defines it:

> This protestant ascendency means nothing like an influence
> obtained by virtue, by love, or even by artifice and seduc-
> tion . . . It is neither more nor less than the resolution of
> one set of people in Ireland to consider themselves as the
> sole citizens in the commonwealth; and to keep a dominion
> over the rest by reducing them to absolute slavery under a
> military power; and thus fortified in their power, to divide
> the publick estate, which is the result of general contribution,
> as a military booty solely amongst themselves.[5]

These opinions are repeated by Burke in various letters to his
son Richard, who was Agent for the Catholic Committee in
Dublin. It is an 'Ascendency of Hucksters', a 'Jobb-Ascendency', a
'junto of Robbers'. In 1867 Gladstone, during a famous speech at
Wigan, was to refer to the Ascendency as that 'tall tree of noxious
growth, lifting its head to heaven and poisoning the atmosphere
of the land so far as its shadow can extend'.[6] From the beginning,
Burke asserted that the Catholics of Ireland must be fully admitted
to political and civic life if the country was ever to be stable and
prosperous. Equally, the Ascendency must be uprooted and replaced

---

[4] *The Works of the Right Honourable Edmund Burke*, 8 vols. (London, 1877), vol. 5,
p. 440.
[5] Ibid., vol. 6, p. 65.
[6] John Morley, *Life of Gladstone*, 2 vols. (London, 1903), vol. 2, p. 252.

by a 'true aristocracy'. The American and the French revolutions made his demands more urgent, for Ireland had immense strategic importance for the British Empire. Its instability was, he claimed, the product of British policy. Ireland, a 'much Slandered, and Injured Country',[7] was not, as official propaganda would have it, discontented with good government. Instead, he declared:

> there is an interior history of Ireland – the genuine voice of its records and monuments – which speaks a very different language from those histories from Temple and Clarendon. These . . . show . . . that these rebellions were not produced by toleration but by persecution; that they arose not from just and mild government, but from the most unparalleled oppression.[8]

The admission of British guilt and responsibility, the need to extirpate the Protestant Ascendency, the retention of Ireland within the Empire, the relief of the Catholics – these are the main planks of British liberalism in the nineteenth century. They all came from Burke's writings. Arnold acknowledged the debt time and again and, in 1881, went so far as to produce an anthology, *Edmund Burke on Irish Affairs*, in the preface to which he wrote:

> Our neglected classic is by birth an Irishman; he knows Ireland and its history thoroughly . . . He is the greatest of our political thinkers and writers. But his political thinking and writing has more value on some subjects than on others: the value is at its highest when the subject is Ireland. The writings . . . show at work all the causes which have brought Ireland to its present state. The tyranny of the grantees of confiscation; of the English garrison; Protestant Ascendency; the reliance of the English Government upon this ascendency and its instruments as their means of government; the yielding to menaces of danger and insurrection what was never yielded to considerations of equity and reason; the recurrences to the old perversity of mismanagement as soon as ever the danger was passed – all these are shown in this volume; the evils, and Burke's constant sense of their gravity, his constant struggle to cure them.[9]

[7] *The Correspondence of Edmund Burke*, Gen. Ed. Thomas Copeland, 10 vols. (Cambridge and Chicago, 1958–78), vol. 1, p. 202.
[8] *Works*, vol. 6, p. 65.
[9] Matthew Arnold, *Edmund Burke on Irish Affairs* (London, 1881), p. vii.

Arnold, learning from Burke, recognizes that good government could stifle the Irish demand for self-government. But this version of killing Home Rule by kindness was an old Burkean policy adopted more than a century too late. Neither Gladstone nor Morley had the imagination to realize that the failure of Liberal policies made the idea of a separate Irish nationality more appealing to those who sought for an explanation of that failure. If the policy was, from the British point of view, right and reasonable, then its failure must have its roots in Irish difference. Arnold helped this notion on its way by his sponsorship of the Celtic element in literature and by his sympathy for a nation which found intolerable the rule of the philistine English middle classes.

Even now it is difficult to overestimate the importance of Arnold's Oxford Lectures, *The Study of Celtic Literature*. Published in 1867, the year of the Fenian Rising and of Gladstone's speech at Wigan (not to mention *Das Kapital*), they depict the nineteenth-century idea of the Celt with a clarity outstripping even Renan, whose *Poetry of the Celtic Races* was not translated into English until 1893. Of course, every virtue of the Celt was matched by a vice of the British bourgeois; everything the philistine middle classes of England needed, the Celt could supply. (The reverse was also true.) The dreamy, imaginative Celt, unblessed by the Greek sense of form, at home in wild landscapes far from the metropolitan centres of modern social and political life, could cure anxious Europe of the woes inherent in Progress. The Scholar Gypsy of Europe, the Celt is already encroaching upon the territory of Yeats and Synge – where folk-tales are preferred to the 'English diet of parliamentary speeches and the gutter press', where speech is highly flavoured, where peasants, be they Christy Mahons or figures from a Jack Yeats painting, have the vigour and vitality the anaemic city dweller has lost. But the main point about this vitality is its racial basis. The genius of the Celtic race produces imaginative intensity, a domestication of poetry into the fabric of daily life. Standish O'Grady, Pearse and Daniel Corkery come to mind as readily as Yeats and Synge. The mutation from the Celtic to the Gaelic Revival is quick, subtle and, in the end, sectarian.

The sectarian element was bound to appear. Given that the Protestant Ascendency was so 'noxious' and the Catholic majority so repressed, any proposed solution was likely to attribute to the Catholics a new prominence, political or cultural. Arnold contributed to this, although he had to use Burke to do it. In 1878 he

25

published his essay 'Irish Catholicism and British Liberalism' in John Morley's *Fortnightly Review*. Indeed over the next three years he published so much on Irish questions that his next volume was called *Irish Essays* (1882). Much of it was taken up, like the central article, with the Irish university question. Unsurprisingly, therefore, Arnold is profoundly attentive to the issue of Catholicism in relation to Dissent, the enemy of Irish claims for a Catholic university. The main proposition is that: 'The opinion and sentiment of our middle class controls the policy of our statesmen towards Ireland.'[10]

Since the middle class is benighted, so is the policy. The result is shameful to England. But the source of that shame for Arnold is the inextinguishable bigotry of the Protestant middle classes towards any concession to Catholic Ireland. The religious question in both islands becomes bound up with the racial difference: 'Nothing is more honourable to French civilisation than its success in attracting strongly to France – France, Catholic and Celtic – the German and Protestant Alsace. What a contrast to the humiliating failure of British civilisation to attach to Germanic and Protestant Great Britain the Celtic and Catholic Ireland.'[11] Racial and religious distinctions are used by Arnold to explain the kind of racial and religious discrimination practised by the British in Ireland. His plea is the Burkean one for 'healing measures', for the abolition of this kind of injustice. Yet the ground of his argument concedes the principle that in Ireland there is a collision between two racial types and two religions. Celt and Teuton, Catholic and Protestant, confront one another. Arnold's attack on the hard and dull English civilization is extended to include the Protestants of Ulster whom he sees as representatives of the English middle classes, the Murdstones of the nineteenth century:

> But the genuine, unmitigated Murdstone is the common middle-class Englishman, who has come forth from Salem House and Mr. Creakle. He is seen in full force, of course, in the Protestant north; but throughout Ireland he is a prominent figure of the English garrison. Him the Irish see, see him only too much and too often . . .
>
> The thing has no power of attraction. The Irish quickwittedness, keen feeling for social life and manners, demand

---

[10] *The Complete Prose Works of Matthew Arnold*, ed. R. H. Super, 11 vols. (Ann Arbor, 1968–76), vol. 9, p. 322.
[11] Ibid., vol. 9, p. 322.

something which this hard and imperfect civilisation cannot give them. Its social form seems to them unpleasant, its energy and industry to lead to no happiness, its religion to be false and repulsive.[12]

So the romanticizing of the Celt becomes, in effect, the romanticizing of the Irish Catholic. Burke's attack on the Protestant Ascendency is incorporated into Arnold's attack on the English middle classes and the Protestant garrison in Ireland. Race, politics and literature visibly enter into a combination which the Irish Revival took as part of its cultural base.

It is possible, therefore, to trace a line of filiation from Burke's early Tracts to Arnold's essays of 1878–81. Arnold updated Burke's thought to take account of the conditions which were already bringing about the second Celtic Revival. But in doing so, he gave fresh emphasis to the sectarian features which were part of the Irish political situation by providing them with a cultural myth. Burke and Arnold seem to be unlikely grandparents to the Irish Literary Revival. But the facts of the case seem to warrant this conclusion. As a result, our idea of the Celtic tradition, in so far as it affects our reading of Yeats, Synge and others, is modified. The ideas of continuity and of betrayal persist, but they have become associated with the experience of sectarian division in such a way that continuity has become the preserve of the Catholic Celts and betrayal the role of the Protestant garrison. For this we have to thank one of the greatest of English literary critics writing under the influence of the greatest of Irish political thinkers.

[12] Ibid., vol. 9, pp. 277–8.

27

2
the literary myths
of the revival

Perhaps the most seductive of all Yeats's historical fictions is his gift of dignity and coherence to the Irish Protestant Ascendency tradition. This was, in itself, a considerable achievement on behalf of a group which Standish O'Grady described in 1901 as 'rotting from the land in the most dismal farce-tragedy of all time, without one brave deed, without one brave word'.[1] We tend perhaps to forget just how much retrospective glamour the Ascendency has gained from the Yeatsian version of its achievement in literature. The literary tradition has absorbed this fiction as a vital and even unquestionable imaginative truth. As a consequence, we fail to see that the heroic impulse which rather ambiguously transforms the physical-force tradition in politics (as in 'Easter 1916' or in 'The Statues') also produces the intellectual chauvinism of that Yeatsian recitation of the great eighteenth-century names – Berkeley, Burke, Swift, Goldsmith and Sheridan.

Briefly, Yeats claims that the eighteenth-century Irish writers have in common a specifically anti-modernist outlook. Berkeley's refutation of Locke, Swift's attacks on the Royal Society and on the mercantile system, Goldsmith's lament for the old way of life destroyed by 'luxury' and the agrarian revolution and, above all, Burke's great tirade against the French Revolution, were all, in his view, attempts to stem the 'filthy modern tide' for which empiricism, science and parliamentary democracy were responsible. It had been a standard charge since the first generation of Romantic writers, that Locke and/or Newton were to blame for the afflictions of modernism. This was as much a stock response for literary men as was the attribution of Europe's political

[1] Standish O'Grady, *Selected Essays and Passages* (Dublin, 1918), p. 180.

28

problems to Voltaire and Rousseau by political commentators. 'C'est la faute à Voltaire, c'est la faute à Rousseau' was a refrain adaptable to almost any persuasion. Yeats's selectivity is revealed in his omission from the Anglo-Irish pantheon of John Wilson Croker – the outstanding Government spokesman against the revolution, France and the new 'Jacobinical' world.[2] Croker's hostility to the new literature (especially towards Shelley) probably disqualified him in Yeats's eyes. But this one example reveals what an oddly construed Anglo-Irish tradition we are offered. It is more comprehensible as a version of the Romantic polemic against the Enlightenment than as an account of Irish intellectual history in the eighteenth century.

Yeats, however, was unique in attributing the shared antimodernism of his eighteenth-century heroes to their Irishness. The Irishness is, for him, partly genetic, partly environmental:

> Born in such a community, Berkeley with his belief in perception, that abstract ideas are mere words, Swift with his love of perfect nature, of the Houyhnhnms, his disbelief in Newton's system, and every sort of machine, Goldsmith and his delight in the particulars of common life that shocked his contemporaries, Burke with his conviction that all States not grown slowly like a forest tree are tyrannies, found in England the opposite that stung their own thought into expression and made it lucid.[3]

This particular version of eighteenth-century literary and intellectual history is manifestly absurd. In that short paragraph, Yeats misreads Berkeley and Swift, makes Goldsmith appear far more eccentric and controversial than he actually was, attributes to England a role in Burke's thought which really belongs to France – and yet he manages to escape derision. This is because he provides himself with the exit much favoured by poets since the Romantic revival, especially by those irresistibly drawn to the mythologizing of history. Very simply, we are told not to take such myths *as* history: they are myths *of* history. In *A Vision*, speaking of his 'circuits of sun and moon', Yeats asks that we

---

[2] Myron F. Brightfield, *John Wilson Croker* (London, 1940). See also Croker's *Essays on the Early Period of the French Revolution* (London, 1857), and L. J. Jennings (ed.), *The Correspondence and Diaries of the late Right Honourable John Wilson Croker*, 3 vols. (London, 1884).

[3] *Essays and Introductions* (London, 1961), p. 25.

learn to regard them as 'stylistic arrangements of experience'.[4] On that level, the hermeneutic value for Yeats of his circuits and of his version of the Protestant Ascendency is undeniable. But it should be very clearly recognized that, in relation to history, these things are metaphors, lending to widely dispersed materials a provisional coherence.

This part of Yeats's writings does not then, in any serious sense, constitute a reading of history, even though the first to be so fooled was Yeats himself. When he told the Irish Senate that the Anglo-Irish were 'no petty people', he was evidently not thinking of the John Wilson Croker type. He was translating into a proud assertion an almost comically absurd historical fiction. Unfortunately, the fiction has been believed. Yet its absurdity does not render it futile. It may not be a very persuasive reading of history but it is fascinating in the manner of Romantic aesthetics. In Coleridge, in Blake, in Carlyle, in William Morris, history is essentially engaged with the fortunes of the Imagination and, therefore, almost indistinguishable from aesthetics. The various histories we have inherited from the *Prophetic Books* or the *Philosophical Lectures* or, indeed, from the essays of T. S. Eliot as well as Yeats, are at root theories of the imagination expressed in historical terms. More simply, they are aesthetic theories rendered as stories of which Yeats's Ascendency is one of the more notable examples. This particular story has won a measure of acceptance equal to Arnold's story of the Celt. One flatters the Protestant, the other the Catholic and both depend upon the notion that there is an identifiable and commonly shared racial component – Irishness – which expresses itself in hostility towards the modern world.

Yeats's account of the Anglo-Irish tradition blurs an important distinction between the terms 'aristocracy' and 'Ascendency'. Had he known a little more about the eighteenth century, he would have recognized that the Protestant Ascendency was, then and since, a predominantly bourgeois social formation. The Anglo-Irish were held in contempt by the Irish-speaking masses as people of no blood, without lineage and with nothing to recommend them other than the success of their Hanoverian cause over that of the Jacobites. This is evident in the poetry of men such as Daithi O'Bruadair and Aodagain O Rathaille who lived through the first and most painful phase of the Whig Settlement in Ireland. But much later in the century Burke also

[4] *A Vision* (New York, 1961), p. 25.

went to great lengths to distinguish what Yeats ignored. Ireland, Burke claimed in his *Letter to a Peer of Ireland on the Penal Laws against Irish Catholics* (1782), had an oligarchy without an aristocracy. The Protestants in Ireland are, he claims, plebeian. And:

A plebeian obligarchy is a monster: and no people, not absolutely domestic or predial slaves, will long endure it. The Protestants of Ireland are not *alone* sufficiently the people to form a democracy; and they are *too numerous* to answer the ends and purposes of *an aristocracy*. Admiration, the first source of obedience, can only be the claim or the imposture of the few. I hold it to be absolutely impossible for two millions of plebeians, composing certainly a very clear and decided majority in that class, to become so far in love with six or seven hundred thousand of their fellow citizens, (to all outward appearance plebeians like themselves, and many of them tradesmen, servants, and otherwise inferior to some of them,) as to see with satisfaction, or even with patience, an exclusive power vested in them, by which *constitutionally* they become the absolute masters; and, by the manners derived from their circumstances, must be capable of exercising upon them, daily and hourly, an insulting and vexatious superiority.[5]

Nevertheless, it is this group which Yeats refers to as an aristocracy and it is to Burke and others he looks for an intellectual justification for this description. It may be argued that he had more grounds for his view of the Ascendency by the twentieth century. Yet Yeats's defence of this 'aristocracy' is developed in the twenties and thirties, after its defeat and, as O'Grady had pointed out, its rather ignoble demise. Since the death of Parnell, modern Irish writing has been fond of providing us with the image of the hero as artist surrounded by the philistine or clerically-dominated mob. This is a transposition of the political theory of aristocracy into the realm of literature and it has had, since Yeats, a very long run in Irish writing. The Big House surrounded by the unruly tenantry, Culture beseiged by barbarity, a refined aristocracy beset by a vulgar middle class — all of these are recurrent images in twentieth-century Irish fiction which draws heavily on Yeats's poetry for them. Since Elizabeth

[5] 'A Letter to Sir Hercules Langrishe', in *The Works of the Right Honourable Edmund Burke*, 8 vols. (London, 1877), vol. 3, pp. 304–5.

Bowen's *The Last September* (1929) to more recent novels such as Aidan Higgins's *Langrishe, Go Down* (1966), Thomas Kilroy's *The Big Chapel* (1971), John Banville's *Birchwood* (1973) and Jennifer Johnston's *How Many Miles to Babylon?* (1976), the image and its accompanying themes have been repeated in a variety of forms. The power of this tradition is reflected in the work of English writers who set their novels in Ireland. Two remarkable examples here would be Henry Green's *Loving* (1933) and J. G. Farrell's *Troubles* (1972). The irony is that the Yeatsian view of the Irish Catholic middle classes is so similar to the Irish Catholic view of the eighteenth-century Protestant Ascendency. Yeats was so eager to discover an aristocratic element within the Protestant tradition and to associate this with the spiritual aristocracy of the Catholic and Celtic peasantry – defining aristocracy in each case as a mark of Irishness and Irishness as a mark of anti-modernism – that he distorted history in the service of myth. This myth of history, the bequest of some of his greatest poems and of his highly eccentric essays, is a subtle and adaptable figure of thought, as a careful reading of 'Nineteen Hundred and Nineteen' or of 'Meditations in Time of Civil War' reveals. Yeats's poetry constitutes the real link between the Irish nineteenth-century novel and its twentieth-century counterpart. The experimental tradition which includes Joyce, Flann O'Brien and Beckett is clearly distinct in many ways from this Yeatsian inheritance. But in John Banville's fiction we can see how the traditional imageries of the Irish novel can be wedded to the experimental tradition.[6] The survival of the Big House novel, with all its implicit assumptions, is a tribute to the influence of Yeats and a criticism of the poverty of the Irish novelistic tradition. In fact the Big House is now more concerned with tourism and tax concessions, with the preservation of the artifacts of 'culture', than with power or value. In fiction, it is an anachronism. The over-extension of the Yeatsian myth of history into fiction helps us to see what an odd and protean thing it is and how far removed it has become from contemporary reality. In seeing this, we might finally decide to seek our intellectual allegiances and our understanding of our history elsewhere.

Yeats is not the only example of a writer making history palatable by imaging it as a version of the personality. Synge and Austin Clarke also come to mind. Synge's West, and Clarke's medieval, monastic, Ireland are not historically accurate so much

[6] See especially *Birchwood* (London, 1973).

as imaginatively useful in yielding a sense of the artist's enterprise in a world which, without these metaphorical suasions, would remain implacably hostile. The sweet-tongued vagrants of Synge's world are memorable Irish versions of the Baudelairean *poète maudit* – healthier and folksier no doubt, but estranged in a similar way. Equally, we can see that the randy clerics of Clarke's beehive-hut civilization signal a reconciliation between religion and sexuality, Clarke's most obsessive concerns, which twentieth-century Ireland had, in his view, failed to achieve. These images do not operate as ideals, nor do I insinuate that they are to be deplored because they distort social and historical fact. But it is surely remarkable that the treatment of history as metaphor by these writers enables them to mount an attack upon the small and squalid soul of the modern bourgeois by glamorizing either the Ascendency, the peasantry or the medieval clergy. In other words, the desire to see Ireland as 'a country of the imagination' led to a conclusion that was identical with its premise. And that was the old Romantic premise that the world could be seen, falsely, in a bleak Newtonian light or, truly, in a pre-Newtonian aura. The destruction of aura, the argument runs, has been brought about by the development of modern science and its evolution into philosophies such as dialectical materialism which Yeats, in an astonishing and garbled paragraph, claims 'works all the mischief Berkeley foretold'.[7] This Romantic-aesthetic heritage, with which we still struggle, clearly harbours the desire to obliterate or reduce the problems of class, economic development, bureaucratic organization and the like, concentrating instead upon the essences of self, community, nationhood, racial theory, Zeitgeist. Yeats had demonstrated throughout his long career that the conversion of politics and history into aesthetics carries with it the obligation to despise the modern world and to seek rescue from it. His sympathy for fascism is consistent with his other opinions, although he is, in the end, loyal to his early conception of an aristocratic society dominated by 'some company of governing men'.[8]

O'Connell and Parnell had mobilized Irish political energies into national movements. Yeats mobilized Irish cultural energies in a

---

[7] *Essays and Introductions*, p. 401.
[8] 'Michael Robartes: Two Occult Manuscripts', ed. W. K. Hood, in *Yeats and the Occult*, ed. George Mills Harper (London, 1976), p. 219.

similar way, enhancing the distinction between Irish and English culture and providing the leadership to make this institutionally effective. The élite company which he envisaged would govern a community rather than represent a public. Therefore his aristocratic views needed reinforcement from the belief in the possibility of such a community in Ireland and, of course, the peasantry were there to supply it. The astonishingly swift decline of the Irish language in the years after the Famine and the increasing prominence of shopkeepers, publicans and innkeepers in the Land League and Home Rule movements were clear indications that Yeats's view of the peasantry was outmoded by the 1870s.[9] Their language was dying, their social formation had been drastically altered, their nationalism was fed on the Young Ireland diet of Thomas Moore, James Clarence Mangan and the pervasive emblems of harp, wolfhound and round tower. In addition, the literature of the Gaelic civilization was making its way into Yeats's and indeed into the national consciousness in the form of translation, most of it inept. Yeats came at the end of a long line of amateur antiquarians, most of whom regarded the translation of Gaelic poetry into English as a contribution to the enlightenment of an English (or English-speaking) audience on the nature of the Irish Question. Charlotte Brooke's *Reliques of Irish Poetry* (1789), James Hardiman's *Irish Minstrelsy* (1831), Samuel Ferguson's *Lays of the Western Gael* (1867) and even Douglas Hyde's *Love Songs of Connacht* (1894) helped to consign Gaelic poetry to the bookshelf, transforming it into one of the curiosities of English literature.[10] They were little more than obituary notices in which the poetry of a ruined civilization was accorded a sympathy which had been notably absent when it was alive. The same can be said for Standish O'Grady's *History of Ireland: Heroic Period* (1878–80), the work which so coloured Yeats's mind that he believed all modern Irish writing owed part of its distinctive tincture to that source. Much of what Yeats believed about the Irish peasantry, its past and its native literature, was formed by the literature produced by the more cultivated sections of the nineteenth-century landlord class. The paradox does not seem to have troubled him unduly.

[9] R. Theodore Hoppen, 'Politics in Mid-Nineteenth-Century Ireland', in *Studies in Irish History*, eds. A. Cosgrove and D. McCartney (Dublin, 1979), p. 222.
[10] See Cathal G.O Hainle, 'Towards the Revival: Some Translations of Irish Poetry 1789–1897', in *Literature and the Changing Ireland*, ed. Peter Connolly (London, 1982), pp. 37–58.

Nevertheless, it might trouble his readers. The flimsy basis upon which Yeats built his conception of the Ascendency and of the peasantry ultimately affects his poetry and drama. All his ideas and images of tradition and communion are predicated on the idea of spiritual loneliness. Even when he sees himself as being in some sense the inheritor of Young Ireland, he envisages the crisis of his own times as one in which the individual is liberated from conformity, in which the lonely aristocratic spirit can survive only because it lives within an organic community:

> Ireland is passing through a crisis in the life of the mind greater than any she has known since the rise of the Young Ireland party, and based upon a principle which sets many in opposition to the habits of thought and feeling come down from that party, for the seasons change, and need and occupation with them. Many are beginning to recognise the right of the individual mind to see the world in its own way, to cherish the thoughts which separate men from one another, and that are the creators of distinguished life, instead of those thoughts that had made one man like another if they could, and have but succeeded in setting hysteria and insincerity in place of confidence and self-possession.[11]

His heroes – Parnell, John O'Leary, Synge and Hugh Lane – were all men whose aloofness and loneliness were a product of their immersion in some aspect of the national consciousness. They were embodiments of individuality, enemies of individualism; aristocrats, not democrats. Three of them, Parnell, Synge and Lane were at the centre of three great controversies – the O'Shea divorce case, the *Playboy* riots and the Lane bequest. In each instance, Yeats viewed them as heroic and aristocratic figures attacked by the plebeian mob. Events like these, and the carnage of the First World War and of the revolutionary period in Ireland 1916–22, deprived him of that sanguine spirit which had informed his early writings, especially those essays in which he declared his faith in the sense of a beginning which the revived Ireland of his youth provided. Thereafter, from about 1913 onwards, he is, like so many of his Edwardian contemporaries, preoccupied with gloomy predictions and fears of the end of civilization.[12] Perhaps

---

[11] *Plays and Controversies* (London, 1923), p. 198.
[12] Samuel Hynes, *Edwardian Occasions* (London, 1972), pp. 1–12.

Yeats had a more pronounced sense of disappointment than Wells, Conrad, Forster, Shaw or Galsworthy precisely because he had so recently entertained such high hopes for his country. The frailty of his conception of the Irish tradition and community made its collapse inevitable. Yet, in Auden's famous phrase, Ireland did 'hurt' him 'into poetry', not by being mad but simply by being other than he had imagined. After the death of Swinburne in 1809 Yeats, with the Bullen edition of his *Collected Works* published in 1908, was the senior poet of the English-speaking world. At the age of 43 he already appeared to be 'one of that generation of massive late Victorians who were to dominate our literature'.[13] At the age of 50 he had become one of the great modernists. It is in 1915 that his poem 'Scholars' opens Pound's *Catholic Anthology*, followed by 'The Love Song of J. Alfred Prufrock'; it is in 1922, the *annus mirabilis* of the modern movement, that his *Later Poems* appeared. With an almost inexhaustible resourcefulness, he maintains the privileged role for Ireland in his thought, contrasting the self-sacrifice of Easter Week with the mindless slaughter of the trenches, using the bitterness of the Civil War as the ground for a great threnody on the disappearance of the civilization of the Big House, the Anglo-Irish spirit and, by extension, of Western Christendom itself. But in the thirties Yeats's fidelity to his governing ideas of aristocracy and community was to betray him into absurdity through his association with the fascist Blueshirt movement. Romantic Ireland was dead and gone but Yeats seemed to be less ready to believe this in 1933 than he had been in 1913.

Still, the power and influence of Yeats's versions of Irish community and tradition remain, no matter how insubstantial their basis in our contemporary understanding of history. They retain their life because they are rooted in his poems and plays although our inclination is to think of the poems and plays as rooted in them. The principle of continuity which he established in literature, stretching from Swift to the Revival, and that which Pearse established in politics, stretching from Wolfe Tone to the men of 1916, are both exemplary instances of the manner in which tradition becomes an instrument for the present. Without such a tradition, or the idea of it, history appears gapped, discontinuous, unmanageably complex. The period between 1880 and 1940 made a fetish of continuity in part because the generation

---

[13] Cyril Connolly, *Previous Convictions* (London, 1967), p. 252.

before had witnessed the final rupturing of the Gaelic civilization. The glamorization of the Celt and of the Ascendency was an attempt to reconcile on the level of myth what could not be reconciled at the level of politics. It was, in effect, an Arnoldian 'healing measure' which failed. It offered the Irish the opportunity to be unique but refused them the right to be independent on the grounds that independence would lead to a loss of their uniqueness. Yeats's unhappiness with the new Irish state stemmed from this. In refusing to accept an Ascendency-led cultural nationalism of Yeats's sort, with its aristocratic claims, post-Treaty Ireland effectively put an end to the Revival, a fact for which many of its writers and artists have not forgiven it. The great myths had gone. The best of the poets after Yeats quickly learned that the local and the ordinary defined the horizon for literature as it did for politics. With the emergence of Patrick Kavanagh, the new state found its characteristic, if adversary, voice. The day of the literary peasant and of the aristocratic hero was over. It was not Eman Macha but Armagh which the dawn light revealed to the poet from County Monaghan. Moreover, there was a political border between them.

3

yeats and the idea of revolution

Yeats began his career by inventing an Ireland amenable to his imagination. He ended by finding an Ireland recalcitrant to it. His readiness to include the actuality of modern Ireland gave substance to his intricate system of symbols. But in the end the actuality overbore the symbolism, and left his poetry hysterical when he let his feeling run free of the demands of form, and diagrammatic when he imposed wilfully formal restraints upon his feeling. 'The Statues' best exemplifies this dilemma. In no other poem did he more eagerly seek an accommodation between his occultist system and his vision of Ireland. The demands of that poem are great and its ambition, especially for 'We Irish', almost measureless, but its rhetoric is strained, spoiled by a kind of oratory which arises from convictions that lie outside the poem's range of reference. I want to discover the sources of such strain. We can find them, I would suggest, by tracing back his ideas of Ireland and of revolution. Where they converge, Yeats's energy expands; but when the convergence is willed or forced against the grain of actual circumstance or of authentic feeeling, then we hear the strident oratory of a man for whom the notion of authority has become effete and has been replaced by an authoritarian technique.

Yeats was, from the beginning, one of that long line of European Romantic writers who combined a revolutionary aesthetic with traditionalist politics. The homeland of that combination was Germany and the authors who most clearly enunciated its implications were Nietzsche and, later, Thomas Mann. We know, of course, that Nietzsche was important to Yeats. In him, and in Blake and Shelley, Yeats found his dominant theme – that of regeneration. Like these three writers, he spoke of it in a now highly familiar idiom – the idiom of release from the manacles forged by the conspiracy between British empirical philosophy and urban industrial capitalism:

> Locke sank into a swoon;
> The Garden died;
> God took the spinning-jenny
> Out of his side.

('Fragments')

For Yeats the miracles of technology had already lost their aura inside the dreary frames of empiricism.

To support his theme of regeneration, Yeats ransacked the fields of history and magic, and he used his highly eclectic knowledge in these fields to construct a history of philosophy which was also a philosophy of history. Just as Coleridge had emphasized a peculiar concept of Englishness, so too did Yeats – except that Yeats used the older, Romantic conception of an Englishness that had existed before Locke, Hobbes and Bacon in order to give edge to his own concept of an Irishness that had always been opposed to the empirical tradition.

Berkeley, Swift and Burke composed for Yeats an Irish Ascendency tradition of 'idealism' which he then associated with the folk tradition in Ireland, claiming that each refuted science by its apprehension (although differently articulated in each case) of mystery and of death. The peasant and the aristocrat, kindred in spirit but not in class, united in the great Romantic battle against the industrial and utilitarian ethic. The energizing principle for Yeats in this late confection of Romantic notions was clearly that Ireland was the only place in Europe in which the aristocratic and peasant element had a fair chance of winning.

Yeats added a certain melodrama to the situation by always investing it with a sense of crisis. Ireland was not only a special country. It was one where the great battle must be won precisely because it had been so totally lost elsewhere. Ireland was, for him, a revolutionary country for the very reason that it was, in the oldest sense, a traditional one. History, viewed as crisis, became politics – the politics of his own day and of his own country. But Irish politics enacted for him the great cultural battle of the era between Romantics and Utilitarians. He enforced this reading time and again. It is therefore very difficult, once we acknowledge this fact, to misread the various 'political' poems he wrote, even though some commentators have made it look easy.

Yeats had no idea or attitude which was not part of the late-Romantic stock-in-trade. He was different in the fervour of his convictions, not in their form. His sense of crisis allowed him to see the archetypal patterns of history emerging out of the complexities of contemporary politics; it exposed for him the intimacies which bonded magic and art together; it gave Ireland's technological and economic backwardness the benefit of a spiritual glamour which had faded from the rest of Europe, as if it were a vestigial Greece in a sternly Roman world.

So we find in Yeats (as in Joyce) a version of racial history which is married to (or at least gives support to) a theology of art. Of course we have in Joyce's work that which is importantly absent from Yeats's – middle-class Catholic Ireland. Joyce is one of the greatest and one of the last writers in the bourgeois tradition. Yeats, on the other hand, despite his own middle-class origins, wished to exile himself and his ideal version of society as completely as possible from the bourgeois world. Yet we should be careful when speaking of this wished-for exile. It is the kind of thing which we would properly associate with, say, Baudelaire or with Oscar Wilde. But in Yeats's case we can be led to believe that his condemnation of the middle classes is the inevitable social extension of his aesthetic. His theory of the imagination, as we have seen, has certain aristocratic, even authoritarian implications. But it would be too bland to infer these from a poem like 'September 1913':

> What need you, being come to sense,
> But fumble in a greasy till
> And add the halfpence to the pence
> And prayer to shivering prayer, until
> You have dried the marrow from the bone?
> For men were born to pray and save:
> Romantic Ireland's dead and gone,
> It's with O'Leary in the grave.

Although one could find a dozen other instances of Yeats's contempt for the middle-class attachment to praying and saving, we must recognize that it represents for him something more devastatingly barren than these habits would indicate. In his early essays, gathered together in *Ideas of Good and Evil* in *The Cutting of an Agate*, he distinguishes between the 'three types of men (who) have made beautiful things' (aristocrats, countrymen and artists) and those others who 'being always anxious, have come to possess little that is good in itself'. Artists, we are told, are 'the priesthood of a forgotten faith' and are opposed to the 'makers of religions who have established their ceremonies, their form of art, upon fear of death, upon the hope of the father in his child, upon the love of man and woman'.[1] The condescension of tone and the undergraduate hauteur of these essays betray their literary origins. But the basic attitude remains intact in the savage and bitter poems of his last years. Common to the early essays and late poems is the belief that those others, the middle classes, are unredeemable from the things of earth because of their fear of death. More precisely, Yeats believed they had neutralized death as an imaginative and physical reality. This, I believe, is a governing feature of Yeats's thought and experience. His abhorrence of the neutralization of death in the middle-class consciousness led him towards disciplines and interests in which the notion of death was pre-eminent and the contemplation of it a crucial activity.

Reincarnation seems to have been the most fervently held of all Yeats's private beliefs. By virtue of it, death was both contemplated and overcome. Politically, one could say that the revolutionary thrust of his attack on empiricism and its social constellation in the middle classes was constantly parried by his defence of traditional social and religious systems which were, for him, valuable because they were reverential towards the notion of reincarnation. Like Greece, Ireland was for him a holy land because the spirits of the dead were given imaginative housing on every rath and hill. The haunted groves and sacred woods of the earth were made accessible either by folk belief or by art. The artist stood at the crossroads between the aristocrat and the countryman, combining aristocratic form with emotion of multitude. Unlike the bourgeois, he outfaced death and by so doing acknowledged in the world a dimension other than the secular. Ireland became for Yeats the embodiment of such beliefs and attitudes.

But Yeats's world and that of the Romantic movement in general is not really quite so different from its bourgeois counterpart as it would have liked to be. Neither world will yield to the fact of extinction; each preserves, in different ways, belief in the eternity of the world and in the eternity of consciousness. Both are rooted in the fear of death. The opposition between the city of

[1] *Essays and Introductions* (London, 1961), pp. 251, 203.

art and the decaying body in 'Sailing to Byzantium' cannot be resolved because the city, in order to be supreme, must outface the fact of bodily extinction. And it cannot. The poem is in that respect unresolved, but it is not irresolute. In fact, it is the very resolute nature of Yeats's honesty and his will to overcome what is unconquerable in experience – its very extinction – which makes the poem a great one. In the end, Yeats's demand is that art or history rescue consciousness from death; but this is a demand neither art nor history can bear. For although each may be said to embody the principle of eternity, that embodiment is perceptible to an individual who *personally* by his death contradicts that principle even though, in a representative way, as *Homo sapiens*, he may be said to confirm an eternal process. It is precisely that gap between personal experience of transience and the conviction of an eternal realm, which exercises Yeats to his most magnificent frustrations and contradictions. Can 'ancestral night' really, in the words of 'A Dialogue of Self and Soul' 'Deliver from the crime of death and birth'? A play like *Purgatory* and the whole cycle of Cuchulainn plays also remind us of this dispute. In *A Vision* Yeats said that Cuchulain 'should (and could) earn deliverance from the wheel of becoming by participation in the higher self, after which he should offer his spiritual history to the world; instead, he condemns himself to a career of violent and meaningless action, and this is responsible for the developing tragedy of his life'.[2] Unlike Hamlet, Lear or Ophelia, Cuchulain is not 'gay'. He does not escape from the wheel of eternal recurrence into the eternal haven of art. He is the man of action whose action is always incomplete because it has not become a thought. Yet if we read 'The Death of Cuchulain' or 'A Dialogue of Self and Soul' carefully, we would, I suggest, come away puzzled and torn by their contradictions. We would find the whole sequence of contradictions epitomized in *A Vision* and in certain passages in *Explorations*.

We can put the matter simply. Death renders life meaningless unless life achieves a form which death cannot alter. For Yeats, that form is art, phase fifteen of the circle of the moon. Otherwise, life is a recurrent cycle of meaningless action (perhaps the basic Yeatsian view of history). Yeats would therefore seem to be saying that the act of taking thought is, as such, the act of recognizing the meaning of death. But the world cannot (in all

---

[2] *A Vision* (New York, 1961), p. 257.

logic) contain a consciousness which can realize its own separation from the world. For such a consciousness has obviously something beyond the world as its horizon and limit. This, for Yeats, is the triumph of great art. To realize death is to see life simultaneously in personal and in historical terms; the confluence of these is the aesthetic form. Time loses its rigorous sequentiality and becomes plastic, dramatic. So many famous poems dwell on past moments which are emblems of the future, 'Leda and the Swan' being perhaps the most famous. Yeats saw the constant remaking of the self as the effort to escape two things – a meaningless recurrence like that which afflicted Cuchulain, and a meaningless extinction like that which afflicts all men. In the first case we have unsatisfied history; in the second, unsatisfied life. Bringing the two together, conjoining the personal with the historical, gave a man the balance, the equipoise and the immortality of art. The achievement of Yeats here is reminiscent of what Valéry said of Mallarmé: 'A man who measures himself against himself, and remakes himself according to his lights, seems to me a superior achievement that moves me more than any other. The first effort of humanity is that of changing their disorder into order, and chance into power. That is the true marvel.'[3]

So, by contemplating death, by bracketing the personal and the historical, Yeats evolves for us the notion of an art which articulates itself in great, changeless masterpieces but which reaches the point of articulacy through the process of changing, remaking and making of the personality of the artist. It is a true dialectic, by virtue of which the term changelessness finds its meaning in its opposite, change; in which eternal recurrence discovers itself through the concept of eternal fixity; in which the wheel of becoming turns into the phase of being. This is, *in nuce*, a theory of human freedom realized under the aegis of death. It is the mode of thought which we might more readily, perhaps, associate with Heidegger, all the more so nowadays since such a theory has become associated, in the case of both these men, with a savage politics. Yeats did give substance and support to the philosophy of fascism. It is a fact to which we should afford some further attention.

From *Michael Robartes and the Dancer* (1921) to the end of his life, Yeats's lament for the loss of his own bodily, especially sexual, powers coincides with his lament for a civilization that

---

[3] A. E. Mackay, *The Universal Self: A Study of Paul Valéry* (London, 1961), p. 43.

was also hurtling towards its own death. The bird of subjective consciousness was being replaced by the beast of mass or objective consciousness. To put this into the idioms which he increasingly came to favour – Ireland and Europe had fallen into the cycle of meaninglessness (usually indicated in Yeats by random violence). The past had its proleptic emblems here, Leda and the Virgin. But the queen of the new dispensation would be impregnated by no swan or dove, but by the brutish swineherd. The offspring would be a rough beast indeed. The association of sexuality and violence is not a new one with him, but it once had a more perfumed, Pre-Raphaelite fragrance (as in a poem of 1902, 'Adam's Curse'). But if we think, for contrast, of the ominous silence of 'Long-Legged Fly' (1939), we begin to sense the distance between poetry of personal crisis and a poetry which has become saturated with the sense of a public apocalypse. Yeats's personal lament for the decay of his body coinciding with his coming into his imaginative strength, reinforced the antinomies of body and soul, spiritual and material, which had proliferated in his early poetry. They had, by the twenties, become elements in a personal crisis as well as constituent parts of a speculative symbolic system. During and after this decade, the twin issues of sexuality (the personal crisis) and Ireland (the historically unique culture) are cherished by him as sources of value and of feeling. Balancing them, or threatening to overcome them, are the opposing forces of a very Burkean mob and Carlylean democracy.

Sexuality and death, posed against the mob and democracy – surely this almost too easily offers us another instance of the Romantic gift for the interiorizing of values and the apotheosis of solitude in the face of a mass civilization? When Crazy Jane faces the Bishop we also witness biology against theology, outsider against institutional figure, sacred energy against routine force. Yet this folk figure with the aristocratic vocabulary is, like her male counterpart, the Wild Old Wicked Man, a rather one-dimensional creature compared to the personae of some of the great poems like 'Among School Children' or 'Nineteen Hundred and Nineteen'. The ballad form of the poems does not consort very happily with their inclination towards sententiousness. We are left hovering between a strange metaphysic of sex and a folk mythology. A short piece like 'The Lover's Song' of 1938 might illustrate this:

Bird sighs for the air,
Thought for I know not where,
For the womb the seed sighs.
Now sinks the same rest
On Mind, on nest,
On straining thighs.

No more than Yeats, we still do not know where thought sighs
for. It has no natural goal or aspiration like bird or seed. But it is
appropriate that the image of sexual exhaustion should be the
analogy for a loss of intellectual direction.

Yet a host of poems – the Crazy Jane verses, 'The Statues', 'The
Municipal Gallery Revisited', 'News for the Delphic Oracle',
'Cuchulain Comforted', 'Under Ben Bulben', 'The Circus' Animals'
Desertion' – makes it clear that the sexual theme and its relation
to death can only be understood in the context of the other
theme to which we have recurred – that of Ireland. There is no
doubt that Yeats wanted to save Ireland from democracy. He
wanted the Irish to remain a people and not become a mob, a
people living imaginatively on their local history and stories
instead of on the English diet of parliamentary speeches and the
gutter press. In his notes to *Words Upon the Window Pane*, he
wrote:

> The fall of Parnell had freed imagination from practical
> politics, from agrarian grievance and political enmity, and
> turned it to imaginative nationalism, to Gaelic, to the ancient
> stories, and at last to lyrical poetry and drama.
>   . . . What shall occupy our imagination? We must, I think,
> decide among these three ideas of national life; that of
> Swift; that of a great Italian of his day; that of modern
> England.[4]

Clearly, in the end he chose an Irish version of Mazzini's Italian
nationalism. He was always liable to choose Italy, but especially
so when the choice was between it and modern England. As for
Swift's spirit, he, Yeats, would incarnate that, thereby bringing
about the desired fusion between Ascendency values and a
nationalist culture based on the folk. It seems clear too that for
him this version of Mazzini led visibly to Mussolini and that Irish
nationalism became increasingly transfigured in his imagination

---

[4] *Explorations*, selected by Mrs W.B. Yeats (London, 1962), p. 343.

by the sacrifice of Easter Week into a movement opposed to everything that middle-class England, Arnold's philistines, stood for – Utilitarianism, Statism, the greasy till. Ireland's recent history was a gesture in defiance of the Lockean-Benthamite tradition. It was what the French Revolution had been for English poets before the invasion of Switzerland or the September massacres.

The men of 1916 had offered their deaths to history. In doing so, they had broken the cycle of eternal recurrence. Their consciousness of themselves became the consciousness of the race. Irish difference, Irish uniqueness, the basis, after all, for the Gaelic-nationalist claim to independence, had been mediated through death. Yeats's aesthetic became, then, more and more politicized under the pressure of the crisis which had afflicted his country. It could not but emerge as a conviction that the Irish had a crucial, redemptive role to play in the recovery of European civilization from barbarism. Easter Week made the Great War look like a mindless, despiritualized carnage. Cuchulain's (and, by extension, Ireland's) cycle of recurrence became finally complete in the sacrifice of Pearse. What stalked through the Post Office was a new and specifically Irish version of modern, existential heroism.

But here we see Yeats in desperate straits. He is translating into politics the implications of his aesthetic. He denies, for instance, the bourgeois character of the Irish rebellion in order to preserve it as an aristocratic emblem caught in the tide of bourgeois life. He took the racial element in Irish nationalism, separated it from the class element, and made the former supreme. His version of the Irish past became a rationale for his version of the Irish future. But his apocalyptic sense, always easily ignited anyway, was consumed by the spectacle of the Great War and the Irish struggle of 1916–22. Ireland's future history was thus projected across the terror of the Second Coming. It is surely an irony of some magnitude that Yeats's politics should now make him appear an emblem or symptom of the Rough Beast's arrival rather than its hostile prophet. But this is, in fact, the case. His idea of Revolution is, in the end, no more substantial, politically speaking, than that of D'Annunzio. It was history illuminated by a brilliant temperament. We measure that brilliance by the effulgence of the poetry he produced. Yet at the same time, we realize that his temperament has itself become part of our history and of our understanding of ourselves.

The question that remains is how this temperament can be described. In political terms we need to know if it can seriously and accurately be described as fascist. Although we have some important poems after 1929, it is perhaps in his plays that Yeats reveals most fully the effect upon his work of his fully matured political and aesthetic opinions. Yet what do we make of *A Full Moon in March* (1935) in which the Queen holds the severed head of the Swineherd above her head before they sing their reciprocal songs of 'desecration and the lover's night'? If we return to an essay written in 1901, entitled 'Magic' and collected in *Ideas of Good and Evil*, we come across a story that might help to lighten the strange opacity of this play. Yeats tells us there of a vision he had during a séance, in which a medical man, who had just lectured on the dissection of the human body, was discovered unwrapping a clumsy doll model of the human form, the result of his attempting 'to make human flesh by chemical means'. But the man sickened as the object took upon itself an evil life, drawing for its energy upon his terror. Finally he had to sever the head of the image from its body, but as he did so he fell back 'as if he had given himself a mortal wound, for he had filled it with his own life'.[5] He was never completely well again and became accursed among the townsfolk and among his own students.

This is a Frankenstein-like story the significance of which for Yeats lay in the fact that the creator of the chemical body was trying to do by naturalistic means what could only be done imaginatively. The experiment therefore had evil results. In *A Full Moon in March*, however, the story gains its full symbolic growth. Frankenstein, Salome and Irish folk-tale are combined into the crucial image of an act of decapitation which is also an act of love. Sex and violence produce poetry. Aristocrat and peasant produce, out of a violent fusion, art. This play enacts for us the Yeatsian ideal of the growth of consciousness in Ireland. The Queen's apathy and the Swineherd's body are both destroyed. In the wake of that destruction they learn to sing to one another. Ireland had to die before it could be regenerated. Yet in its regeneration it became not a fascist, but a colonial, culture. Like the call to Irish poets in 'Under Ben Bulben', the Queen and the Swineherd in this play cry for the famous Unity of Being within a Unity of Culture. They sing the song of the self-cancelling antinomies, of the dialectic in which each positive finds its expression

---

[5] *Essays and Introductions*, p. 32.

through the negative of the other. In *A Full Moon in March* the 'drunken, vainglorious lout' of the Swineherd is changed utterly. The play is a ritual enactment of Yeats's version of the Irish revolution.

In this play, as in his poem, he seeks an identity for himself which will also be the identity of his race. The quest for the grail of 'Irishness' is not, however, to be confused with the cruder racial theories so pervasive in the Europe and Ireland of the thirties. Yeats had learned the notion of an essential racial 'signature' both from his Anglo-Irish mentors and from the English Romantics. National identity is a concept often occasioned by the belief, on the part of the conqueror as much as on the part of the conquered, that there is some identifiable, genetic or cultural 'difference' between the two groups. Matthew Arnold, after all, had said this often enough about England and Ireland in his Irish essays. There are more recent examples. V. S. Naipaul writes in *An Area of Darkness* of how the English left behind in their twentieth-century colonies one of their most enduring inventions – a concept of Englishness. One of its affectations was that 'of being very English, of knowing nothing at all about India, of eschewing Indian words and customs'.[6] If we substitute Ireland there for India, we can easily recognize the symptoms. The whole Irish revival is a reaction against this attitude, a movement towards the colony and away from the mother-country, a replacement of 'Englishness' by 'Irishness'. Yet we must remember that for Yeats and Synge in particular the Irish maintained their especial quality precisely to the degree that they had remained loyal to those old beliefs and that old eloquence which had formerly characterized the seventeenth-century English. This is the Coleridgean notion of the English community rephrased in an Hibernian idiom. The colony, Ireland, has now become the motherland of historical memory. The actual motherland, England, has become degraded past recognition. We thus discover in Yeats the process of a complex act of colonial repossession, linguistic symptoms of which are to be heard also in Synge's Preface to *The Playboy of the Western World* when he says: 'It is probable that when the Elizabethan dramatist took his ink-horn and sat down to his work he used many phrases that he had just heard, as he sat at dinner, from his mother or his children. In Ireland, those of us who know the people have the same privi-

---

[6] V.S. Naipaul, *An Area of Darkness* (London, 1964), p. 210.

lege.' 'Those of us who know the people' – a perfect colonial phrase. Yeats considered himself to be one of those too; he wasn't, in that sense, one of 'the people'. His so-called fascism is, in fact, an almost pure specimen of the colonialist mentality. Even the comparison Synge makes with a Merrie England of bygone days is one that had almost become *de rigueur* among English Romantics from Blake and Coleridge to William Morris and W.B. Yeats. The call to Englishness has been a persistent one for almost two centuries. We find its contemporary forms in Donald Davie's espousal of Thomas Hardy; in Geoffrey Hill's *Mercian Hymns*; in the poetry of Ted Hughes. When transferred to Ireland, such a search for a national signature becomes colonial, on account of the different histories of the two islands. The greatest flowering of such a search has been Yeats's poetry.

To describe Yeats's politics, and to a large extent his achievement, as colonial is not at all to diminish it. His career is, especially in its close, marked by incoherence and by an almost wilful mysticism. Yet his demand was always that Ireland should retain its culture by keeping awake its consciousness of metaphysical questions. By doing so it kept its own identity and its links with ancient European culture alive. As always with Yeats, to be traditionalist in the modern world was to be revolutionary. This is not the sort of opinion that we can any longer attribute to an outdated nationalist position. It is a conviction which has a true revolutionary impact when we look at the history of the disappearance from the Western mind of the sense of eternity and of the consciousness of death. It is a history coincident with the history of modern capitalism. The greasy till is, after all, spiritually empty. Theodor Adorno put the issue like this in *Negative Dialectics*:

> What in a highly unideological sense ought to be the most urgent concern of men has vanished. Objectively it has become problematical; subjectively, the social network and the permanently overtaxing pressure to adjust leaves men neither the time nor the strength to think about it. The questions are not solved, and not even their insolubility is proven. They are forgotten, and any talk of them lulls them so much more deeply to their evil sleep.

It is out of that evil sleep that Yeats saw his Rough Beast arise. He wanted to take Ireland into awareness with him. In its consciousness of death, the culture would become truly alive. To quote Adorno again:

> We might be tempted to speculate . . . whether the turn in evolutionary history that gave the human species its open consciousness and thus its awareness of death – whether this turn does not contradict a continuing animal constitution which prohibits men to bear that consciousness. The price to be paid for the possibility to go on living would be a restriction of consciousness, then, a means to shield it from what consciousness is, after all, the consciousness of death.[7]

As against that we remember Yeats's words:

> Consume my heart away; sick with desire
> And fastened to a dying animal
> It knows not what it is; and gather me
> Into the artifice of eternity.
>
> ('Sailing to Byzantium')

He was a revolutionary whose wars took place primarily within himself; and he knew that in the end, struggle as he might, it was a losing battle. Not even art could quite compensate for that. We can close on the poem 'The Four Ages of Man' from the 1934 sequence *Supernatural Songs*:

> He with body waged a fight,
> But body won; it walks upright.
>
> Then he struggled with the heart;
> Innocence and peace depart.
>
> Then he struggled with the mind;
> His proud heart he left behind.
>
> Now his wars on God begin;
> At stroke of midnight God shall win.

---

[7] Theodor W. Adorno, *Negative Dialectics*, trs. E.B. Ashton (London, 1973), p. 395.

4

synge and heroism

It is generally accepted that Synge's most important works are distinguished by a linguistic richness and vitality which derive from the combination of Gaelic and English speech habits and literary conventions.[1] Synge was uniquely equipped to exploit the fading potential of the Irish language as a regenerator of an English which seemed to him asphyxiated by the formal apparatus and the narrow preoccupations of realism and naturalism. His work, like that of Yeats, declares the need for a new horizon, a new language, by a reincorporation of the past into the present through art. But before he could discover the new language or the new art he had to discover the new Ireland. To do that, he had to forsake his Protestant, evangelical beliefs and attitudes. In his *Autobiography* he says: 'Soon after I relinquished the Kingdom of God I began to take a real interest in the kingdom of Ireland. My politics went round from a vigorous and unreasoning loyalty to a temperate Nationalism. Everything Irish became sacred.'[2]

The salvational vocabulary of the *Autobiography*, and especially of this section, is remarkable. In a short space we have the following sequence of words: radiance, beauty, intangible glory, transfigured, pilgrim, divine ecstasy, puberty, primitive people, adoration, divinity, kingdom, God, Ireland, sacred, human, divine, goddess. Synge was saved again, re-baptized in the faith of a utopian conviction: his new, Irish community was to be a liberation from the repressive inherited workaday world of his class, religion and political attitudes. A persistent feature of his new faith was his enhancement of the 'primitive' feelings. He believed they

[1] See Declan Kiberd, *Synge and the Irish Language* (London, 1979).
[2] *The Collected Works of J.M. Synge*, ed. Robin Skelton, 4 vols. (London, 1962–8), vol. 2, p. 13.

were released in the young by the death of the old. At the age of 10 he wandered in the woods at Rathfarnham with his first girlfriend. An aunt had just died:

> The sense of death seems to have been only strong enough to evoke the full luxury of the woods. I have never been so happy. It is a feeling like this makes all primitive people inclined to merry making at a funeral.
> We were always primitive. We both understood all the facts of life and spoke of them without much hesitation but with a certain propriety that was decidedly wholesome. We talked of sexual matters with an indifferent and amused frankness that was identical with the attitudes of folk tales. We were both superstitious, and if we had been allowed . . . we would have evolved a pantheistic scheme like that of all barbarism . . . The monotheistic doctrines seemed foreign to the real genius of childhood in spite of the rather maudlin appeal Christianity makes to little children . . .[3]

Thus Synge's career seems at first to have been dominated by a series of actual escapes and symbolic reorderings. He moved from unionism to nationalism, from respectability to the theatre, from English to Irish, from decadence (in literature) to an originary primitivism, from class to folk community, from the bourgeoisie to the peasantry, from his own ill-health to the glamorization of physical well-being and of youth. The list of transpositions could be extended but the general direction remains the same. A joyless, repressive regime, linguistically anaemic, gives way to a joyful, liberating order, linguistically rich, even luxurious. The claustrophobic fears discernible in a work like *Étude Morbide* are alleviated time and again by the thought of open spaces, open and candid speech, and, above all, by the openness of a small-scale civilization like that of the West of Ireland to the European past. When Pat Dirane finished a story, Synge, who was well versed in the contemporary researches into the oral traditions of Europe, wrote: 'It gave me a strange feeling of wonder to hear this illiterate native of a wet rock in the Atlantic telling a story that is so full of European associations.'[4]

Even so, Synge never loses sight of the constrictions of peasant life. All his work recognizes the link between constriction and

[3] Ibid., vol. 2, p. 7.
[4] Ibid., vol. 2, p. 65.

intensity and shows a desire to escape from the intensities of the personal life, which can become merely neurotic or worse, into the 'naturalness' of the folk life, which can retain intensity and remain communal. The psychological finesse of his autobiographical writings and of the literature of decadence (Baudelaire, Huysmans, even Zola) is, in his own view, symptomatic of an illness, a closure within the self characteristic of the late-bourgeois era. Ireland's nationalism offered an escape into health, sanity and community, but for Synge nationalism was a moment of resistance to the inevitable transformation of traditional life, not a programme of redemption for it. In this his nationalism deviates in a radical manner from that of Pearse who sought, in a new educational system and in a new ideology of cumulative rebellion, the instruments for the re-establishment of a lost cause.

In Synge, the cause is always lost. The order of things is not regenerated. Traditional Irish life, in Wicklow or in the West, is changed only to the extent that it becomes conscious of its bereavement from authentic value. In *The Playboy of the Western World*, Pegeen Mike's desolate cry of loss brings to an end the prospect of a glorious future with Christy Mahon, one which Christy had invoked by articulating a vision of pastoral romance which properly belongs to the old Gaelic past. The failure of the community to bring the past Eden into a utopian future marks the boundary line of nationalist and romantic desire. The vagrant hero or heroine fades into legend or fantasy. The community remains; more deeply stricken, more visibly decayed. The traditional conflict between youth and age, so evident in *The Playboy*, *Deirdre of the Sorrows* and *In the Shadow of the Glen*, gives the social victory to age, the existential victory to youth. Society is not redeemed, and the traditional function of comedy remains incomplete. Synge is not writing out the failure of heroism. He is registering its failure in regard to society or, conversely, society's failure in regard to it.

This is one of the themes of Yeats and Joyce too. The hero betrayed or expelled by a community (which has itself conspired to create the idea of heroism as a means to its own salvation) is a literary trope. In it we see the suppression of its own utopian vision of itself by a community which did not have 'courage equal to desire'. Synge himself became one of the lost heroes in Yeats's pantheon, especially after the *Playboy* riots in 1907 and the performance of *Deirdre* in 1910. In fact Yeats's search for the ideal audience is part of his interpretation of the meaning and reception of Synge's drama. The meaning was heroic, the reception base. Thus, a new audience was needed, one to which heroism would come naturally. This is not a distortion of Synge. Rather it is a true perception of the plight of the hero in his plays. Yeats's own repeated attempts to conceive of Cuchulain as a hero who could participate in the mind of the present generation, Pearse's assertion of Cuchulain's presence, and their mutual castigations on the community which could not receive these demanding exemplars, are repeated, with variations, by Joyce, O'Casey, George Moore and others. There was no audience for heroism when it became flesh.

The complexity of Synge's plays is in part focused for us by their ostensible adherence on the one hand to an oral tradition which prizes story, an institutionalized narrative, and on the other to a written tradition which prizes textuality, a linguistic production which calls attention to its own nature rather than to any narrative end for which it is merely an instrument. Synge was aware of the blend of opposites in his work. He read it sometimes as a blend of the Irish and English elements: 'With the present generation the linguistic atmosphere of Ireland has become definitely English enough, for the first time, to allow work to be done in English that is perfectly Irish in essence, yet has sureness and purity of form.'[5] Sometimes it was a blend of the lyric and epic impulses:

> Lyrics can be written by people who are immature, drama cannot. There is little great lyrical poetry. Dramatic literature is relatively more mature. Hence the intellectual maturity of most races is marked by a definite moment of dramatic creation. This is now felt in Ireland. Lyrical art is the art of national adolescence. Dramatic art is first of all a childish art . . . without form or philosophy; then after a lyrical interval we have it as mature drama dealing with the deeper truth of general life in a perfect form and with mature philosophy.[6]

These remarks return us to the traditional linguistic and literary origins out of which his drama grew.

But the programme, which envisages the fusion of diverse elements, is not identical with the plays, which enact the contra-

[5] Ibid., vol. 2, p. 384.
[6] Ibid., vol. 2, p. 350.

dictions between them. Story is one thing and Synge's modifications of the folk stories that supply his plays help us to understand the inevitable difficulties of his position. Once the oral
tradition is written, it is transformed. Synge is involved in an act
of translation as much as the nineteenth-century rewriters of
Irish poetry into English. Thus the oral tradition, the story, is
there as a moulding presence, as a guarantor of universal validity,
giving sanction to the fiction but not having sanction within
itself. (Joyce used *The Odyssey* in a comparable way in *Ulysses*). The
oral hinterland lends prominence to the mode of telling the story
which Synge turns into a virtuoso performance. The balance
between the 'epic' story and the 'lyric' performance, between the
'maturity' of the old tale and the 'adolescence' of the actors
within it, is an expression of Synge's desire to incorporate the
present (as something that had never happened before) into the
past (as something in which the present *had* happened before) in
such a way that the audience would be left to contemplate 'purity
of form' or, in Yeats's words, 'an eddy of life purified from
everything but itself'.[7] In consequence, there would be in such
works something more than the disengagement from the petty
concerns of everyday life which both Synge and Yeats desired.
There would be, finally, a disengagement from history, achieved
by the constant relocation of the specific sequence of incidents in
the frame of the universal, human condition. So the oral or
mythic readings of the plays emerge: *In the Shadow in the Glen* is a
rewriting of the old story of the marriage between January and
May; *The Playboy* is a rewriting of the Oedipus myth; *Riders to the
Sea* is a version of man's tragic struggle against the inevitability of
death. Such readings would be encouraged by the almost total
absence of historical references in Synge's plays and by the
luxurious presence of a self-consciously 'poetic' language.

Man and Nature, it would seem, are the protagonists in this
new, post-Christian art:

> The religious art is a thing of the past only – a vain and
> foolish regret – and its place has been taken by our quite
> modern feeling for the beauty and mystery of nature, an
> emotion that has gradually risen up as religion in the
> dogmatic sense has gradually died. Our pilgrimages are not
> to Canterbury or Jerusalem, but to Killarney and Cumberland
> and the Alps . . .

[7] *Explorations* (London, 1962), p. 154.

> In my plays and topographical books I have tried to give humanity and this mysterious external world.[8]

It is appropriate that Synge should provide this connection between art and tourism. For, though he was a serious scholar of the Irish language and of Irish literature and the oral tradition, he was also a visitor to a culture which had already degenerated into the quaintness of the preserved species, quarantined in its own beautiful and economically unproductive landscape. The refreshment which the landscape of famous beauty-spots gave to the exhausted sensibilities of the urban weekend visitor is transposed by Synge into a linguistic key, with the exhausted English language gaining a new vitality from its recourse to famous beauty-spots in the Irish language – its folk-tales, its poems, its brilliant but almost occluded literary achievement. As in Lady Gregory, Douglas Hyde, Yeats and others in the literary world, as in the world of Franco-Germanic philology, the concentration of interest was on the language of this dying community and, in the case of the writers, on what could be rescued from it for the contemporary moment. It was an *elixir vitae* for a decadent civilization. But Synge consistently emphasized that its natural home was in art. He wanted a revival of the English, not of the Irish, language. The Gaelic League, seeking the re-establishment of the Irish language, could perhaps

> keep the cruder powers of the Irish mind occupied in a healthy and national way till the influence of Irish literature, written in English, is more definite in Irish life, and then the half-cultured classes may come over to the side of the others, and give an intellectual unity to the country of the highest value.[9]

It is not clear from this passage who the 'half-cultured classes' and 'the others' were, but it is a safe bet that neither of them were Irish speakers. The goal of art was culture; its means was the creation, through a language in which Irish and English were reconciled into a new balance and beauty, of a cultivated audience.

The idea of the new Ireland was predicated on the replacement of politics and history by art. This is a version of Sir Samuel Ferguson's cultural conservatism duplicated by a much greater writer. A peasantry blessed by refinement, an aristocracy free

---

[8] *The Collected Works of J.M. Synge*, vol. 2, p. 351.
[9] Ibid., vol. 2, p. 386.

from decadence, both distinct from the crude citizens of the towns – these are the recognizable ideals of the Anglo-Irish writers from Ferguson to the present day. It is a weary theme, employed with unwearied persistence, the burden of the Victorian traveller's tale of distant, exotic places. In *The Aran Islands* we read:

> The absence of the heavy boot of Europe has preserved to these people the agile walk of the wild animal, while the general simplicity of their lives has given them many other points of physical perfection. Their way of life has never been acted on by anything much more artificial than the nests and burrows of the creatures that live round them, and they seem in a certain sense to approach more nearly to the finer types of our aristocracies . . . than to the labourer or citizen, as the wild horse resembles the thoroughbred rather than the hack or cart-horse. Tribes of the same natural development are, perhaps, frequent in half-civilized countries, but here a touch of the refinement of old societies is blended, with singular effect, among the qualities of the wild animal.[10]

The distinctive fact about Synge and about the writers of the period in which he lived was that the country in which they conducted this species of spiritual tourism was not a far-off region. It was their own.

So in the plays we find ourselves confronted by discontinuities. Their narrative form is oral, that of the folk-tale; their narrative mode is literary, that of the specialized language. Their background is Nature, open, wild and romantic; their foreground is Society, closed, decayed and utilitarian. The rituals of a community are invoked but the loneliness of individual heroism prevails. Mythical figures are remembered, historical detail is blurred. Love is an enchantment, marriage a travesty; lies become truths, dreams become realities; vagrancy is a virtue, settlement a vice; the heart's a wonder but there are no psychological problems; authority is pervasive but anarchy also prevails. Each play presents its own peculiar form of discontinuity, but they all have in common the story of a fantasy – Christy Mahon's fantasy about the killing of his da, Maurya's fantasy in *Riders to the Sea* about having one son preserved, Martin and Mary Doul's fantasy in *The Well of the*

---

[10] Ibid., vol. 2, p. 66.

Saints about their own splendid appearances – which is, first, rebuked by fact and then, in the next instant, legitimized as belonging or contributing to a higher truth than mere fact could ever reach. This double fold in the stories allows us to think of them as something more complex than exercises in a kind of cultural *bovarysme*, since they both share in and castigate illusions. Finally, the illusion must be ratified by something larger than realism. Mesmerized by an eloquence which begins in illusion but which continues after the destruction of illusion, we are forced to concede to the imagination a radical autonomy. It insists on its own truth not by ignoring fact but by including it and going beyond it. The imaginary, overtaken by the real, becomes the imaginative.

The dynamic force which makes this possible is language. People talk themselves into freedom. No longer imprisoned by sea or cottage, by age or politics, the Synge heroes and heroines chat themselves off stage, out of history, into legend. Yet they leave behind them a community more hopelessly imprisoned than ever. In one sense, we can read this as a criticism of the community's hopelessness as a receptive audience for heroism. But it is also an acknowledgement that heroism of this sort is a hopeless means of reviving the community. The central discontinuity is there. Synge's drama affirms and denies the value of the heroicizing impulse of the Revival. It produces the hero out of the 'organic' community but leaves the community empty and exhausted. The glorious language is not a signal that all is well. Self-realization involves social alienation. Those who walk away from society and those who remain within it represent two kinds of value which are not reconcilable.

An examination of the text of *The Playboy* reveals these tensions operating at the deepest level. Key-words – *lonesome, afeard, decent, sainted* – and their associated epithets, such as *queer* and *dark*, so dominate the rhythms of speech that they give it the regularity of chant. The adoption of the present habitual tense, so common in the Irish language, into the present participle in English also helps to give regularity and continuity to the speeches, allowing for a smoothness in the transitions not native to either language. 'If I am a queer daughter, it's a queer father'd be leaving me lonesome these twelve hours of dark, and I piling turf with the dogs barking and the calves mooing, and my own teeth rattling with fear.'[11] The wonderfully lubricated syntax and the grammatical

---

[11] Ibid., vol. 4, p. 63.

nonchalance of Synge's writing certainly abet the impression of naturalness which is so important in these plays. But the ever enfolding repetitions, the picking up of one phrase by a number of speakers, the alliterative patterning ('dews of dawn', 'wonders of the western world', 'a high wave to wash him from the world'), enforce the contrary impression – of artificiality, of design. The more brilliant the artifice, the more natural it appears to be. Yet the conciliation between these things is not only a matter of cadences; it also involves meaning. The key words which generate the play's meanings provide us with no sense of final conciliation. At the simplest level we can, by their light, pick out the main movement in the play. Beginning in anonymity and squalor, Christy moves, via eloquent fiction, to fame and glory. For a moment he is offered the sidetrack temptation of the Widow Quin, notorious not famous, shrewd not glamorous. Resisting that, he is finally brought down by the reappearance of his father, only to rise again above father, above the villagers, and leave 'master of all fights from now'. Lonesomeness, tempted by decency, becomes individuality. Decency, with its saints and cardinals, popes and peelers, wakes and marriages, is left behind.

Yet it is a strange kind of decency which, for instance, demands that a dispensation be sought from Rome for the marriage of Pegeen and Shawn (because they are related) and at the same time approves of a son who boasts how he killed his father. It is an odd fact that a play which seems at one level to promote the comic idea of the subversion of adult authority and the liberation which is its consequence, should be so sparing in its references to the oppressions and dangers of authority itself. We hear of priests and of peelers and of a thousand militia ' – bad cess to them! – walking idle through the land';[12] we hear of hierarchies of potentates, religious and secular, of God in his golden throne, of St Peter in his seat, and we smile at the fearful anxieties of a Shawn Keogh who is terrified at the very name of Father Reilly, the parish priest. The poverty and the limited incestuous nature of the society is hinted at on several occasions. Yet famine, eviction, military oppression and landlordism, the characteristic facts of late-nineteenth-century Irish rural existence for the peasantry are almost entirely repressed features of the text. The peasant society that Synge knew was dying because it had been atrociously oppressed – not because it had lost contact with the

[12] Ibid.

heroic energies which its early literature had once exhibited. Synge aestheticizes the problem of oppression by converting it into the issue of heroism. The oppression is finally understood as self-inflicted by the community, because it insists on the lower-class realism of fact and refuses the aristocratic symbol of imaginative truth. It is strange to see this mutation of politics into literature against the background of the County Mayo which had produced Michael Davitt and the Land League, Captain Boycott and some of the worst agrarian unrest in late-nineteenth-century Ireland. The heroic figures of the Revival's imagination are social as well as literary constructs. They are leaders of their people in the sense that Lecky imagined the eighteenth-century landlord to be: 'The Irish character is naturally intensely aristocratic; and when gross oppression was not perpetrated, the Irish landlords were, I imagine, on the whole very popular, and the rude, good-humoured despotism which they wielded was cordially accepted.'[13]

This Trinity College view of Irish history was extended and enriched by Synge and by Yeats into a myth of union between peasant and aristocrat – leading to the emergence of heroism, spiritual leadership, still aristocratic in tone, Anglo-Irish in content, but frustrated by the intractable facts of a situation which Michael Davitt had more accurately described in his book *The Fall of Feudalism in Ireland* (1904). The dispossession of the landlords, the breaking of the political power of the Ascendency (urged by Burke over a century before) and the deep material and cultural impoverishment of the peasantry which was a direct result of the exercise of that power, are the central political facts of Synge's mature life. The attempt to recover a new ideal of heroism from the reintegration of the shattered Gaelic culture with the presiding English polity is no more than the after-image of authority on the Anglo-Irish retina.

It is therefore quite proper to resign ourselves to the mythic interpretations of Synge's plays. In *Riders to the Sea*, the extreme poverty of the islanders, the carefully annotated disintegration of their traditional habits, the colour symbolism of black and white, grey and red, the sheer marginality of existence, can be embraced under the aegis of Sea and Death. Maurya is the voice of humanity uttering its resignation to an incurable human plight. In her, quietism is heroic. Within this frame, every object – the clothes of the drowned Michael, the white boards for the coffin, the cake on

[13] W.E.H. Lecky, *Leaders of Public Opinion in Ireland* (London, 1872), p. 252.

the griddle – shines with the pathos of the human artifact in the fact of the hypnotic and obliterating force of the sea.

Similarly, in *Deirdre of the Sorrows*, the betrayal of Naisi and his companions by Conchubor, already foretold, gives Deirdre the opportunity to satisfy her desire for death and for the escape from old age. The political fact is minor in contrast to the 'metaphysical' fact. As she says with her last breath: 'It's a pitiful thing, Conchubor, you have done this night in Emain, yet a thing will be a joy and triumph to the ends of life and time.'[14]

Deirdre, like Maurya and Christy, is a natural symbolist. The purity of action emerges only when it is drawn from the sheath of history. Then it glitters through all ages. But *Deirdre* is a costume drama with no image of the 'natural' to rescue it from its heavy Celtic brocade hangings. Synge's fascination with obliteration, with being open and free, closed and imprisoned, dominates the action.

NAISI: There's nothing surely the like of a new grave of open earth for putting a great space between two friends that love.

DEIRDRE: If there isn't maybe it's that grave when it's closed will make us one forever, and we two lovers have had a great space without weariness or growing old or any sadness of mind.[15]

Here again, the space that swallows the heroes up is the space that gives them legendary presence. The disappearance of the central figures into death, resignation, or the horizons beyond the cottage or village, is the precondition of that figure's abiding presence in the mind of the community. Real heroism is never in the here and now; it is always in the past of the mind.

In October 1902, George Moore and Yeats presented their *Diarmuid and Grainne* along with Douglas Hyde's *Casadh an tSugáin* (*The Twisting of the Rope*) in the Irish Literary Theatre. Hyde's play was the first to be presented in Irish and it told of a hero repudiated by his community. Synge wrote about the evening for the French newspaper *L'Européen*:

So at the opening of the first piece, it was hard not to smile on seeing all around the hall the fine-looking women of the Gaelic League chattering in abominable Irish to some of the

---

[14] Ibid., vol. 4, p. 269.
[15] Ibid., vol. 4, p. 251.

young clerks and shop assistants who were quite pale with enthusiasm. But it happened that during an interval of *Diarmuid and Grainne*, as was the custom in this theatre, the people in the gallery began to sing some of the old popular songs. Until that moment, these songs had never been so heard, sung by so many people together to the old, lingering Irish words. The whole auditorium shook. It was as if one could hear in these long-drawn-out notes, with their inexpressible melancholy, the death-rattle of a nation. First one head, then another, was seen to bend over the programme notes. People were crying.

Then the curtain went up. The play restarted in a deeply emotional atmosphere. For an instant we had glimpsed, hovering in that hall, the soul of a nation.[16]

It is a famous moment and Synge, with his collector's melancholy, has preserved it for us as a moment of transition, all the more important because he glimpsed in Hyde's play that night the possibilities for a new kind of peasant drama. The soul of a nation and its death-rattle – what are these phrases redolent of more than a wake? As the old language dies the soul passes from its body, is glimpsed in the National Theatre, and disappears for ever. Synge was writing, more truly than he knew, the programme for his own plays.

[16] Ibid., vol. 2, pp. 381–2 (my translation).

5

PEARSE:
WRITING and chivalry

The literature of the Irish Revival is, in essence, an heroic literature; or, more precisely perhaps, it is a literature which draws heavily on the idea that the revival of heroism is a necessary and practicable ambition in Irish circumstances. Padraic H. Pearse belongs to this movement. He is its most famous minor writer and its major revolutionary figure. It is by now a convention to emphasize the call for a blood sacrifice into which Pearse transmuted this heroic aspiration. The former apotheosis of the martyr has now given way to an equally extreme denunciation of the pathological elements involved, elements which our recent history has enabled us so penetratingly to observe. There was also a cult of violence deeply cherished before the First World War both in Germany and in England, a cult that died very suddenly in 1916 on the Somme, less than a year after its Easter 1915 apogee, when Dean Inge read Rupert Brooke's 'The Soldier' from the pulpit in St Paul's, *The Times* reprinted it, and when Brooke, soon after, hallowed it all even further by dying from blood poisoning while on active service in the Aegean. There was a legend of England as well as a legend of Ireland in those years and they were both intimately associated with the idea that war and violence were in some sense redemptive and cleansing experiences.[1]

The year 1916 effectively destroyed the legend in England; it confirmed it in Ireland. Pearse is a crucial figure if we are to understand this difference. In Irish political mythology, Arbour Hill, where the executed leaders of 1916 are buried, became the 'corner of a foreign field/That is forever England'. By now, of

[1] Some of this material is based on Paul Fussell, *The Great War and Modern Memory* (London, 1975); Bernard Bergonzi, *Heroes' Twilight* (London, 1965), pp. 32–59.

course, party political considerations have irreparably distorted our view of this almost absurdly literary legend and have managed to obscure the emotional and intellectual innocence which led him, as it led Brooke and Grenfell and others in England, to an early death. Violence was glamourized in the literature of the Edwardian and Georgian eras for two reasons: one, because it had not been experienced in any noticeable way by these generations; two, because it was regarded as a great and manly simplifier of problems which were by then, on every level, threatening to become almost infinitely complex (as indeed they were). In England particularly there had always been an emotional need, strongly fed by Kipling, for a demonstration of imperial might and an anxiety, dating from the Boer War, that when it came to a crisis the Empire might not. Julian Grenfell, a poet almost as famous and as ubiquitous in the popular anthologies as Rupert Brooke, wrote in August 1914, from South Africa:

> And don't you think it has been a wonderful and almost incredible, rally to the Empire; with Redmond and the Hindus and Will Crooks and the Boers and the South Fiji Islanders all aching to come and throw stones at the Germans. It reinforces one's failing belief in the Old Flag and the Mother Country and the Heavy Brigade and the Thin Red Line, and all the Imperial Idea, which gets rather shadowy in peace time, don't you think? But this has proved real enough.[2]

In Ireland, the only mythology which could compete with this imperial one was the nationalist ideal. They were, in some respects, remarkably similar. Each lived in the conviction that there was a sleeping giant, liable to be raised to life again by the spectacle of the Hun at the Gate or by the Fenian Dead. In Ireland, though, a specific form of nationalist recovery had begun to take place, particularly after the death of Parnell. Yeats and Synge both speak of a quickening in Irish cultural life; both place its birth in the 1891–1901 decade. For a long time, Pearse felt it too. Like them, he regarded it as essentially cultural in its nature. For him, its centre was the revival of the language. For them, it was centred in the revival of the literature in English, deeply indebted though that was to the language revival. At first, Pearse was too narrowly educated to give Yeats and Synge credit for

[2] Quoted in Bergonzi, *Heroes' Twilight*, p. 47.

their achievement. But as his horizons broadened with experience he acknowledged their contribution. By that time, though, he was already turning from the commitment to a cultural regeneration towards a belief in the necessity for a political resurgence. Politically, Ireland was still asleep. Yeats could recall the glories of the Ascendency tradition. But Burke and Swift were, for Pearse, politically irrelevant compared with Tone, Davis, Lalor, Mitchel or Emmet. The claim of the Revival was that Ireland was culturally distinct from England. Pearse took this notion to its literal conclusion, that Ireland should also become politically distinct. His idea was that the achievement of political separatism could only be produced by the recovery of a nobler and more spiritual ideal than that which prevailed in the lower-middle-class Ireland which he knew. The source of this spiritual authority was in the old Celtic civilization; its modern prophets were the revolutionary leaders of the past century; its modern inheritor was the contemporary generation. Pearse's evangelism against mean spiritedness, cowardice, caution, commercial wisdom, is precisely the old Victorian-Romantic crusade against the spiritual atrophy of middle-class rule.

I mention Arnold deliberately here because he had three important convictions in common with Pearse. The first was that there was an identifiable Celtic element in European civilization, visible more in literature than in political institutions, hostile of its nature to the practical and unimaginative English spirit which the middle classes so perfectly embodied. The second was that the English could not successfully legislate for Ireland unless they changed into something more 'Celtic' or, as Arnold would more usually have said, more 'Hellenic'. The third was that education of a more liberal sort could foster the growth of the nobility and imaginative grace England so sorely lacked. In other words, both Arnold and Pearse believed in the link between education and the recovery of an old nobility of the spirit which had been stifled by the development of modern social, economic and political institutions. But Pearse's idea of the old Gaelic or Celtic civilization and Arnold's matching idea of the civilization of Ancient Greece or of the 'Celtic spirit' can easily be dismissed as flimsy and even grotesque in their main elements. The point is, though, that they were both instrumental ideas, fictions which had the creation of a regenerated society as their aim. Both men were teachers with society as their audience and the idea of civilization as their subject. They were morally passionate about the need for their ideas; the truth of those notions which they promoted was for them dependent on the precision of their diagnosis of their societies, not upon strict historical evidence. The idea of Celtic civilization, to be found in variant forms in Arnold, Renan, Yeats, Synge and in many others, writers and scholars, was one Pearse would have found difficult to miss. Equally, though, once discovered, he found it impossible to resist.[3]

The idea of Celtic or of Irish difference was not, however, one upon which Arnold or any other Victorian would have based the political demand for separatism. The immense cultural influence of Arnold's thought is pervasive enough to embrace Pearse and Pearse's one disciple in literary criticism – Daniel Corkery. Politically speaking, it is almost negligible. Arnoldian cultural notions were part of the rich mixture indulged in by Yeats and other members of the Irish Revival. Their political implications were invisible to Pearse. He did not perceive that the fact of Irish difference was something the English took considerable pleasure in repeating. It was one of the assurances of their Englishness, the deviancy that defined the norm. In a recent book called *On Revolution*, Peter Calvert has spoken of the ways in which the idea that the Irish were different helped to intensify the sense of solidarity and homogeneity upon which the English prided themselves.[4] But to an imperial people, cultural difference was certainly no ground for political separation. Rather the reverse. Cultural difference enriched the imperial fabric while contributing to the centre's reputation for and sense of near-infallible political wisdom. This was especially true in relation to Ireland, part of the United Kingdom and therefore not recognized as a colony in the real sense of the word. Although there was certainly a considerable logic in Pearse's position, his writings show little sense of the complexity of the relationships which had perforce grown between Ireland and England. Like those English writers – Chesterton among them – who were associated with the Georgian movement in verse and with Little-Englandism in politics, Pearse was a kind of Irish Georgian writer, a Little-Irelander in politics, part of the long literary reaction against the clamant imperialism of Henry Newbolt, William Watson, Alfred Noyes and, let it be said, Ulster Unionists. This anti-imperialist literature, whether Irish or English,

---

[3] See Matthew Arnold, *English Literature and Irish Politics*, ed. R.H. Super (Ann Arbor, 1973), vol. 4 of *The Complete Prose Works of Matthew Arnold*. On Renan, see *The Poetry of the Celtic Races and Other Studies*, trs. W.G. Hutchinson (London, 1896).
[4] P. Calvert, *On Revolution* (Oxford, 1970), p. 172.

is imbued with a deep pastoral innocence and a fervent, almost religious nationalism. 'England' and 'Ireland' are almost sacred words in such writing. It is full of a cultural home-sickness, although the longing for that cultural home was the more intensely felt in Ireland as it was there the more culturally remote. Pearse's school at Rathfarnham, haunted by the ghost of Emmet, and Yeats's tower at Thoor Ballylee, haunted by the idea of a spiritual aristocracy, are symptoms of this, not equalled in English experience.

A powerful teacher is like a propagandist in at least one important respect – he restricts himself to a very small vocabulary. Equally, he has the skill and the ingenuity to manipulate it in a nearly endless variety of ways, saying the same things over and over again with such urgency that the words seem to fulfil an already implicit logic. Pearse is such a teacher and his writings bear witness to it. He began, as I have said, as very much an Irish Georgian writer. That is to say, he exploited, as they did, a kind of pastoral sentimentality, associating strong feelings with words and images that had already secreted to themselves a certain cultural longing. 'Ireland', 'The Gael', phrases such as 'the antique faith' or 'the high and sorrowful destiny of the heroes'[5] have the grand resonance that we associate also with some of the early poetry of Yeats. The Celtic Twilight was, after all, Ireland's version of the Georgian movement. A long passagework of such words and phrasings runs through all Pearse's writings, lending them that curious air of having combined the power of ancestral voices with literary respectability. For such writing is routine in its vocabulary and in its invocations; yet Pearse cannot be fairly accused of being nothing more than a writer of pastiche. For two other factors must be taken into consideration. First, his writing is didactic in its intent; and second, as a consequence of that, his writing is most successful when it departs from the more accepted and specifically literary modes of the play or of the poem and becomes a direct form of address to a particular audience. Pearse is at his best, in other words, as an orator and as an essayist. As a poet and as a dramatist, he is easily and perhaps mercifully forgotten.

The didactic intent in the writing makes itself quickly evident in the highly simplified patterns of its syntax, its constant reiteration of key words, its incantatory rhythms, its dependence upon a few

---

[5] *Collected Works of Padraic H. Pearse: Political Writings and Speeches*, ed. Desmond Ryan (Dublin, 1917–22), pp. 4, 58. There are numerous other instances of this kind of phrase.

basic images and its abundant use of the superlative. The forensic appeal is always more pronounced than the cogency of the argument. The emotion is, so to speak, already there. The function of the language is to provoke it anew in the audience. The novelty of the author's suggestions achieves a kind of legitimacy when it assumes for itself the spiritual authority of an ancient tradition. As an example, take the following passage from chapter V of *The Murder Machine*; Pearse is speaking against the tendency to make the relationship between teacher and pupil a merely businesslike transaction:

> Against this trend I would oppose the ideal of those who shaped the Gaelic polity nearly two thousand years ago. It is not merely that the old Irish had a good education system; they had the best and noblest that has ever been known among men. There has never been any human institution more adequate to its purpose than that which, in pagan times, produced Cuchulainn and the Boy-Corps of Eamhain Macha and, in Christian times, produced Enda and the companions of his solitude in Aran. The old Irish system, pagan and Christian, possessed in pre-eminent degree the thing most needful in education; an adequate inspiration. Colmcille suggested what that inspiration was when he said, 'If I die it shall be from excess of the love that I bear the Gael.' A love and a service so excessive as to annihilate all thought of self, a recognition that one must give all, must be willing always to make the ultimate sacrifice – this is the inspiration alike of the story of Cuchulainn and of the Story of Colmcille, the inspiration that made the one a hero and the other a saint.[6]

Although the idea of education espoused here would still be considered at least decorously progressive, the sentiment of this and similar passages is remarkably remote from us. The idolatry of the hero, be he Cuchulainn or Christ or a very Pearsean blend of the two, is so insistent that it becomes a form of indoctrination. But the odd and powerful thing about Pearse was the way in which he made heroism practicable for his audience. He was not an inspired writer; but he taught the doctrine of inspiration with extraordinary effect. Education, the Gaelic polity, love, excess, inspiration, sacrifice – the pagan warrior, the Christian saint – the

---

[6] Ibid., pp. 24–5.

modulation from 'an adequate inspiration' to 'a love and a service so excessive' – these are all marks of that devotional and homiletic appeal which Pearse addresses to his audience.

The point of Pearse's sermons was simple: Ireland was a nation that sought to become a state. Several times before, the translation had been tried by revolution. The time to do so had come round again. He clothed this message in what he called 'figures drawn from the divine epos'.[7] Much of his persuasive strength lies in the rich vocabulary of baptism, vocation, holiness, prophecy, service and martyrdom which dominates his work and gives to his conception of the nation and of the state its powerful charismatic appeal. The early Romantic idea of the Christian essence of the state and its hostility towards the secular liberalism that derived from the French Revolution are both to be found, perfectly preserved, in Pearse's writings. His attitude towards English Liberalism is very much like that of Synge towards English realism in drama. Both sought a new richness, a more generous spirituality; both forged a new language designed to catch the heart of a race which had for too long been overborne by a dreary and philistine rationalism. Pearse was too much the teacher not to have his texts; he did not stress a spiritual condition so much as a spiritual tradition. In his essay on Thomas Davis, 'The Spiritual Nation', he writes: 'nor can I convince myself . . . that there is actually a mystical entity which is the soul of Ireland, and which expresses itself through the mind of Ireland. But I believe that there is really a spiritual tradition which is the soul of Ireland.'[8]

Such belief warrants the Corkery-like distinction which Pearse draws in 'Ghosts' between the tradition of Burke, Berkeley and Swift and that of Tone, Davis, Lalor and Mitchel: 'I am seeking to find, not those who have thought most wisely about Ireland, but those who have thought most authentically for Ireland, the voices that have come out of the Irish struggle itself.'[9] In conservative, romantic politics, authenticity is always a higher value than wisdom since it comes from immersion and intimacy, not from detachment and estrangement. Pearse's attitude here is not anti-intellectual; it is opposed to a particular notion of the intellect and favours a more total participation, a sense that nationhood is a mysterious condition and not a practical problem.

The biblical and prophetic force of what Pearse has to say is

[7] Ibid., 'The Coming Revolution', p. 92.

[8] Ibid., p. 301.

[9] Ibid., p. 246.

enhanced by his recognition that his beliefs are, first, true and, second, shared only by a minority. The spectacle of the few true believers against the despiritualized many was powerfully attractive to Pearse. The sowing of the seed, the preservation of the flame, the fostering of the pure and the true in the midst of the contaminated and false are all favourite tropes in his writings. His reading of Irish history depends upon a distinction between the Celtic Old Testament Prophets such as Cuchulainn or Colmcille and the New Testament Baptists such as Tone and Mitchel.[10] He is not just a Messianic author; his view of the Messianic tradition glorifies the purity of a minority view of things, unpopular because true, true and therefore unpopular. Again, we see that authenticity is preferable to wisdom, is more like prophecy than analysis and is more inclined to action than to passivity. Above all, it should be obvious that the action of the minority tradition in history has the effect, when successful, of converting the majority to its authentic view of things, thereby making the idea of the nation coincident with the reality of the state.

Pearse's version of heroism is, then, closely supported by his notion of the pure, prophetic minority tradition which will, by a sacrificial act, convert the majority from a state of nationhood into the condition of a state. The people possess the longing for statehood but in an inarticulate, blind fashion. One person, born among the people, defines this longing in words and satisfies it in action. The single hero incarnates the potential of his race. In his plays and poems Pearse gives a steadily increasing prominence to this kind of Messianic populism in the form of MacDara of *The Singer*, Giolla na Naomh of *The King* and Ciaran of *The Master*. These are also, respectively, a son, a child and a teacher. The directness of the autobiographical inference should not however obscure for us the fact that all of Pearse's heroes are in service to a social group – family, school, monastic community – as well as to an ideal. He had less admiration for the lonely individual leaders like O'Connell and Parnell, both of whom would have seemed, on the face of it, likely candidates for someone in search of a tradition of heroic spiritual authority. Instead, Pearse chose leaders of, or outstanding members from, organized groups such as the United Irishmen, the Young Irelanders, the Fenians and the IRB.

---

[10] Cf. 'From a Hermitage' in *Political Writings and Speeches*, p. 168, where he calls Mitchel's *Jail Journal* 'the last gospel of the New Testament of Irish Nationality, as Wolfe Tone's Autobiography is the first'.

The cabal or revolutionary group was his idea of the political family out of which the blessèd redeemer would emerge. His politics had, indeed, a populist basis but, on top of that, he had the standard faith in the power of the tightly bonded revolutionary élite group of intellectuals who are the articulators of the implicit desires and sentiments of the great mass of the people. The Catholicism of the Irish middle classes differentiated them, as Cardinal Newman had pointed out in 1855, from their Continental class-fellows.[11] It may help to account for the fact that Pearse spoke the language of Christian, European conservatism and used the methods of radical European revolutionaries. When we remember that this peculiar heritage was intermingled with the new 'Celtic' consciousness which the literary revival and the revival of the language had helped to crystallize, as well as with the schoolboy militarism of the period in European literature, then we have a clearer idea of Pearse's formation and influence as a writer. His work has great appeal for adolescents and is easily dismissed by those for whom cynicism has become the alternative. At times, it is possible to feel that we are reading the words of a genuine revolutionary; at other times, we are hearing the accent of the scoutmaster. If Pearse fails to inspire, he is almost sure to embarrass his reader.

A vocabulary deeply dyed by religious feeling, a syntax of a simple and repetitive structure, well-designed for purposes of oratory, a determination to heighten the sentimental appeal while minimizing the rational cogency of an argument or discussion – these are easily identified features of Pearse's writings. The number of clichés is extraordinary: Pearse's contemporaries are always his generation; his men are always virile; his goals are always noble; his ideals are always noble or high or of the highest or of the noblest; his English are always the Gall, his hopes immortal, his convictions absolute, splendid or sure. Pearse has some peculiar uses of the definite article ('having done the clear, clean, sheer thing')[12] and has also a tendency to over-use the

---

[11] In a speech to the School of Science of the newly created Catholic University of Ireland: 'Here then is one remarkable ground of promise in the future of Ireland, that that large and important class, members of which I am now addressing – that the middle classes in its cities, which will be the depositaries of its increasing political power, and which elsewhere are opposed in their hearts to the Catholicism which they profess – are here so sound in faith, so exemplary in devotional exercises, and in works of piety.'

[12] 'Why We Want Recruits' in *Political Writings and Speeches*, p. 121.

word 'thing' ('a thing upon which I stake all my mortal and all my immortal hopes').[13] These ordinary and innocuous words can, by their very frequency, give the impression of something physically there; they lend certitude to the vaguest references or notions. Speaking in June 1913 at Wolfe Tone's grave in Bodenstown, Pearse said:

> This man's soul was a burning flame, a flame so ardent, so generous, so pure, that to come into contact with it is to come into a new baptism, into a new regeneration and cleansing. If we who stand by this graveside could make ourselves at one with the heroic spirit that once inbreathed this clay, could in some way come into loving contact with it, possessing ourselves of something of its ardour, its valour, its purity, its tenderness, its gaiety, how good a thing it would be for us, how good a thing for Ireland.[14]

One year later, in June 1914, he wrote of the Fenian spirit in these terms:

> that virile fighting faith which has been the salt of all the generations in Ireland unto this last. And is it here even in this last? Yea, its seeds are here, and behold they are kindling: it is for you and me to fan them into such a flame as shall consume everything that is mean and compromising and insincere in Ireland and in each man of Ireland – for in every one of us there is much that is mean and compromising and insincere, much that were better burned out. When we stand armed as Volunteers we shall at last be men, and so shall be able to come into communion of thought and action with the virile generations of Ireland: to our betterment, be sure.[15]

The repetitions and the effective use of accumulated epithets and clauses, especially in the familiar triadic pattern, are evident enough here. But surely, with that, we have a powerful imagery of communion and purgation (seeds and flames with their natural sexual connotation) cast in a prose moulded by ideas of austerity, chastity, honour, nobility. It is as though we are being invited to entertain a warm notion of fusion along with a cold notion of

---

[13] 'Peace and the Gael' in ibid., p. 293.
[14] 'How Does She Stand' in ibid., pp. 56–7.
[15] 'From a Hermitage', pp. 205–6.

aristocratic disdain. A steely destiny is formed in the heat of history. The prose avails of religious and sexual connotations to produce a kind of fervour not very far removed from what used to be called 'muscular Christianity'. Of course the fact that the process of sublimation is going on here is less important than the fact that its appeal was so powerful.

The purpose of such writing and speaking is that of provoking feelings which, it is assumed, are already there. It does not create or interrogate a complex of experience. Feeling is referred to *en bloc*, as something which is atmospherically shared by all. Argument is at a minimum; rhetorical intensification is the chosen mode of progress. Contradictions are there only to be absorbed. In *Peace and the Gael* (December 1915) Pearse wrote:

> Always it is the many who fight for the evil thing, and the few who fight for the good things; and always it is the few who win. For God fights with the small battalions. If sometimes it has seemed otherwise, it is because the few who fought for the good cause have been guilty of some secret faltering, some infidelity to their best selves, some shrinking back in the face of a tremendous duty.[16]

The definite article has its work cut out for it here, but note how easily it yields its prominent place to the word 'some' which, with the help of some sibilant alliteration, helps us to feel that the absolute statement which has suffered a drastic qualification is nevertheless still absolute. 'The few' still remain etched out against the murky background of 'some secret faltering' or 'some infidelity' or 'some shrinking back'. Pearse was not a clear thinker, but he was a man of very definite opinions. His writings are a weapon for the furtherance of his convictions, not in any sense an activity in which the process of arriving at a conviction is displayed. For like Tone, he was 'Thinker and doer, dreamer of the immortal dream and doer of the immortal deed'.[17]

The final retrospect on Pearse's writings is obviously supplied by Pearse's actions. Even in his death cell he continued to use his writing in the service of the cause he died for. All the famous poems, 'The Mother', 'To My Mother', 'The Wayfarer', are written in a slightly anachronistic, almost self-consciously poetic and biblical phraseology ('A splendid thing which shall not pass

[16] Ibid., pp. 215–16.
[17] Ibid., p. 55.

away') which is nevertheless impressive in light of the fact that he knew he would die. As poems they are not particularly good. But the quality of the writing is a minor consideration against the fact that they were written at all, written *then*, an example of literature in service up to the last moment and, of course, in service to something more important than itself. For all his sentimentality and for all his literariness, Pearse is a strictly utilitarian writer. He wrote to teach and move his audience. In that respect, he was successful. He also practised what he taught. In that respect, his class is still in session although the conditions which made him so influential during his lifetime and for a period after his death have indeed 'changed utterly'. As he rightly said: 'Methinks I have raised some ghosts that will take a little laying.'[18] Methinks, indeed.

[18] Ibid., p. 255.

6
JOYCE and stephen:
the provincial intellectual

Despite the vast quantities of exegetical study expended on *Ulysses*, little of it has to do with what Joseph Frank in his famous essay of 1945 called 'the perceptual form of Joyce's novel'. The questions we put surely need not concern the winner of the Gold Cup at Ascot in 1904. For the easily discovered answer, no matter how skilfully adapted to a critic's purposes, tells us nothing about the relation of this novel to its English and Continental sources, to its contemporary present or to its future in which, fifty years later, we now live. It is as rash no doubt to attempt to answer these questions as it would be foolish to ignore them.

Part of Joyce's achievement was his successful introduction of erudition into a genre which had not previously borne its learning well. Intellectual vocation had had some grotesque embodiments in English fiction before Joyce took it up. Jude Fawley, Daniel Deronda, Ernest Pontifex, even perhaps Gissing's Harold Biffen, are strange company for Stephen Dedalus, and not even Casaubon, Ladislaw or Dorothea herself makes our sense of recognition any more emphatic. There is Dorian Gray of course, but he reminds us of only one aspect of Dedalus. Artist, rebel, intellectual, dedicated and scholarly fanatic – each one of these poses has a character to represent it. But Stephen contains them all in both *A Portrait of the Artist as a Young Man* and *Ulysses*. He is the first ideologist to appear in English or American fiction, the first protagonist who did not feel it necessary to inform us of his ideas by giving a sermon on the subject. Hardy, of course, comes off worst in such a comparison with Joyce. Chesterton's bright remark has its force: Hardy 'personifies the universe in order to give it a piece of his mind'.

Portrait is the first novel in the English language in which a passion for thinking is fully presented; *Ulysses* is the first novel in which the activity of thought is the central concern and the determining influence on the form. Stephen is remarkable because his capacity for thought is a crucial, not an incidental, feature of his personality. Of those novel-heroes previously mentioned there is not one whose outstanding virtue is his intelligence. If he is intelligent, that is a symptom of the fact that he is admirable in some other, more 'fundamental', respect. Moreover, in Stephen's case, both in *Portrait* and in *Ulysses*, the quality of his mind is one of the novel's formal and therefore moral achievements. By means of it, the novel is made more intelligible. When the quality of the mind of an intelligent hero lapses, the result can be disastrous and perhaps can also be an ominous commentary on the author's capacity to recognize the nature and form of his own intelligence. Lawrence is an outstanding example here. In *Kangaroo*, published only a year after *Ulysses*, we are frequently faced with announcements like this:

> Man that is born of woman is sick of himself, Man that is born of woman is tired of his day after day. And woman is like a mother with a tiresome child: what is she to do with him? What is she to do with him? – Man, born of woman.

Molly Bloom had answers and Stephen and Leopold Bloom had better questions. The search of each of these last two is conducted according to the rules of at least a certain dramatic propriety. Stephen thinks in a manner consonant with his personality and education; so does Bloom. The main point is that their thinking is not a series of solemn propositions, opposed by its nature to their random feelings. Their thinking is a mode of experiencing the world; for Stephen it is the most comprehensive mode, for Bloom, in his incompetence, it is a wished-for mode. It does not lead to discursive, essayistic interludes in the novel but is itself part of the novel's dramatized form. When it does become self-conscious, as in the last two chapters of *Portrait*, we are aware that it is this very consciousness of itself that is being ironically dramatized.

It is, I believe, easier to understand Joyce's achievement in this respect by looking to the Continental tradition of the novel. There the theme of intellectual vocation was much more deeply rooted and was treated with a subtlety quite foreign to the evangelical, female puritan spirit which so dominated the sentimental English novel. Perhaps *Middlemarch* more than any other single work shows how the innate provincialism of the English novel deprived it of a consciousness of itself as a part of a greater European culture. This is something conspicuously present in the French and, even more, in the Russian novel of the nineteenth century. One could not imagine *Crime and Punishment* or *Le Rouge et le Noir* without the idea of Europe, especially Christian Europe, as a living force in them, in their traditions, and in the minds of their creators. But *Emma* and *Great Expectations* and *Middlemarch* survive happily, and more modestly, apart from that idea. Not until an American, Henry James, arrived on the scene was the novel in English Europeanized, and the Irishman Joyce countered this achievement by anglicizing the European novel.

He had the instrument to do so in his own and in his country's Catholicism. The Irish version was not of the kind to create in its young men the frisson of aesthetic pleasure that passed for conviction among French *décadents* such as Huysmans. In *En Route*, for instance, Durtal has the great advantage over Stephen Dedalus of starting in a Gothic cathedral in which the *De Profundis* and the *Dies Irae* are being magnificently played and sung. The church is before him in all its historical splendour and the setting supports the exclamation:

> Ah! la vraie preuve du Catholicisme, c'était cet art qu'il avait fondé, cet art que nul n'a surpassé encore! C'était, en peinture et en sculpture, les Primitifs; les mystiques dans les poésies et dans les proses; en musique, c'était le plain-chant; en architecture, c'était le roman et le gothique.[1]

Dedalus never had this seduction to yield to or to overcome. Yet Huysmans is interesting and important for Joyce, much more I would think than Wilde could have been, because the French author combined various forms of what one might call liturgical aestheticism with realism. (Valéry, after all, thought that Huysmans' work had 'marqué les limites du naturalisme'.) Besides, Joyce inverts the typical attitude of a Huysmans or of a Wilde by the remarkable sensory hostility he has for a Catholicism that simultaneously fascinates him intellectually. Unlike Huysmans, he was not a man to Catholicize art in the name of the liturgy. Instead, he was to become the artificer of Catholicism, making of the religion a subject matter which had within it a number of organizing principles which he, Joyce, could put into operation for his own purposes.

---

[1] J.-K. Huysmans, *En Route* (Paris, 1895), p. 10.

The advantages he gained from this fate or this decision (or both) were many. The greatest was that by it he entered into the mainstream of the European consciousness, not simply because he was of Catholic origins but because his Catholicism granted him an awareness of the European heritage from which he was in other respects separated. The story of the Greek wanderer Ulysses and a selective version of Roman Catholic history are the two major outlines that emerge through that palimpsest of cultural maps, the landscape of Dublin. Joyce's great contemporary, Thomas Mann, another novelist devoted to the epic analysis of a cultural disintegration, spoke also of the importance of these two aspects of the European experience. In an essay written in 1934 he emphasized the importance and vitality of a European culture which is based on classical antiquity and Christianity. Mann's comment is useful in helping to place Joyce. For the latter is obviously a European novelist in the sense that Mann is and in the sense in which Mann conceives of the idea of Europe:

> Say what you will: Christianity, the flower of Judaism, remains one of the two pillars upon which Western culture rests, the other being Mediterranean antiquity . . . The critique of the twentieth century upon the Christian ethic (not to speak of dogma and mythology); the changes that come about naturally with the flow of life; no matter how deep these go, or how transformingly they work, they are and will remain superficial effects. They can never touch the binding authority of the cultural Christianity of the Western world, which once achieved cannot be alienated.[2]

There is a great difference between Huysmans' response to the culture of Christianity (in terms of its architecture, music and literature) and Mann's concept of 'the cultural Christianity of the Western world'. It is not wholly explained by referring to the political conditions in Germany that year and the consequent defensive assertion of value against barbaric forces. To understand the difference fully, I believe we must recognize the role Joyce has played between the era of Huysmans and that of Mann. Joyce registered, particularly in *Ulysses*, a mutation in European culture. He attempts to understand the experience of cultural disintegration by forging classical antiquity and Christianity into a fable of their

---

[2] Thomas Mann, 'Voyage with Don Quixote' in *Essays by Thomas Mann* (New York, 1957), p. 356.

collapse which would nevertheless be an ordered fable, one in which organization and disorganization would confront one another. Of course organization must win since we are reading a novel and one rightly famous for the high articulacy of its form. But, on the other hand, we witness through that form a failure in which Stephen and Bloom share. We also share in it, suffer perhaps from their sharing in it, but do not suffer it ourselves. The sense of disorganization is therefore all the more present to us because of the high degree of organization the novel reaches in presenting it to us. The problem is, how is this achievement to be described? Can it be recognized in terms of what preceded and of what succeeded it? I believe that it can, and that the first step towards seeing how is to acknowledge the extent to which *Ulysses* broke the provincial bonds of the main tradition of English fiction. In doing so, it introduced into the European novel a parodied form of the English novel, to the final and mutual benefit of both.

In 1800 Madame de Staël explained the English predominance in the novel by pointing to the particularly important role which family life played in English culture.[3] Her implicit comparison is always, of course, with France; at this stage she is still almost completely ignorant of Germany. The novel, she explains, is a particularly modern literary genre fitted by its nature to express the delights and tensions of married (or unmarried) love. Because of this familial bias women played a vital role in the development of the novel, both as authors and readers. They had more freedom and education in England than elsewhere. They therefore wrote and read novels about the family life which they dominated. There are flaws in this argument, but its general truth seems to be unquestionable. The English novel displays a liking for and an interest in domestic bliss which no other novelistic tradition can equal. Madame de Staël was willing to attribute this to England's Protestantism. So, too, during and after the Revolutionary and Napoleonic Wars were the English, since their Protestantism and their chauvinism combined nicely in the image of family Bible-reading round the fireside. With the rise of the Victorian middle classes there also came into being a powerful censorship of the treatment of domestic love in literature by setting, in Chesterton's words, 'certain verbal limits' which ensured 'that every writer

---

[3] Madame de Staël, 'Essai sur les fictions' in *Oeuvres de Mme de Staël*, 2 vols. (Paris, 1832), vol. 2, p. 25.

shall draw the line at literal physical description of things socially concealed'.[4] This cosy moralism, this strain of familial sentimentality and hearthside English scenes get full expression in Dickens, and from him they radiated even more strongly through the English novel of Joyce's youth.

This is the provincial tradition which he inherited. The force of anti-French propaganda in the early part of the century had been such that the writer, especially one distinguished by his 'ideas' (usually little more than anti-conventional social sentiments of as great an antiquity as the conventional ones he opposed), was still liable, when he appeared in the English novel, to be thought of as foreign, sexually promiscuous or outspoken, elegant in peasant surroundings, Bohemian in middle-class situations. Figures as relatively minor as Lydgate or Fitzpiers are good examples of the type, although Heathcliff and Rochester belong to this category too. Their Byronic ferocity separates them, of course, from the others, and is perhaps all the more impressive because it is a function of their personalities as such and not merely an indication of the fact that they are artists and therefore odd or different.

The standard approach to the writer, epitomized in a novel like Gissing's *New Grub Street*, was to picture him as torn between the demands of the market and of art. Almost nothing of this survives into Joyce, either in *Portrait* or in *Ulysses*. Joyce changes the wearisome, discursive idiom by which the act of writing and the fate of being a writer were seen as social activities which led to social problems. In his work, writing becomes an existential act; being a writer becomes an existential state. Even more, Stephen in *Ulysses* is not a writer at all. He is an intellectual, concerned to define himself in terms which are more extensive and precise than those available to the common man, Bloom. As in *Portrait*, our sense of Stephen is controlled by the fact that he must find an epistemology of art before he can write. Writing does not depend on certain well-worn rebellious attitudes towards convention. It depends on the questioning, at a high pitch, of the nature of the relation between the perceiving artist and the perceived world; and the relation between this and the transposition of it into fiction. To be an artist, one must be an intellectual first. Valéry had anticipated Joyce in this, in some ways, but it is in conjunction with Valéry that Joyce's conception of the role of the artist needs to be understood. Stephen Dedalus is closer to Monsieur

---

[4] G.K. Chesterton, *The Victorian Age in Literature* (London, n.d.), p. 99.

Teste than he is to any figure in English fiction. *Ulysses* is, after all, the greatest novel in the Symbolist tradition. And the Symbolists were, after all, French.

So, the British tradition which Joyce inherited was in a peculiarly emphatic state of provincialism, proceeding as it was, with a sort of insolent mediocrity, to lose itself in what Chesterton described as 'a thing being everywhere called "Art", the Greek Spirit, the Platonic Ideal, and so on'. These elements persist, of course, in Joyce, but not in that isolation which so dated and disfigures *Esther Waters* or *Dorian Gray*. Indeed, Moore and Wilde, more than most, entirely fulfilled the coarse public notion of the artist as a sort of Frenchified dandy – the notion which was so prevalent a part of the long propaganda war between England and France in which these two were comfortably ensnared. Because of it, they do not belong to the modern movement in any real sense. They are minor nineteenth-century figures with all the major nineteenth-century features. Joyce incorporates these features in Stephen's aesthetic aspirations and goes far beyond in setting these aspirations in a wide European context which, by virtue of its Catholic overtones, and by virtue of its literary tradition, is uniform with the young man's personal experience.

The most salient fact about *Ulysses*, however, is that it breaks the basic mould of the bourgeois novel in England, the family unit in terms of which all social groupings had been previously seen, and substitutes for it, first a parodied version of the family, and second the strange isolated figure of the outcast artist to whom exile is a supreme value and simultaneously a great disaster. Stephen's true forerunner is Julien Sorel in Stendhal's *Le Rouge et le Noir*. In *Ulysses*, Stephen is merely an artist figure, not an artist. He is not engaged on any great work of art as such. His interest is in the creation of himself. Unlike Julien he has no astounding national history by which he can achieve self-definition. Where Julien craves relationship through action, Stephen contemplates its necessity inactively. 'Julien était ivre d'ambition et non pas de vanité.' Mathilde wonders, 'S'il y a une révolution, pourquoi Julien Sorel ne jouerait-il pas le rôle de Roland, et moi celui de Madame Roland?'

Julien's Napoleonic image of himself is equalled by Stephen's Daedalan self-modelling; one has social and political overtones, the other classical and aesthetic ones. But the Napoleonic image only has force in a revolutionary situation. France supplied that in good measure. For Stephen the only kind of revolution available to his consciousness was a theological, not a political one – heresy, in other words. As an artist therefore he was not simply a heretic. He was a Napoleon of art; an imperious magical Daedalus who overcame the uproar of the revolution, mastered it and stilled it into the perfect silence of his own magnificent personality. Thus *Ulysses* is a novel speckled with heretical references that co-exist with literary references in a sardonic collusion. Joyce has no French Revolution to look back on like Stendhal; he has no Nazi terror to face like Thomas Mann; but he has, in the heretical tradition of Catholicism, his own great image of disintegration which can be allied to his own and to his country's experience; and he has, in the English provincial novel, as in the Irish middle-class scene, the social unit in terms of which the disintegration can be both mirrored and viewed. Inevitably then, the family is parodied in *Ulysses*. Its renowned unity and bliss is to be exploited there for the purpose of giving shape to a sense of breakdown for which all European history provides the material.

Conceiving of Joyce in this way allows us to recognize him as the creator of a hero, Stephen, who occupies in modern European culture a position exactly half-way, morally speaking, between that of Julien Sorel and that of Adrian Leverkühn. Stephen's break with the acknowledged pieties of family life is, in terms of English fiction and Irish Catholicism, exactly like Leverkühn's break in *Dr Faustus* with traditional tonality in terms of the German musical tradition. Stephen's parody of the image of the family in the Trinity and the Holy Family is, like Leverkühn's parody of Beethoven's Ninth Symphony in the cantata *The Lamentation of Dr Faustus*, an ironic exploitation of cultural and traditional images. If we remember that Leverkühn was to some extent at least modelled in his capacity as a musician on Arnold Schoenberg, the following remark by Mann has a sharp relevance:

> For there's no question about it: Music as well as the other arts – and not only the arts – is in a crisis which sometimes seems to threaten its very life. In literature that crisis is sometimes concealed by an ironic traditionalism. But Joyce, for example, to whom I am closer in some ways than might appear, is quite as outrageous to the mind trained in the classical romantic, realistic traditions as Schoenberg and his followers. Incidentally, I can't read Joyce either, if only because one has to be born into English culture to do so.[5]

[5] *Letters of Thomas Mann*, 2 vols. (London, 1970), vol. 2, p. 465.

This seems true. English, not Irish, culture is important here, because it is fundamentally English culture, especially in its literary aspect, which is being parodied, even though the context is an Irish and European Catholic one.

So instead of Napoleon or Beethoven, Roland or Nietzsche, Joyce has God the Father or Shakespeare, Sabellius or Arius, Christ or Parnell as the figures against which his hero defines his relationship to all that surrounds and all that resides within him. Of course these cultural heroes whose names are totemistic operate in the various novels at a level of high irony or, sometimes, gross sarcasm. Comparisons with names like these are odious for provincial youths. Altamira's conversation, however, gives Julien a glimpse of the way by which the gap between an ideal and a mediocre reality might be leapt. 'Faut-il voler, faut-il se vendre? pensa Julien. Cette question l'arrêta tout court. Il passa le reste de la nuit à lire l'histoire de la Révolution.'

In the first chapter of *Ulysses* Stephen allows the witty but shallow Irishman, Mulligan, and the dull Englishman, Haines, to expound mock-versions of his programme in self-definition, thus escaping mockery himself by his usual tactic of a silence which satirizes them by its implicit refusal to commit itself to words, even while acknowledging that the words of others are fair approximations. So we have Mulligan talking about Hamlet and Shakespeare and algebra to make fun of Haines; and Haines making fun of himself by talking about 'The Father and the Son idea. The Son striving to be atoned with the Father', while Mulligan finally sings the ballad of Joking Jesus which incorporates the same kind of relationship. The humour reflects on the subsidiary characters; the implicit seriousness of the enterprise is preserved, by his weary hauteur, with Stephen. And in *Dr Faustus*, the same kind of cross-referencing between, for example, Christ, Beethoven, the Garden of Gethsemane, and Adrian's bitter 'sleep in peace' in the *Lamentation*, is developed for the same ironic-tragic effect. It is, indeed, noticeable that each of these diabolic heroes, Julien, Stephen and Adrian, is not only set against more traditional but ineffectual characters like Monsieur de la Mole, Bloom and Zeitblom, but also that each has a Mephistophelean comrade like Altamira, Mulligan or Adrian's very real devil (whose demonism is refracted through a variety of subsidiary characters like Breisacher). In this intermediate personality we see tradition debased and revolution vulgarized. The hero can thus, by simple contrast and satirical commentary, appear the more formidable by having the inherent weaknesses of his position absorbed by someone else. There is a kind of undergraduate insolence and cleverness natural to Stephen's attitude, but Mulligan bears the blame for most of it.

Ulysses has the parodied family as its central metaphor and the stream-of-consciousness as its central technique. The two naturally have a close relationship. But first, it is worth looking at the various deformations to which the traditional family unit is subjected by Joyce. Stephen's family is broken. He has betrayed his mother and been betrayed, or at least disillusioned, by his father. He regards himself as a son who must create his own parents, since his actual parents, and Ireland and Catholicism, his symbolic parents, are unsatisfactory. He is a heretic in the sense that he conceives of (literally) the child-parent relationship in a non-traditional manner. Hence his links with Photius, Valentine, Arius, Sabellius, all of them heretics with respect to the dogmatically accepted relationship between God the Father and God the Son. This theological question of the Trinity is itself parodied on the human level by the relations between the members of the Holy Family. 'Qui vous a mis dans cette fichue position?' 'C'est le pigeon, Joseph.' The pigeon, or dove, representing the Holy Ghost, and inspiration, links both the Trinity and the Holy Family, *via* the bird image, which is reminiscent of Daedalus and his son Icarus, to the artist who is parent to his own work. The Word takes flesh, the inspired artist or Virgin gives birth to a cultural hero like Christ or Icarus or Hamlet. And, of course, as there is a sense in which Christ is his own father, theologically speaking, so is Hamlet his own father artistically speaking. Consequently the image which grows out of the multiple parodies of family relationship is that of the embryonic growth of the artist, of literary tradition, of Mrs Purefoy's baby, of heretical tradition to the point where parturition is achieved and we are presented with the finished thing . . . the work of art, the epic myth crystallized around the Icarian, Christ-like hero, Stephen.

That is largely Stephen's view of the situation, not Joyce's. For Bloom is also a member of a family which suffers breakdown. He is a father who has lost a son, a husband who has lost a wife, a Jew who has lost his homeland, his tradition, his own father through suicide and apostasy. He is a son without a father, and a father without a son. He is Christ and Joseph simultaneously, but not continuously for he is unable to grasp the various relationships in which he has become entwined. Yet although the patterns are blurred to him the substance of relationship, sympathy, is in his possession. With Stephen, the reverse is true. He sees all the patterns but understands them to be founded upon a void into which he might sink:

> A father, Stephen said, battling against hopelessness, is a necessary evil. He wrote the play in the months that followed his father's death. If you hold that he, a greying man with two marriageable daughters, with thirtyfive years of life, *nel mezzo del cammin di nostra vita*, with fifty of experience, is the beardless undergraduate from Wittenberg then you must hold that his seventyyear old mother is the lustful queen. No. The corpse of John Shakespeare does not walk the night. From hour to hour it rots and rots. He rests, disarmed of fatherhood, having devised that mystical estate upon his son. Boccaccio's Calandrino was the first and last man who felt himself with child. Fatherhood, in the sense of conscious begetting, is unknown to man. It is a mystical estate, an apostolic succession, from only begetter to only begotten. On that mystery and not on the madonna which the cunning Italian intellect flung to the mob of Europe the church is founded and founded irremovably because founded, like the world, macro- and microcosm upon the void. Upon incertitude, upon unlikelihood. *Amor matris*, subjective and objective genitive, may be the only true thing in life. Paternity may be a legal fiction. Who is the father of any son that any son should love him or he any son?

This passage is central. Generally, we are told that Bloom is the true hero of *Ulysses* because of his seeking for relation, his sympathy and his final reconciliation with Molly after the meeting with Stephen. Such a reading has undoubtedly its persuasive aspects, but it does not satisfactorily explain the fact that Bloom's relationships are all abortive, even if touchingly so; and it leaves Molly's soliloquy high and dry at the end of the novel, an unnecessary appendix to Bloom's triumph. But if instead we think of Bloom as a sympathetic man who is defeated – let's not make too much of that breakfast in bed – the novel assumes a more ample and satisfying shape. The defeat is at least pathetic, almost tragic, certainly complete. For the father has found no son, the son no father. The myth of the madonna, the virginal chastity so grotesquely epitomized in Gerty McDowell, is rejected. There is no Holy Family myth re-established in a bourgeois setting here. Instead we have a negotiated and calculated peace between the middle-class Jew and his Irish wife. The family unit does not exist except in comic terms. It is replaced by the Trinity in which each man is his own father, each man is, like Stephen, *sui generis*, alone and doomed, if he is to be fully human, to realize himself by giving birth to a full conception of himself as artist does to hero. The Trinity and Shakespeare and Daedalus are analogues for Stephen's search for a rationale and a technique by which he might realize his own identity. This is the novel's concern and this concern surely explains its executive brilliance.

The form of the novel is a disruption of the linear form assumed by the bourgeois familial novel of the Victorian era. Its various complicated and cinematic techniques are devoted to the elucidation of a new experience of what appears from the familial point of view to be a diabolical resolve to live alone, but is in fact not so much a choice as a necessity. How, after all, do Bloom and Stephen part? Like men in a Beckett novel: 'Standing perpendicular at the same door and on different sides of its base, the lines of their valedictory arms, meeting at any point and forming any angle less than the sum of two right angles.' Bloom remains to feel 'the cold of interstellar space', remember the dead, see the dawn, bump his head on re-entering the house, and so on. Stephen has gone. We are in a world of objects, bowing again under the hailstorm of data, remembered and freshly experienced, a comic, gargantuan and meaningless world. Only Molly's delight in the processes of love and femaleness, delight in fecundity itself, is left. But the delight is without a goal unless Stephen can contrive one for it. Bloom cannot.

The catechism of the Ithaca chapter takes the naturalism of the nineteenth-century novel to the point where it becomes a parody of itself. Malraux has a fine phrase for this sort of thing when he is talking about the cinema: 'Photography . . . has no scope for fiction.' By this he means that the simple recording of what happens is futile. It does not constitute art because it denies the possibility of structure. Editing is what makes the film an art form, because it substitutes the artist's ordered meaning for the camera's orderly lack of it. But there are also techniques like that of the close-up or the long shot which break up the defined space of the photograph (still or moving) into different levels, so that there is a system of cross-referencing immediately available by means of which we can be presented with a complicated and continuous meaning.

Naturalism has been as native to the novel as to the film. Its inherent tendency towards documentary inertness, one well demonstrated at the close of the nineteenth-century (Gissing and Zola), is evaded by Joyce even while he manages at the same time to retain all the sensory immediacy which naturalism was able to grant. He did this, of course, by his adoption of the stream-of-consciousness technique, whereby we are allowed to re-experience the exact effect of what the characters experience while, at the same time, by the breaking of levels or cross-referencing, we understand its significance more fully than they can. Stephen and Bloom each represent the extremes towards which Joyce's techniques tend to veer. Stephen is forever speaking in terms of a patterned, Bloom in terms of a patternless, experience. Both, of course, are caught in the total fiction. R. P. Blackmur described its formal tension best, perhaps, when he spoke of Stephen's gesture of aesthetic disdain as a means of repudiating the world and Bloom's realistic description as a means of recovering it. The two movements are interlocked in a tension which we can casually ascribe to Joyce's love-hate relationship to Dublin, and more fully now perhaps to an attitude towards a cultural crisis which had overtaken his social class, leaving him to find a means of identity outside the decayed social frame into which he, like so many other Europeans, had been born.

But there is a paradox here. The stream-of-consciousness technique is reputedly one by means of which the author absents himself from his fiction – comparatively speaking at least. It is certainly held to be at one end of the narrative spectrum which is closed at the other by the convention of the omniscient author. This is the basis for Joseph Frank's discussion of Joyce in his essay on spatial form. Yet a close reading of *Ulysses* does not support either Frank or the general idea of what the stream-of-consciousness method entails. One reason for this is, I believe, that Joyce uses the technique for largely satirical purposes and in doing so converts its renowned aims to others quite opposite. He differs from Dujardin, Richardson, Virginia Woolf, Thomas Wolfe, Faulkner and others in that he does not use the method straightforwardly by imitating the voice of his characters as he depicts their inner consciousness. He caricatures them. He uses them as a ventriloquist uses his dummy, pretending that they are speaking while at the same time letting us see how skilled he is to make us so believe. The consciousness of Gerty McDowell, for instance, is very cruelly caricatured by allowing her pap-fed romanticism to run its arc of desire like the rocket or like the Mass being said in the nearby chapel. Obviously she is not aware of these parallels. Bloom merely pronounces some of them. The author is the controlling agent here even while pretending not to be. Joyce is most present when apparently quite absent. The effect is the well-known satiric one generated by Swift on various occasions: the reader is lulled into thinking he is listening to the hack writer or to Gerty when in fact many signs in the narrative indicate Swift and Joyce. The whole secret is of course one of disguised tone, at which both authors are masters.

Even when the caricaturing intent has gone and we are in a more simply imitative situation, the system of different referential levels keeps the satiric bias prominent. Stephen is always being seen in the context of Bloom and Bloom in the context of Stephen, so that the author and reader enjoy an advantage over the character even while the pretence, the fiction, is that the reader is himself subject to the inconsequence of the character's consciousness. The stream-of-consciousness technique then is one which usually dwells on the random and minute or apparently minute detail. But in Joyce the detail is constantly controlled by the satirical purpose. The solipsism of the novel is not so much a peculiar characteristic of its people; it is representative of their state. This is the cultural phenomenon analysed by a narrative device which nevertheless insists that we recognize the degree to which solipsism has become a necessary assumption for the act of communication. Joyce plays up this paradox endlessly.

The satiric approach he adopted in this novel gives it a formal coherence which is the result of great wealth of detail being married to multiple interpretative patterns in and through the nature of the main protagonists, Bloom and Stephen, and not imposed by any solemnizing need on the author's part to defend a particular ideology or attitude. Again, the most immediate comparison would be with the persistent ironic tone that pervades Mann's work and lightens its massive structure by its fine tact and balance. Goethe's almost overpowering presence in *Lotte in Weimar* is restrained by the delicate mockery of the Goethean style in that novel. Shakespeare is not an overbearing presence in *Ulysses* because the context is always placing him into a dense pattern of popularization, quotation, insult, biographical extravagance and humour.

The erudition displayed in the novel is also palatable because it is so consistently and often so comically functional. Joyce has had a more pervasive influence on the modern novel than has Mann because his treatment of isolation produced a hero who, in the various misreadings we give him, is an iconoclastic young rebel devoted to great and precise learning for the sake of expressing his sense of futility. He shows how bankrupt the tradition is by quoting time and again from its once-solvent account to remind us that he knows what was. And what is. Stephen may be less attractive than Bloom but he is more of an object-lesson. He seems to prove that, in this apocalyptic situation, art is either the only effective therapy or possibly the only therapy, effective or not, although sympathy and pleasure are minor possibilities. Art as therapy creates virtuosity; one form of virtuosity is eccentric learning brought in from all points of the compass to a very highly defined and modern centre. In such a case, tone is all important. It must be maintained with the continuous delicacy which the overbearing weight of the material demands. Joyce was the first in a now respectably old, modern tradition to sustain this tone to the point of exhaustion.

John Barth has spoken of the literature of exhaustion as if it were a new genre. Perhaps it is. Joyce is certainly its presiding deity. Nabokov's displays of erudition and humour, Beckett's and Barth's constant ducking through epistemological hoops ripped from traditional barrels, Sartre's abandonment of literature for ideology, Borges, Robbe-Grillet, Nathalie Sarraute, all owe much to Joyce and the experimental movement which he began. The one common interest among them is the question of the nature and function of writing itself. Many novels have been written about the act of writing a novel. Some have followed Joyce in their awareness of the fact that a novel is a book and, as such, is condemned, like the dictionary or encyclopaedia but to a lesser degree, to suffer the arbitrary serial nature of print itself. It is also a consistent feature of such writing that its formal controls are so self-conscious that they become a kind of game, one favourite variant of which is to pretend that one is playing without formal controls. The subjectivism of such works is so systematic that the result is an impression of severe impersonality – Beckett and Robbe-Grillet would be perhaps the best examples of this. But *Ulysses* is the earliest such example.

Finally, one has to take into account the kind of criticism which Joyce has provoked. It is as curious in relation to the mainstream of critical writing as was *Ulysses* or *Finnegans Wake* to the mainstream of the novel. But is not a new criticism in any speculative sense. Indeed the kind of speculation one discovers in this field is of a Biblical, exegetical kind, refining certain basic truths out of the text, reading anagramatically, acrostically, allegorically, analogically. On the other hand there is the 'Reader's Guide' sort of criticism, which is really a very elaborate and sometimes useful, sometimes inane, textual apparatus. What strikes one here is how expert the reader has become. We already talk glibly of Joyce experts, Proust experts and so on. Something is obviously both wrong and inevitable here. It is wrong because one senses the loss of distinction between the author and his public. Joyce becomes the preserve of his experts, not the property of the world public. In a beautiful essay, published in 1936, Walter Benjamin described this phenomenon in relation to film. One passage (in *Illuminations*) ran:

> Thus, the distinction between author and public is about to lose its basic character. The difference becomes merely functional; it may vary from case to case. At any moment the reader is ready to turn into a writer. As expert, which he has become willy-nilly in an extremely specialized work process, even if only in some minor respect, the reader gains access to authorship. In the Soviet Union work itself is given a voice. To present it verbally is a part of a man's ability to perform the work. Literary licence is now founded on polytechnic rather than specialized training and thus becomes common property.[6]

The truth of this for Joyce criticism is all too apparent. His *Ulysses* is a complicated score that can be played in as many ways as there are conductor-experts – the Dublin expert, the Jesuit specialist, experts in the classical references, the literary allusions, the Irish history. Every reader is an expert in Joyce depending on the reader's speciality. This is not so much a tribute to Joyce's omnivorous knowledge as it is to the strange epic and yet democratic form of his work. It is, after all, the odyssey of a specialist, Stephen, and the *homme moyen sensuel*, Bloom.

It is a secret book and yet an open one, culminating with its fascinating formal propriety in a soliloquy which is also an interior monologue, a public and a private act simultaneously. We will continue to accumulate our specialist knowledge of what the text conceals. But everything it conceals it also reveals if only

[6] *Illuminations* (London, 1970), p. 234.

we look long and sharply enough. Joyce is one of the liberators of the mass consciousness of the twentieth century. He exemplifies it in its sympathetic inconsequence in Bloom and in its splintered but undeterred specialisms in Stephen. Their obsessions are ours, as they are Leverkühn's and Julien Sorel's. When all coherence is indeed gone, and the family, the revolution, the musical tradition have all been transmogrified into something else, what is to be done? Even to understand is not enough. One must live through the collapse, alone. The loneliness is the basis for pride; but it has its intolerable aspects. 'Qu'on m'aime', says *notre paysan, notre provincial*. 'Qu'on m'aime'.

7

JOYCE AND NATIONALISM

It is well known that Joyce, like Stephen Dedalus, considered himself to be the slave of two masters, one British and one Roman. It is equally well known that he repudiated the Irish Literary Revival, going so far as to characterize 'Gogarty and Yeats and Colm [*sic*] the blacklegs of literature'. Repudiating British and Roman imperialisms and rejecting Irish nationalism and Irish literature which seemed to be in service to that cause, he turned away from his early commitment to socialism and devoted himself instead to a highly apolitical and wonderfully arcane practice of writing. Such, in brief, is the received wisdom about Joyce and his relationship to the major political issues of his time. Although some revision of this estimate has recently begun,[1] it remains as one of the more secure asumptions about his life and work.

It is, however, seriously misleading to view Joyce in this way. His very real disaffection with politics, Irish or international, enhanced his sense of isolation and was translated into his creed of artistic freedom. Since history could not yield a politics, it was compelled to yield an aesthetic. In this process, disaffection became disdain, political reality dissolved into fiction, fiction realized itself purely in terms of its own medium, language. As a consequence, the finite nature of historical fact was supplanted by the infinite, or near-infinite, possibilities of language. Language was cast into a form which would extend the range of possible signification to an ultimate degree of openness, thereby setting itself against the closed world of limited and limiting historical fact. Stephen Dedalus, in the course of his history lesson, wonders about the brute facts of the deaths of Pyrrhus and Caesar: 'They are

[1] See Colin McCabe, *James Joyce and the Revolution of the Word* (London, 1978), and Dominic Manganiello, *Joyce's Politics* (London, 1980).

not to be thought away. Time has branded them and fettered they are lodged in the room of the infinite possibilities they have ousted. But can those have been possible seeing that they never were? Or was that only possible which came to pass?' The finite has replaced the infinite. Minor modifications are, of course, possible. In *Ulysses*, we learn that Bloom perhaps 'gave the idea for Sinn Fein to Griffith' or that he may have picked up Parnell's fallen hat and returned it to him after a fracas. But this is harmless embroidery. Parnell's downfall and death is a brute fact that Joyce found it more difficult to counter. He took if from the world of history and re-established it in the world of fiction by unfettering it from actual circumstances and making of it a maieutic image which helped him to understand what he already knew – that in Ireland possibility would always be humiliated into squalid fact. The more squalid the fact, the more finite it seems. Joyce's Dublin was, after all, a carefully composed image of squalor and the 'naturalism' of his rendering of the city claims our assent because it is so unflinching in the face of all that is mean and unpleasant.[2]

History, then, must be countered by fiction. But the fiction, to perform its necessary function, must have broken its traditional affiliations with history. Plot and theme, those elements which produce the story, are to be subdued, even abolished, and replaced by language. Even though language will inevitably carry the traces of these story patterns, it will not allow them to dominate. The last six sections of *Ulysses* upset many of the expectations raised by the preceding twelve because they abort the story element in order to redeem the status of language. Even the story of Stephen's or of Bloom's consciousness is a kind of internal history. We are deprived of that too. In *Ulysses* and, more so in *Finnegans Wake*, Joyce manages to achieve interrelationships between the various elements in the novels which cannot be effectively demonstrated in a summary of the stories of the works. Mere story ousts too many possibilities which language retains.

A history as calamitous as Ireland's could certainly do with some countering, but Joyce was by no means the first Irish writer to feel this. In 1907 he spoke of Ireland's claim, articulated in the nineteenth century, to a renewed cultural identity: 'the Irish nation's insistence on developing its own culture by itself is not so much the demand of a young nation that wants to make good in the European concert as the demand of a very old nation to

[2] See J.C.C. Mays, 'Some Comments on the Dublin of *Ulysses*' in *Ulysses, Cinquante Ans Après* (Pan's, 1974).

renew under new forms the glories of a past civilization.'[3] Among
his contemporaries, Yeats and Pearse were the most articulate of
the cultural nationalists, systematically rereading the past in
order to supply a model for future development. The differences
which separate them are less important than the similarities they
share. Both sanctified Ireland as a legendary and revolutionary
place which was again about to take her place among the nations.

Nationalism, as preached by Yeats or by Pearse, was a crusade
for decontamination. The Irish essence was to be freed of the
infecting Anglicizing virus and thus restored to its primal purity
and vigour. The Gaelic League pointed one way towards this
restoration – the recovery of the Irish language and the displacement, partial or total, of English. Pearse concentrated on the
educational system, the famous Murder Machine as he called it,
and its replacement by one known to the Gael of Celtic times,
nobler, more liberal, more suited to the national temperament.
Yeats and Synge looked to the emergence of a new literature in
English vivified by the linguistic energies of an Irish civilization
not yet blighted by the inanities of 'parliamentary speeches and
the gutter press'.[4] The presiding opposition between a 'spiritual'
Ireland and a 'mechanical' England lent itself to an immense
number of subsidiary variations – sexual purity as opposed to
sexual squalor, ancestral faith as opposed to rootless urban alienation, just rebellion as against imperial coercion, enduring faith as
against shallow modernism, imaginative vitality as against dehy-
drated utilitarianism. History too could be realized in a new form.
Pearse's line of heroes (Tone, Emmet, Davis, Lalor, Mitchel) and
Yeats's line (Berkeley, Swift, Burke, Goldsmith) both had their
justification in their essential contact with the spirit of Irishness
which was retained by the mass of the people.

It would be inaccurate, however, to claim too close a kinship
between Pearse, Yeats and Joyce in this respect, even though all
three do visibly share in the heroicizing spirit which informed the
whole Irish Literary Revival. In 1914, in a speech delivered in
New York, Pearse spoke of patriotism in terms which are precisely
those rejected by Stephen Dedalus in his *non serviam*:

> For patriotism is at once a faith and a service . . . a faith
> which is of the same nature as religious faith and is one of

[3] *James Joyce: The Critical Writings*, eds. E. Mason and R. Ellmann (London, 1964),
p. 157.
[4] W.B. Yeats, *Explorations* (London, 1962), p. 42.

the eternal witnesses in the heart of man to the truth that we are of divine kindred . . . So that patriotism needs service as the condition of its authenticity, and it is not sufficient to say 'I believe' unless one can say also 'I serve'.[5]

Such belief and such service as Pearse demands repelled Yeats as much as it did Joyce. It refused freedom to the mind. It had, in Yeats's words, pedantry not 'culture' as its distinguishing mark and for him 'Culture is the sanctity of the intellect'.[6] In his Journal, for 12 March 1909, he wrote:

There is a sinking of national feeling which is very simple in its origin. You cannot keep the idea of a nation alive where there are no national institutions to reverence, no national success to admire, without a model of it in the mind of the people. You can call it 'Kathleen-ni-Houlihan' or the 'Shan Van Vocht' in a mood of simple feeling, and love that image, but for the general purposes of life you must have a complex mass of images, making up a model like an architect's model. The Young Ireland poets created this with certain images rather simple in their conception that filled the mind of the young – Wolfe Tone, King Brian, Emmet, Owen Roe, Sarsfield, the Fisherman of Kinsale. It answered the traditional slanders on Irish character too, and started an apologetic habit, but its most powerful work was this creation of sensible images for the affections, vivid enough to follow men on to the scaffold. As was necessary, the ethical ideas involved were very simple, needing neither study nor unusual gifts for the understanding of them. Our own movement began by trying to do the same thing in a more profound and enduring way.[7]

But, Yeats goes on to say in a famous passage, the appearance of Synge's work persuaded him that the Revival 'must be content to express the individual'. 'The Irish people were not educated enough to accept as an image of Ireland anything more profound, more true of human nature as a whole, than the schoolboy thought of Young Ireland'.[8] All this appears in the midst of Yeats's attack on the journalistic spirit which had infected the

[5] Collected Works of Padraic H. Pearse: Political Writings and Speeches, ed. Desmond Ryan (Dublin, 1917–22), p. 65.
[6] W.B. Yeats, Memoirs, ed. Denis Donoghue (London, 1972), p. 179.
[7] Ibid., p. 184.
[8] Ibid.

Gaelic League and the national movement as a whole, degrading it to little more than an exercise in chauvinism.

Despite the differences which separate them, Yeats and Joyce repudiate the more pronounced forms of political nationalism – those associated with Pearse and with the journalism of newspapers like D. P. Moran's *The Leader* – on the same grounds. It is, in effect, too crude, too schoolboyish, too eager to demand a spirit of solidarity and service that has more in common with propaganda than it has with art. But whereas Yeats did indeed give up, to some extent, 'the deliberate creation of a kind of Holy City in the imagination' and replace it with images of enduring heroism and not-so-durable authority, Joyce remained faithful to the original conception of the Revival. His Dublin became the Holy City of which Yeats had despaired.

Joyce had been as fascinated by the career and achievement of James Clarence Mangan as Yeats had been by William Carleton. For Yeats these writers were premonitions of what was yet to come. But for Joyce, Mangan was in fact the finished product, the figure in whom 'an hysterical nationalism receives its final justification'.[9] His two lectures on Mangan (1902 and 1907) are highly ambivalent, for he is sympathetic to this *poète maudit* in so far as he portrays the plight of the artist in Ireland, and unsympathetic to him in so far as Mangan remained subject to those environing forces which he, Joyce, must elude. Joyce is as willing as is Pearse to speak of Ireland's soul, to speak of the nation as a spiritual entity, and to conceive of her plight as one in which something ethereal has been overwhelmed by something base. In his review of Lady Gregory's *Poets and Dreamers*, published in 1903 under the title *The Soul of Ireland*, he wrote of Ireland's 'one belief – a belief in the incurable ignobility of the forces that have overcome her',[10] although the same article characteristically reveals his acid contempt for the Gregorian old men with 'red eyes and short pipe'.[11] Joyce, in other words, believes in Ireland and the sorry tale of her doomed spirit through the ages. His conception of history is dominated by the idea of the noble spirit debased by ignoble domination and demeaning circumstance. Like Pearse, he assumed that there was a necessary connection between belief

[8] Ibid.

[9] Joyce, *The Critical Writings*. p. 186.

[10] Ibid., p. 105.

[11] *A Portrait of the Artist as a Young Man*, ed. Chester G. Anderson (New York, 1968), p. 251.

and service. The question was, then, to what should the service be given: Church, Nation, State? Refusing all of these left him with the idea of service to art.

Still, while the service is to art, art is itself in service to the soul of Ireland. This soul is still uncreated. It is the function of true art to create it — a function all the more necessary since all other forms of Irish activity had failed by producing a debased version of that spiritual reality. Whether it was in Mangan or in Lady Gregory, in the Citizen or in Buck Mulligan, in Arthur Griffith or in John Redmond, Ireland found herself travestied. The new day that threatened to dawn was always an Ivy Day, or a Day of the Rabblement, and its light would always break on a committee room or a theatre shadowed by betrayal. Until, that is, the fictive day of 16 June 1904. Joyce, in other words, put his art in service to something which would be created only by that act of service. The absence of Ireland would be overcome in his art; there it would achieve presence. But the presence is itself dependent on the conviction that, before Joyce, there was nothing. The desire of nationalism pales in comparison with this desire. An act of writing which will replace all earlier acts; which will replace all politics; which will make the ignoble noble; which will make history into culture by making it the material of consciousness — this extraordinary ambition is at the heart of Joyce's enterprise. Yeats had it and gave it up for the theme of individuality, despairing of Ireland's incompleteness. But for Joyce, that incompletion was the very ground of his art. The unfinished and the uncreated culture provided the opportunity for the most comprehensive, the most finished, the most boundlessly possible art. The colonial culture produced imperial art. A culture which had never known the idea of totality was to be embodied in art. Further, it could produce such art precisely because it was so bereft. Only a minority culture could seek an articulation of itself as a total culture. Pearse and Yeats knew this. In that respect they were nationalists. But such articulation had to be achieved by a process of repudiation, the rejection of all previous abortive attempts, the incorporation of them as imperfect paradigms and the extension of the ironic conception of the paradigm and the harbinger into a principle of structure. Yeats and Joyce knew this and in that respect they went beyond nationalism into a universalism for which history, myth and legend supplied the imagery merely. The supreme action was writing.

Therefore in Joyce we can never forget the primacy of writing as action. Its early 'scrupulous meanness' in *Dubliners*, the delicate fission in *Portrait* between the narrative and the narrated voice of Stephen, the interior monologues and parodies of *Ulysses*, the multilingual voices of *Finnegans Wake*, all coerce the reader into accepting the text as writing which is calling attention to its written nature. Even the plots of these books, in so far as they can be said to have plots, are so designed that their interconnections are aggressively verbal, insisting on the linkages of words rather than on the illusion of events. Joyce dismantles the agreed relation between author and reader whereby fiction was allowed autonomy as story. Instead, he insists on the dependence of the story and of the very idea of fiction upon language. Given that, he can then make language constitutive of reality not merely regulative of it. Irish nationalism was one of the forces which enabled him to do this, largely because it had been trying to do that itself for over half a century before Joyce wrote.

Since the last decade of the eighteenth century Ireland had learned to believe in the relationship between literature and rebellion as a natural one. Burke had pointed to the influence of men of letters on the French Revolution, blaming them for the introduction into European politics of an element of abstract ideological fury which had never existed before. Nineteenth-century Ireland tended to follow the remedy promoted by Coleridge in his completion of Burke's thought – the establishment of an intellectual clerisy as an integral part of the structures of the state, safeguarding the historical continuity and cultural complexity of the nation's heritage. In Ireland this led to the foundation of the *Dublin University Magazine* and the attempt by Sir Samuel Ferguson to create a cultural identity for all the factions of Irish society, past and present, by conjoining a conservative Tory politics with a cultural nationalism. But since the Irish situation was a semi-colonial one, the aspiration towards cultural identity could not be indulged without involving itself in the aspiration towards political identity. Thomas Moore's sentimental songs helped to create that atmosphere of misty nostalgia in which the ballad, especially the political ballad, became a more effective stimulator of national consciousness than the essay, poem or novel. But poetry did tend towards the ballad form as the only one in which the two impulses, political and cultural, were effectively fused. Otherwise, poetry ran the risk of becoming 'literary', out of touch with the deepest aspirations of the people. The myth of Mangan takes its origin from this complex of factors, all the more enhanced by the Young Ireland movement's disagreement with O'Connell and its consequent tendency to move towards violent rebellion and away from constitutional agitation. Thus, the Irish intelligentsia was split into two factions – one, led by Ferguson, which was pro-union, politically conservative, and romantic-nationalist in the cultural sense; the other, anti-union, politically separatist and also romantically nationalist. Yeats brought these two streams together in his life and work. Joyce repudiated both.

This is not to say he was not interested. Joyce recognized the importance of Arthur Griffith's Sinn Fein movement and how formidable 'this last phase of Fenianism' was in having 'once more remodelled the character of the Irish people'.[12] Parnell and O'Leary, the constitutional and the physical force movements and their interaction on one another under the pressure of Westminster and the Vatican, absorbed a good deal of his attention. The Ireland that sought to remodel herself while 'serving both God and Mammon, letting herself be milked by England and yet increasing Peter's pence' was, nevertheless, politically vibrant, not at all like the Yeatsian version of an Ireland that turned its attentions to art after its disillusion with politics after Parnell. But if Yeats's Ireland was one in which the Celtic past was to be embraced, Joyce's Ireland was one in which spiritual reality did not yet exist. Stephen Dedalus's diary records: 'Michael Robartes remembers forgotten beauty and, when his arms wrap her round, he presses in his arms the loveliness which has long faded from the world. Not this. Not at all. I desire to press in my arms the loveliness which has not yet come into the world.'[13]

The relationship between literature and politics was not, for Joyce, mediated through a movement, a party, a combination or a sect. For him, the act of writing became an act of rebellion; rebellion was the act of writing. Its aim was to bring into the world a loveliness that still did not exist. Such writing therefore achieves its aspiration by coming into existence. It serves only what it is. Between the idea of service and the idea of the thing served, the distance has disappeared. In pursuing this conception of the artist and art, Joyce was presenting himself, via Stephen Dedalus, with a specifically Irish problem which had wider implications. How was he to create as literature something which would otherwise have no existence and yet was believed to exist

[12] Joyce, *The Critical Writings*, p. 191.
[13] *A Portrait of the Artist as a Young Man*, p. 251.

already? The idea of Ireland still uncreated, awaited its realization. The minority culture desired total embodiment.

But its embodiment in literature inevitably meant its embodiment in the English language. This was a central paradox. For English literature supplied Ireland with no serviceable models for imitation. Irish experience, different from English and anxious to assert that difference to the ultimate extent, needed a new form of realization which would not only differentiate itself in formal terms from its English counterpart, but would also have to do so while fretting in the shadow of the colonizer's language. In accepting these challenges, formal and linguistic, in accepting the unique role of the artist in whom a minority culture, characterized by incompleteness and fracture, would achieve completeness and coherence, Joyce necessarily became a rebel against all that preceded him.

His rebellion took three forms, corresponding to the three forces from which he had to extricate himself. The Roman imperium he overcame by inversion, taking the idea of priesthood and dedicated vocation and applying it to a secular art. The British imperium was overcome by parody, taking the tradition of literature as it had expressed itself in the novel, and scrutinizing its silent assumptions. The Irish imperium he overcame by exile, refusing the various forms of commitment and renewal which it preached and preferring instead isolation. But these three forms of rebellion – exile, parody, vocation – were strategies of displacement, not radical amputations. The Church, the English literary tradition and Ireland all remained as forces in his imagination. They operated under the aegis of irony, but the irony depended on their presence. Joyce was always to be the Irish writer who refused the limitations of being Irish; the writer of English who refused the limitations of being an English writer; the priest who refused the limitations of the conventional priesthood. His loyalty to himself was measured by the disloyalty he displayed towards the forces which had moulded him. It is not, therefore, surprising that he should have been obsessed by the notion of betrayal. Betrayal for the sake of integrity is his form of displacement and also lies at the source of his ironic method. Stephen betrays his mother and becomes superbly ironical at the expense of those who, like Buck Mulligan, wish to confront him with this fact. For Mulligan does not see the integrity which Stephen seeks through this betrayal. Instead, Mulligan reveals himself to be treacherous, for he is blind to the existence of integrity as a possibility. Ill-formed, he has no part in that loveliness which still does not exist, although its presence is often sentimentally invoked. Mulligan's Hellenism, the Citizen's Celticism, are twins. They indicate the existence of an ideal which they fail to embody. Bloom, the victim of so many betrayals, by father and by wife, embodies integrity without knowing what it is. Stephen, the sponsor of so many betrayals, knows what it is without embodying it. Each is the fulfilment of the other's desire.

Yet *Ulysses* is not primarily concerned with the alienation of these two men from their native culture. Although they are both in a minority – each is indeed a minority of one – they are not provincial as the other Dubliners are. To be excluded from parents, lovers, ideologies, and yet to be in some way respected as out of the ordinary, is the fate of the Universal Man in the local culture. They are concerned with the Mystery of Being, not with the mystery of being Dubliners or of being Irish. The relationship between parent and child is one which they understand as part of an ever-present identity and anxiety. For others, it is an historical relationship. Historical relationships are determined by the fidelity shown towards them. Whether it is the history of the Fenians or of the development of English prose, of the history of Dublin or of church dogma or one's own family, the idea of sequence demands that one should conform to the pattern of the past so that, in doing so, the pattern becomes extended or fulfilled in oneself.

Stephen and Bloom, however, try to avoid sequence and to replace it with simultaneity. For them, history is not a record of facts but the material of their consciousness. The act of reflection constantly moulds the past into the present. Their present determines the past. Their history is always the present. The interior monologue or stream-of-consciousness method is appropriate to them. For in it, the kaleidoscope of past and present can be constantly shaken to form transient patterns which are not essentially historical but psychological. The apparently uncensored reflections of Stephen and Bloom allow for the emergence of ostensibly inconsequential or random associations, all the more attractive because they are, so to speak, 'unofficial' versions of history (Bloom's vision of the Middle East, Stephen's version of Shakespeare and *Hamlet*) but also cryptic because they seem to be so arbitrary. It would be possible to speculate upon Joyce's increasing interest in the liberty bestowed upon an author by the exploitation of these uncensored states of consciousness. Below the threshold of complete wakefulness, there is a universe of associative patterns which, in their unofficial way, might be more real or universal or simply more interesting than the world of recorded fact can provide. But Joyce is not simply opening a Pandora's box. Whatever emerges has to be named, organized, 'placed' in some context of relation. The mode of Stephen's thought, or of Shem's, might reveal something of that character's personality, type or bias. But it is most remarkable for the way in which it established itself as only one mode among others in a larger discourse which is meaningful to the reader in a way not available to the putative character. The loss of censorship in relation to a single consciousness demands the articulation of a final, all-encompassing orderliness in which the uncensored reflections finally lose their cryptic, arbitrary status. In getting rid of the 'author' at one level, Joyce re-establishes him more emphatically at another. His chaos is local; his order is universal.

Although a dreamer like HCE is both narrator and narrated, the very scope of his consciousness, which embraces world history, indicates his universal status. Yet his universality, precisely because it avoids the stable identifications which are possible in the local Irish context – that of Irish nationalism – produces a form of consciousness which is essentially esoteric. The Universal Hero, in other words, can only be read by a specialist audience. He does not produce a universal language. Instead we are given a language in which the desire for universality expresses itself, paradoxically, in the most arcane form imaginable. In breaking away from the restrictions of a local nationality and from the kinds of identity conferred upon him by tradition, Joyce achieved a language which, by the sheer number of its polyglot associations, appears to be all-inclusive and yet which, by the sheer complexity of its narrative orders, manages to be almost wilfully exclusive. A text like *Finnegans Wake* is characterized by a dispute between the anarchic possibilities of its vocabulary and the despotic demands of its various structuring paradigms. On occasion, we can perceive that the male voices seem to adhere to a form of discourse which is seeking to achieve discrimination and pattern, while the female voices tend towards an undifferentiated mode of discourse in which discriminations are blurred and in which the very process of language being formed is revealed to us. This is also, to a lesser extent, true of *Ulysses*, in which Molly's coda to the novel restores us to the surging principle of existence itself, free from the helpless orderings to which Stephen and Bloom have tried to subject it. Of course, in each work, the sexual differentiation is important, since it is aligned with the opposition between ordered

102

discourse and discourse which attempts to elude order. Nevertheless, the central problem remains insolubly there. The difficulty of
these texts is an indication of Joyce's failure to discover for
Universal Man a language comparable in its serviceability to the
language for local man which had been developed by writers like
Pearse. The 'schoolboy thought' of Young Ireland was replaced by
the language and thought of a specialist researcher. In that sense,
Joyce's politics, although it contains the idea of solidarity, also
retains with that the idea of a privileged isolation – the isolation of
the extraordinary individual.

In many ways it is appropriate that, in the twentieth century, a
work of imagination should also be a work of research and that
the burden of research should be imposed upon the reader as
well as upon the author. Yet all the important Irish writers of the
period between 1880 and 1940 were engaged in a kind of
research which produced discourses which had very specific
relationships to the Irish nationalist movement. The language of
Synge and of O'Casey, of George Moore (at least in *The Lake, The
Untilled Field* and in *Hail and Farewell*) and of Yeats is, in many
important respects, quoted language. That is to say, it is offered to
us as a sample of a larger discourse which enfolds and is characteristic of a nation or a group. Nationalism is one of these larger
discourses. It is not simply a way of speaking, but a way of
speaking directed towards a specific goal – the goal of vitality,
reawakening, recovery. The highly stylized writing associated with
all these authors, the fascination with heroism, the extraordinary
individual, the willingness of all of them to subvert that heroism
even while sponsoring it, gives them, when we look at these
characteristics more closely, a striking family resemblance to Joyce.
The absence of such a resemblance would be even more surprising
than its existence, but Joyce did succeed in making the separation
between his work and that of his contemporaries appear more
complete that in fact it is. In *Portrait*, Stephen Dedalus is, so to speak,
quoted into existence by nursery rhymes, political squabbles,
church doctrine, literature. Then he responds by quoting on his
own initiative – Aquinas, the villanelle, the diary. Possessed by
language, he comes to possess it. Pateresque cadences and the
vocabulary of Irish nationalism and of Irish Catholicism combine to
form a new pattern, Stephen's, not reducible to these component
parts yet certainly including them. Stephen endows his existence
with a figurative meaning which might seem to be far in excess of
the resources of his own life to sustain. But his social and political

experience has been of such figurative crises – Ireland and its uncrowned king, Catholicism and its hell of endless torment. In his culture, imagination figured powerfully *as true* what fact could not provide. The crowned king of Ireland, Edward VII, is a sorry figure beside the uncrowned king, Parnell. Even the points of similarity, their sexual escapades, and the different reactions to them, for instance, ironically enhance the contrast.

There are many historical parallels in *Ulysses* and in *Finnegans Wake* which become a source of frustration if taken straightforwardly and yet which have definite ordering functions in the economy of these narratives. The parallel between the Jews and the Irish in *Ulysses* is one well-known instance, ratified by various analogies between Moses and Parnell, the fondness of Irish Home Rulers for this sort of comparison, the extension from that of the Hebraic and Hellenistic contrast, with the Hebraic related to politics, the Hellenistic to art. Yet no matter how urgently we pursue this parallel we can come to no satisfactory conclusion about the bearing it has on the relationship between Stephen and Bloom, or on any other relationship between people in the novel. Equally, while noting its recurrence, and the manner in which it thereby establishes certain patterns throughout the novel, it is impossible to specify for it any particular function other than the sheer function of being there as a possible, but not as a necessary, system of ordering. It has to compete with many others – Bloom's bar of soap, for instance – and it seems to be in the end as arbitrarily introduced as they are. In the same way, Homer's epic is probably less useful to a reader of *Ulysses* than a knowledge of *Hamlet*. A knowledge of Vico's theories, or of Croce's rediscovery of Vico, is helpful for understanding certain important formal aspects of *Finnegans Wake*. But is this knowledge of the same order as that which John Garvin supplies when he tells us about the background to the Maamtrasna murders of August 1882, an incident which also supplies a recurrent motif-phrase to the novel?[14] The switching back and forth from one order or kind of knowledge to another, and the discovery that the knowledge is useful only to a limited and formal degree, never in a substantial, historical sense, leaves the reader in the curious position of realizing that the kind of research which these books demand is itself parodied by the way in which its discoveries are shown to lead nowhere.

[14] John Garvin, *James Joyce's Disunited Kingdom and the Irish Dimension* (Dublin, 1976), pp. 159–69.

Ezra Pound's view of Joyce, although obviously dominated by the development of his own political ideas, is persuasive. In 1922 he wrote:

Joyce has set out to do an inferno, and he has done an inferno.

He has presented Ireland under British domination, a picture so veridic that a ninth-rate coward like Shaw (Geo. B.) dare not even look it in the face. By extension he has presented the whole occident under the domination of capital.[15]

But in 1933, he 'can not see that Mr Joyce's later work concerns more than a few specialists'[16] and claims that Anthony Trollope would have been more alert to the main historical forces of the present than is the Joyce of *Work in Progress*. A more subdued and sustained version of this point is made by Alick West[17] and by Gyorgy Lukács in his essays on Thomas Mann.[18] It is curious to see the right and the left wing combine to accuse Joyce of passivity, indifference to the historical realities of the present, absorption in language as a form of boredom, indifference as a symptom of the decadence of the imperialist era in which subjectivity had become the principle and not the theme of modern literature. Yet the assumption upon which these views rest is the very one which Joyce would have most fiercely challenged – namely the assumption that his fiction stood over against a reality by which it could be tested. Instead, his fiction was creating a reality which otherwise would have no existence and in which the external reality, used so often as a criterion in so-called realistic fiction, would be only one ingredient among others. He had learned from Irish nationalism the power of a vocabulary in bringing to existence that which otherwise had none except in the theatre of words. Joyce, we may say, discovered the fictive nature of politics. His work is, in consequence, an examination of the nature of the fictive – how it is created, how words operate within and without patterns of formal symmetry, how history can be magnified or reduced to archetype, how dream becomes speech and sounds become words, accident becomes design.

[15] *Pound/Joyce: The Letters of Ezra Pound to James Joyce, with Pound's Essays on Joyce*, ed. Forrest Read, with commentary (London, 1968), p. 198.
[16] Ibid., p. 251.
[17] Alick West, *Crisis and Criticism* (London, 1975), pp. 104–30.
[18] G. Lukács, *Essays on Thomas Mann*, trs. Stanley Mitchell (London, 1964), pp. 104–5.

Therefore, to attempt to understand Joyce's relationship to politics or to language in terms of simple oppositions – nationalism outfaced by socialism, socialism outfaced by an apolitical stance, sequence supplanted by simultaneity, design replaced by accident, stream-of-consciousness by ventriloquism or parody – is misleading. No simple opposition and no version of a dialectical tension between these and other principles or attitudes is sufficient to do justice to his fundamental concerns. He belonged to a culture in which there was no congruence between established structures and political or social rhetoric. The various efforts to establish such a congruence were all failures. No group had its ambitions realized. Home Rulers, republicans, unionists, Anglo-Irish, socialists, Irish language enthusiasts, were all disappointed by what finally emerged in the twenties and thirties. Joyce was not directly concerned with these failures as such. He was more concerned with what they indicated about the relation between structure and language. Rather than consign his fiction to any single structure or set of structures, he investigated the activity of structuration itself as it was revealed through the exploration of language, discovering always that there is something excessive in language, something which is of its nature beyond the reach of any structuring principle that can be articulated and yet is within the reach of a structuring activity. For language is itself that structuring activity. Many of the coincidences that surround Joyce's work seem entirely accidental. Much that is discovered is *ben trovato*, not designed. Yet that in itself ratifies the nature of Joyce's enterprise. Language is both arbitrary and systematic. The two features seem to exist in ratio to one another.

So it is with his politics. He repudiated Irish nationalism, socialism, Irish history. He invented the figure of treachery as a way of reading Ireland when he wished to make the repudiation emphatic; a figure of contamination when he wished to make his sympathy with Ireland predominate; a figure of subservience and slavishness when he wished to mix his sympathy with his repudiation. But this is merely a selection of possible figures. Many others are used. Rather than seek one which predominates over the others, we do better to note their variety, the inexhaustibility of the figures, the endlessness of language in creating the very thing to which it apparently refers. Out of Shem's body and biography, world history flows in a continuous unfolding, the very same Shem whom Shaun had berated for having 'kusky-

---

[19] *Finnegans Wake* (London, 1964), p. 176.

korked himself up tight in his inkbattle house'[19] during the War of Independence. Exiled from Ireland's turmoil, ensnared in *Ulysses*,

> this Esuan Menschavik and the first till last alchemist wrote over every square inch of the only foolscap available, his own body, till by its corrosive sublimation one continuous present tense integument slowly unfolded all marryvoising moodmoulded cyclewheeling history (thereby, he said, reflecting from his own individual person life unlivable, trans-accidentated through the slow fires of consciousness into a dividual chaos, perilous, potent, common to allflesh, human only, mortal) but with each word that would not pass away the squidself which he had squirtscreened from the crystalline world waned chagreengold and doriangrayer in its dudhud. This exists that isits after having been said we know.[20]

That which exists depends for its existence on having been said. Even the Ireland of *Ulysses* is included with the Ireland of the War of Independence and the later Ireland of De Valera, after 1932, into the Ireland of *Finnegans Wake*. Ireland, in such a world of words, is a protean sound. Reality is not conferred upon it by Eccles Street or De Valera. Nothing in history, not even the readers of this English, could confine it within any conventional structure of knowledge or understanding. It was and is not 'fettered or lodged in the room of the infinite possibilities they have ousted'. 'You brag of your brass castle or your tyled house in ballyfermont? Niggs, niggs and niggs again. For this was a stinksome inkenstink, quite puzzonal to the wrottel. Smatterafact, Angles aftanon browsing there thought no Edam reeked more rare.'

Indeed nothing reeked more rare. Ireland as an entity, cultural or political, was incorporated in all its mutations within Joyce's work as a model of the world and, more importantly, as a model of the fictive. In revealing the essentially fictive nature of political imagining, Joyce did not repudiate Irish nationalism. Instead he understood it as a potent example of a rhetoric which imagined as true structures that did not and were never to exist outside language. Thus, as a model, it served him as it served Yeats and others. It enabled them to apprehend the nature of fiction, the process whereby the imagination is brought to bear upon the reality which it creates.

[20] Ibid., pp. 185–6.

8
o'casey and yeats:
exemplary dramatists

It is almost superfluous to say that O'Casey, more than any other Irish dramatist (or writer), engaged with Irish and with world politics in a series of particularly fierce battles. It is, I think, necessary to add that there is a coarsening element in his work related to his attempt to make sense of contemporary political situations in the light of an imperfectly conceived moral system. O'Casey does not in any of his plays, and least of all in the three early ones which established his reputation, develop a critique of Irish history or politics, even though he makes gestures in that direction. Politics, as he knew it, was the occasion of his plays; morality was their subject.

He offers morality as a form of behaviour necessarily alternative to the political behaviour of his people, whereas in fact it is neither an alternative nor a necessary corrective. He sponsors, largely through his women, a humanism (with Christian overtones included for the sake of sarcasm or satire) in which one can believe only in so far as it is separated from the political pressures to which his male characters are subjected. Therefore, the humanism has an inbuilt advantage. It is free of all pressure save that of the author's insistence upon it. It is the norm of the 'ordinary' people, i.e. not what people should be like but what they are, fundamentally, like. Every deviation from it, via fanaticism, dream, egoism, is seen as a distortion of the average personality. To so glorify the average is simply sentimentalism; to make Minnie Powell heroic is a sentimental risk only partially justified by the result, which is to make Davoren criminally ridiculous. To construe the average into the heroic at the expense of a political situation against which he is opposed, is propagandistic. It is this role of morality as a form of satiric propaganda which more than anything else makes so much of O'Casey's work linguistically strident and melodramatic. This is not, of course, to say that he should not have analysed or attempted to analyse Irish history and politics in a hostile fashion. But the hostility of his approach should be dramatically incorporated into the humanism to which we are alternatively directed. It is not. Crudely, the recipe is that we should take politics away and supplant it by humanism, even though we have just seen how powerfully humanism can be supplanted by politics. If the latter can happen, and be shown to have happened, the former cannot. The recipe, on his own account, begins to look utopian.

In *Juno* we get a 'great' speech, morality's set piece, deploring the state 'o' chassis separating hearts o' stone' (male) and 'hearts o' flesh' (female). O'Casey, however, is as willing to exploit the comedy of the chaos as he is unwilling to probe the tragedy of the stony-hearted. There is no point in applying labels (tragic, tragi-comic and so forth) to his plays. There *is* point, though, in watching to see how the comedy and tragedy are counterpointed one against the other. The Paycock's fecklessness and irresponsibility seem comic shadow to his son Johnny's cowering nationalism. One ends in drunkenness, the other in death – the drunkenness there, perhaps, to point up the futility of the death. Yet the political death is, dramatically speaking, deserved, while the drunkenness is, in the same terms, excused. It is 'human'. So one concludes that drunkenness is there to present Johnny's death in a hostile, not tragic, manner, as the political manifestation of chaos – and then, to obscure matters further, to occasion Juno's humanist lament for a death from which our sympathy has already bled away. It seems proper that the Paycock should have the last word. The 'chassis' afflicts the play as much as the world. All of O'Casey's gunmen are shadows, and consequently his aggression towards politics is a form of shadow-boxing.

O'Casey does not deny freedom. Rather the reverse; he propagandizes on its behalf. Nevertheless, he *does* deny those necessities – such as political fate – against which, or even in terms of which, freedom has to be defined. It can be strongly argued that the determining forces against which his slum-dwellers must fight are primarily economic. So we have Bentham, with his promise of escape into the petit bourgeoisie, cheating Mary into pregnancy and desertion. The false hopes of the legacy, the bogus theory of energy and the second-rate yogi which he promotes represent the delusions which afflict the Boyles and the Tancreds and all others in the tenement. But Bentham is not an embodiment of these delusions. He is a pallid purveyor of them. Besides, these delusions belong to the sub-plot. They do not primarily focus the play's climax; politics does that. But, as I have said, politics operates in this play merely as a distortion of the human. Moral freedom, or aspiration, as pronounced by Juno, is not discovered in and through conflict with economic or political forces. Dramatically speaking, it is their by-product; 'chassis' is their primary consequence. Yet the dramatic by-product is proffered as the central theme. Something is askew.

An eidetic image is an illusion from the past. To dwell in it is an example of bad faith. O'Casey's eidetic image, which is most marked in his early plays but takes a variety of forms in all of them, is the image of the family or, in another mode, his image of disillusioned romantic love. It is in terms of this image that he reads contemporary politics and, in a way, the development of Irish history. The result is not so much his misreading of these things (although that can be argued) as our misreading of his plays. There are two standards consistently evoked in all O'Casey's work. They are *a)* the dehumanizing effects of visionary dreaming, especially when it takes a political (nationalist) form, and *b)* the humanizing effects of being involved in people rather than in ideas or ideologies, best expressed in the desire for domestic security and bliss which is such a marked feature of his womenfolk. Tangentially one might remark that domestic bliss and its corollaries is as much an 'idea' as nationalism and can take equally fanatic forms (*pace* Nora Clitheroe), but the point nevertheless stands as he makes it, and it is, in addition, the basis for his otherwise odd distinction between heroic women and unheroic men. That in itself probably owes a good deal to Shaw's revision of Victorian drama's shrinking-violet woman and her heroically stupid male counterpart. But Shaw's men and women, in their inverted roles, were successful in an English setting. O'Casey's were doomed to be unsuccessful in the very different Irish one.

The nineteenth-century novel had exhausted the heuristic possibilities of the family with respect to social structures. The artistic mode was institutionalized. By O'Casey's day, the novel, in its major developments, had abandoned the family unit as its social and moral base. The figure of the alienated artist had taken over. The same was and has since been true of drama, except in America; and there are special reasons for American separateness in this regard, most of them already expounded by Robert Warshow. Yet O'Casey takes the family unit and, later, themes of romantic love as the organizing principles of his plays and thus foists upon a complex dramatic situation, to which these principles are inappropriate, a simplistic and deforming kind of moral interpretation. He does not earn his humanistic spurs; he simply wears them as a goad to the inhuman political situation which his plays straddle.

The Plough and the Stars is the one play in which he manages to bring political complexities and moral insight successfully together. The last scene, in which the British Tommies sing 'Keep the 'ome fires burning' in the dead Bessie's living-room, is O'Casey's most powerful single image of the vicious collusion which has taken place between domestic, homely bliss and political and military violence. Outside, Dublin burns. But it is an odd city. It is a metaphorical space in which the virtues of humanity confront the vices of politics. The rudimentary nature of the opposition gives it the appearance of being definitive. Thus, it is a city in which we have had Pearse's ferocious political rhetoric juxtaposed with Rosie Redmond's humanity, much to Pearse's dramatic discomfiture. There Jack Clitheroe has died out of simple egoism and bravura, and not for any political ideal. It is not a city in which politics has any truly social or human basis. Instead, only in repudiation of politics can humanity express itself.

An acceptable and legitimate point of view; but not in these conditions. For the medium through which politics is viewed is the one in which politics does not operate, the apolitical family unit. Thus, the complexities of the political situation are, of their nature, inaccessible to the play except from an unwaveringly satiric viewpoint. The form of the play, moulded by its familial tenement setting, is the form dictated by a moralist's desire to replace politics with an alternative human system. Yet what are the energies, the qualities of this alternative? Pathos is one (Nora's, Bessie's, et cetera), but that is more the failure of quality itself. For what O'Casey has done here is to cast politics in the role of an inexorable fate which exploits the flaws in men's characters for the sake of destroying them. Yet even on this level there is hesitation, since the men are not in any sense heroic or in any tragic way flawed. They are stupid, vain, egotistical, jargon-ridden – or they are those things to the exact degree that they are involved in politics. Their deaths have no meaning. Only the women in O'Casey die meaningfully. But they also die within the framework of that familial unit to which they and not politics, belong. The plays are marvellously contrived devices in this respect. But their analytic power is restrained by the limitations of the device which gives them their rather factitiously tragic atmosphere.

In European theatre generally there has been a marked tendency to distinguish modern drama, in all its forms, from the traditional notions of tragedy. Moreover, as these traditional notions are played with, refashioned, rendered absurdly familiar in shocking new circumstances, the drama has imitated the novel at least to the extent of abolishing the family as the basic social unit and replacing it with the artist hero, the political hero, or the producer hero (another version of the artist). Again, as with the novel, a good deal of energy is thereupon expended in writing drama about the writing of drama; but it is evident that, alongside this epistemological theatre, there has grown up an ideological form of drama in which the basic social unit is the individual and the basic deformity is the traditional social allegiances naturally associated with, for instance, familial bonds, or patriotism, or loyalty to the state. This is a more powerful form of theatre than is available in O'Casey because it questions politics through the medium of all other forms of social relationships rather than selecting one arbitrarily as the source of value.

Despite its esoteric ambitions, its aristocratic gestures and its select audience, Yeats's drama discovers the tragic possibilities of political action and the contemplative alternative to it. This is especially the case in the Cuchulain cycle of plays. Cuchulain should, we are told '(and could) earn deliverance from the wheel of becoming by participation in the higher self, after which he should offer his spiritual history to the world; instead, he condemns himself to a career of violent and meaningless action, and this is responsible for the developing tragedy of his life.'[1] O'Casey too was interested in the spectacle of careers of 'violent and meaningless action' but he rendered it melodramatically as a confrontation between his saved women, that Protestant élite stricken with the grace of humanity in the damned male realm of nationalist politics. The separation between private and public value, which dominates his plays, is nullified in the end because the plays themselves suffer from the separation with which they are preoccupied. They are symptoms, not diagnoses, of a particularly modern affliction. But in Yeats, where the polarity also

[1] W.B. Yeats, *A Vision*, rev. edn (London, 1962), p. 126.

exists (Conchubhair and Cuchulain, Blind Man and the Fool, Virgin and Hero, Subjective and Objective Man, Christ and Dionysus, et cetera) the polarity does not determine the form. The reconciliation between these oppositions is determined by form. The completeness of the Yeatsian form can be understood in terms of ritual. Ritual is social, but extra-linguistic. Theatre is more equipped than any other realm of the arts to present an extra-linguistic form which has nevertheless linguistic elements within it. Yeats's theatre is not for the page rather than the stage since its more fundamental aspect is the placing of language within a presentational image like that of the dance. Language bordered by silence, but the more language for that; that is his aim.

He thus regains lost meanings within a newly discovered form. Observe, for instance, how Yeats presents an historical crisis in *The Resurrection* and compare it with O'Casey on the 1916 Rebellion or on the First World War. Yeats can reach the point at which the passage from the Dionysiac to the Christian rite becomes a metaphor for the polarities of the human imagination; but the play is concerned with the process of becoming between these two, not with one at the expense of the other. The language is correspondingly released to a level beyond the sententious, the level of the apodictic imagination:

> Whatever flames upon the night
> Man's own resinous heart has fed.

The historical separation is subsumed within the form of the play as exhibited in the language of choric ritual. If this is compared to the choric rituals of *The Silver Tassie*, the result is startling. It is O'Casey, not Yeats, who is guilty of literary gestures. His language is so derivative (the rhythms of the Authorized Version, the syntax of Boucicault) that we have to take its meaning on *a priori*, not on dramatic, grounds; and it never comes near the range of Yeats's choric verse which has, with formal tact, been distinguished from his play's prose without ever being dramatically distinct from it. As usual, ritual is the interconnecting link between the two.

In *Red Roses for Me* and *Within the Gates*, *The Bishop's Bonfire*, *The Drums of Father Ned* and *Cock-A-Doodle Dandy*, O'Casey's language goes through a series of deteriorations. It is finally gross, because its idiosyncrasies are not a function of the play's meaning but are, rather, extraneous to it. They operate as local colour in the

113

proposed universal situation, but the universality of the situation is as a consequence localized 'downward' instead of the local situation being universalized 'upward'. The language suffers, in fact, from its very realism. Character is stylized into repetitive patterns of speech; each person is given and holds to a single linguistic profile. In so far as the plays have meaning, we gather it from the relationship of these profiles to one another. Their sharpness may be increased in the course of a play; but their initial disposition to one another always remains the same. The men are still dreamers, the women still realists; sexuality is still life-giving, the Church still death-dealing. The plays rationalize their initial situations; they do not explore them. Politics may be the opposite of humanism, but why? How did it become so? Is it necessarily so? Or is it only true in an Irish context? The plays cannot deal with such questions because they can find no form in which to put them. They find no form because the only language available to O'Casey was the language of a social situation in which the deformed answers had already been given.

In Yeats the drama does not depend for its linguistic base on a social situation which is so specifically portrayed that the language must mimic as realistically as possible the local idioms peculiar to that situation. The boundaries of his language are set by its own energy, not by an artificial and outmoded criterion of naturalism – life-likeness. In fact, that tradition of modern drama in which Yeats has had least influence, that of men like Beckett and Pinter, has parodied that kind of naturalism by taking it to such exaggeratedly logical lengths that it ceases to be 'realistic' and becomes, by reversion, symbolic or comically sententious.

Frequently, discussion of both these dramatists degenerates into a description of one as a communist, of the other as a fascist, and on that basis, judgement is delivered. Such facts (if they are so) have to be carefully handled, and are certainly not unimportant. For, in a way, they bear upon the notion of Ireland, their common possession, and the shape it assumes in their work. Patriotism is not a criterion of literary excellence but its finer forms can be a moulding influence on literary stance. Wallace Stevens, speaking of John Crowe Ransom's relation to Tennessee, said: 'One turns with something like ferocity towards a land that one loves, to which one is really and essentially native, to demand that it surrender, reveal, that in itself which one loves.' And he later continues:

There are men who are not content merely to acknowledge these emotions. There are men who must understand them, who isolate them in order to understand them. Once they understand them it may be said that they cease to be natives. They become outsiders. Yet it is certain, at will, they become insiders again. In ceasing to be natives they have become insiders and outsiders at once. And where this happens to a man whose life is that of the thinker, the poet, the philosopher, the teacher, and in a broad generalized sense, the artist, while his activity may appear to be that of the outsider, the insider remains as the base of his character, the essential person, something fixed, the play of his thoughts, that on which he lavishes his sense of the prodigious and legendary, the material of his imagination.[2]

On these terms I would suggest that Yeats, who stayed at home, was the outsider who nevertheless remained inside, O'Casey the insider who remained outside, separating himself from Ireland in his life as he could never separate Ireland from himself in his art.

Obviously the Yeatsian idea of a theatre had much to do with the Yeatsian idea of Ireland. The cycle of Cuchulain plays, or *The Golden Helmet* and its verse form *The Green Helmet*, with their references to Synge and to Irish squabbles, would be ready instances, out of a great many, which would confirm this. Further, Yeats's career as a dramatist was specifically directed towards the formation of an idea of Ireland in an Irish audience. After the shock of the riot against Synge's *Playboy* in 1907, he turned towards a new audience and a new form of drama. But there was at no point any rupture between the sense of Irish national life and the desire to write plays. Indeed his plays are largely concerned with supplying Ireland with a new self-image, with altering the Davis sensibility into something much more akin to the sensibility first articulated by the Young Irelanders. It was an image of communion predicated on the idea of spiritual aloneness:

> Ireland is passing through a crisis in the life of the mind greater than any she has known since the rise of the Young Ireland party, and based upon a principle which sets many in opposition to the habits of thought and feeling come down from that party, for the seasons change, and need and occupation with them. Many are beginning to recognize the

[2] Wallace Stevens, *Opus Posthumous* (New York, 1966), pp. 260–1.

right of the individual mind to see the world in its own way, to cherish the thoughts which separate men from one another, and that are the creators of distinguished life, instead of those thoughts that had made one man like another if they could, and have but succeeded in setting hysteria and insincerity in place of confidence and self-possession.[3]

Thus the Noh plays, for instance, should be seen in the light of the endless Yeatsian commentary upon the state of the national consciousness. They provide a counter-image of nobility and impersonality against the image of faction and insult which the Parnell, Synge and Hugh Lane controversies had, in Yeats's view, proved sadly characteristic of the new (or was it the old?) Ireland. The gesture the formal apparatus and the tone of Yeats's closet dramas are inspired by a political and cultural intent. They are not esoteric in the sense that they are at some considerable remove from the public domain. They are aristocratic only in the sense that they wish to replace the very idea of a collective public with the idea of a national community in which individuality, not individualism, would be the primary element.

That said, there is no denying that Yeats never really exorcized from his drama the ghost of Villiers de l'Isle-Adam. 'Personal friends and a few score people of good taste' would constitute an odd audience anywhere, and one can hardly imagine the privileged few of a London drawing-room reacting in the approved Japanese manner to the allusions contained in a play like *The Hawk's Well*. Perhaps, in that ambience, it was thought proper to be mystified; certainly, with most audiences, the mystification has remained. It is true, too, as the Celtic scholars tell us, that Yeats consistently softens the harshness and terseness of the ancient sagas. This is not in itself a difficult admission to make, but it does lead many readers on to the conclusion that the world of Yeatsian drama is more blatantly synthetic than anything Thomas Davis could have invented. Thus another charge of 'unreality' is lodged heavily against him. Indeed, his adaptations of Celtic material and Japanese forms are based on a very amateurish and second-hand knowledge of their sources; even his translation of *Oedipus Rex*, played at the Abbey in 1926, was begun under the vague impression that it had some relationship, spiritual of course, with Ireland. But Gilbert

---

[3] W.B. Yeats, *Plays and Controversies* (London, 1923), p. 198.

Murray's repudiation of this idea must have pleased Yeats, even though it did not apparently convince him: 'I will not translate the Oedipus Rex for the Irish Theatre, because it is a play with nothing Irish about it; no religion, not one beautiful action, hardly a stroke of poetry.'[4]

Although Celts, Japanese and Greeks are so strangely adapted by Yeats throughout his dramatic career, it would appear that he rarely wrote 'a play with nothing Irish about it'. There were startling successes in different modes – *The Countess Cathleen*, *Purgatory*, *Words Upon the Window Pane*. There were many failures, although not one of them is unredeemed either by a lyric, a dance, a song. But the important point is that Yeats's dramatic career stands as the most exemplary of all in its desire to reshape Ireland through the appeal of a revivified formality of stage manner which would represent a new formality of social behaviour and relationship. In fact I think it true to say that no drama so clearly offers itself as exemplary of the kind of consciousness which it would like to promote and see prevail. Yeats was a speculator in ideas and in literary forms who was always liable to respond quickly to any sign of oncoming change in the political or literary market-place. But we should remember that, like Ezra Pound, with whom he had a fruitful relationship, he was convinced that a new sensibility was revealing itself in new forms and new languages. Pound, however, was midwife to a cosmopolitan American and European movement; Yeats never ceased to be a cultural nationalist. His Ireland was bathed in the light of the Golden Dawn for much of his career; thereafter it became remarkably similar to the starkly energetic and mythic world of Synge. His plays and poems reveal this transition, but the plays cling to the occult and the theme of national consciousness more fiercely than do the poems.

The Bullen *Collected Works* of 1908 would allow any reader to wonder why Yeats's reputation was at that time so high. Swinburne's death in the following year helped to enhance his presence on the literary scene; but those eight volumes have a very definite and musty Victorian-Edwardian air. At 43 he was already 'one of that generation of massive late-Victorians who were to dominate our literature';[5] at 50 he began to be one of the great modernists.

---

[4] *Letters to W.B. Yeats*, 2 vols., eds. R. Finneran, George Mills Harper and W.M. Murphy (London, 1977), vol. 1, p. 145.
[5] Cyril Connolly, *Previous Convictions* (London, 1967), p. 252.

It is in 1915 that his poem 'Scholars' opens Pound's *Catholic Anthology*, followed by 'The Love Song of J. Alfred Prufrock'; it is in 1922, the *annus mirabilis* of the modern movement, that his *Later Poems* appeared.

In the meantime, Yeats had also managed to become one of the foremost experimentalists in the modern drama. It is rather like watching several careers being carried on at once. Things typical of their period come and go in Yeats's work, picked up, consumed and abandoned in one imperial movement. The preoccupation with the gloomy predictions of the end of civilization, so characteristic of the Edwardian period, is to be found in Yeats but also in Wells, Conrad, Galsworthy, Shaw and Forster.[6] Yet in Yeats it becomes something odd; at first, in the Bullen edition, the sense of an ending is associated with the Country-Under-the-Wave atmosphere of the early plays and poems, pieces which, however wonderful they may be at particular moments, have more than their share of what Pound called 'the abominable dog-biscuit of Milton's rhetoric'.[7] Later, once we can take Virginia Woolf's word for it that 'in or about December 1910, human character changed'[8] and that 'the twentieth century in literature had truly begun, the sense of an ending in Yeats is transformed into a truly apocalyptic vision. Yet, early or late, Yeats still manages to place Ireland at the centre of his premonitory laments and celebrations. His obsession with his native land and culture is not exceeded by Joyce, except for the fact that Joyce liked to preserve the minor decencies of realism, a solecism of which Yeats was never guilty.

No one stated Yeats's achievement as a dramatist more trenchantly than did T. S. Eliot in a talk delivered in honour of Yeats at, very appropriately, the Abbey Theatre in 1940. There Eliot made the point that Yeats did not really master his Celtic legend material until he began to write the Plays for Dancers: 'The point is, that in becoming more Irish, not in subject-matter, but in expression, he became at the same time universal.' And again, in the same talk, Eliot says:

> He cared, I think, more for the theatre as an organ of expression of the consciousness of a people, than as a means to his own fame or achievement . . . the idea of the poetic drama was kept alive when everywhere else it had been

[6] See Samuel Hynes, *Edwardian Occasions* (London, 1972), pp. 1–12.
[7] Quoted in ibid., p. 137.
[8] Virginia Woolf, *The Captain's Death Bed* (London, 1950), p. 91.

driven underground. I do not know where our debt to him as a dramatist ends – and in time, it will not end until that drama itself ends.[9]

And surely here we are given the essential point. Yeats wrote plays which were meant to counter everything that Shaw, Ibsen and Pinero represented; his attitude to the drama of ideas was very much of a piece with the attitude of Virginia Woolf to Arnold Bennett, of Joyce to Zola. Yeats was participating in the modernist repudiation of the kind of deathly realism which he associated with these names at the same time as he was being influenced by the whole literary reaction away from the pallid languages of Georgian poetry, Pre-Raphaelite nuance, sub-Tennysonian reverberation. In other words, while he developed a new and starker realism of language, he repudiated the forms in which realism, as a literary movement and principle, had made its mark.

In this respect he is more acute in his perception than O'Casey whose realism is very much that of the Edwardian dramatists, more hectically coloured indeed than they are by the fever of the Irish political situation. O'Casey's sensibility is that of someone born before the magic mark of December 1910. His mentors are Shaw and Boucicault. He was one of the finest of the Edwardian moralist-dramatists fallen among German Expressionists. But, essentially, his career is that of a powerful dramatic instinct struggling in the toils of anachronistic or unamenable forms. In this respect, he makes a startling contrast with Yeats and could hardly be viewed now as an exemplar save by those who wish to use him as an exponent of pacifism or as a specimen of the proletarian revolutionary. For obvious reasons, Germany has been the country in which these versions of O'Casey have been most popular, although the pacifist O'Casey has fairly recently and not unexpectedly had a vogue in Dublin.

The question which needs answering, however, is this: granted that Yeats was, as a dramatist, part of the modernist avant-garde and that O'Casey was not, is it not nevertheless true that O'Casey dealt more passionately and directly with the Irish situation than Yeats ever did? There seems to be no doubt in most minds that

---

[9] Reprinted in *The Permanence of Yeats*, eds. J. Hall and M. Steinmann (New York, 1950), pp. 337, 342. This volume also includes Eric Bentley's well-known essay 'Yeats as a Playwright' (pp. 237–48), in which he compares Yeats as a dramatist favourably with Eliot.

Juno and Bessie Burgess (although not, surely, the dreary Davoren or the dopey Minnie Powell) are more memorable and now, in the glare of contemporary Belfast, more recognizable figures than the Queens and Swineherds, the Emers and Forgaels of Yeats's dramas. In fact are these women not the living consequence of the pre-revolutionary Countess Cathleen and Kathleen Ni Houlihan, those literary poseurs who perhaps helped send out 'certain men (and women) the English shot'?

The drift of such questions implies that the Yeatsian figures, however avant-garde the form of the plays in which they occur, are essentially literary fabrications beside which O'Casey's women stand, branded with the suffering of the actual. At any rate, my answer to such questions has to be no. They are all of them literary creations and it seems to me that the significance of these heroic O'Casey women or of the non-heroic men is in large part the result of a kind of emotional proselytizing on O'Casey's part, the effect of which is reduced by the contradictory form of the plays in which he relays his missionary appeal. Where Yeats's plays command the audience to participate in a vision of the world, O'Casey's demand that it have or share his opinions about it.

Part of the renewed respect for O'Casey comes from audiences which are more impatient than usual with artists who do not supply an immediate set of approved sentiments for meeting a political crisis. O'Casey seems to do that; Yeats does not. But then it was Yeats who wrote 'Lapis Lazuli'.

> I have heard that hysterical women say
> They are sick of the palette and fiddle-bow,
> Of poets that are always gay,
> For everybody knows or else should know
> That if nothing drastic is done
> Aeroplane and Zeppelin will come out,
> Pitch like King Billy bomb-balls in
> Until the town lie beaten flat.

There is no need to rehearse what is already known about O'Casey's politics and the division in his plays between sympathetic women and egoistic men which makes it impossible for us to conceive of any political commitment not hostile to human feeling. He was a strange sort of pacifist, being inclined to repudiate the violence of his Ireland, not on principle but on the ground that this was not a violence which would lead to any improvement in the lot of those who most needed to benefit from real social and political change. His constituency was tenement Dublin, not the select audience for Yeats's Noh drama. But, while these are certainly views which belong to at least some of the volumes of his *Autobiographies*, they are not at all integral to his plays. Is *The Silver Tassie* an anti-war play, or is it a play about an almost sadistic human selfishness? Or is it essentially about the plight of the demobbed and wounded soldier?

The combination of tragedy and comedy in O'Casey's early work is an unhappy one, since their coexistence renders the first sentimental and the other farcical. They divide from one another so completely that we feel he has managed to divorce rather than reconcile the mixed elements. Whether the oppositions be those of politically egoistic men or heroically humane women, of black clerics or the poetic sex of young lovers, O'Casey can finally deal with them only as schismatic statements in which he takes the side of heresy against official rule. He is in fact a Zhdanovite, making his literature conform to a stereotyped party line, using all the resources of a very stagey Irish rhetoric to support those on the side of Life against the dealers in Death. There is a similarity between his career and that of D.H. Lawrence, in that each of them abandoned the native ground upon which their quarrel with the world began for an exile in which the missionary sense became predominant and sought expression in a crusade – the instinctual life of the dark gods against the white mythologies of officialdom. The fact that O'Casey and Lawrence are generally assumed to be on opposite sides of the political divide makes the similarity all the more startling.

Political thought predicated on utopian premises has to assume a highly utilitarian attitude towards literature. The reduction of the human personality to a stereotype, the homiletic approach to language, the puritan suspicion of formal complexity, are all examples of the reaction against modernism in literature which reached such intellectually bankrupt but politically powerful culminations in the writings of Zhdanov, Stalin and the German fascists. From today's vantage point, O'Casey seems closer to the school of socialist realism than to any other. Even his adaptation of German expressionism is merely the adaptation of a technique; it does not signal a change in sensibility. However progressive his opinions may sound, especially when contrasted with those of Yeats, O'Casey as a writer was part of the reactionary movement against the 'decadence' of literary modernism which is part of the political history of the twentieth century. The world in which his writings are admired is a world which has no time for Joyce, Proust, Beckett or Kafka.

When we look to see which authors have most effectively protested against what Lukács calls 'the dismemberment of human consciousness by capitalism',[10] it is surely to writers like these and to Yeats that we turn. O'Casey spoke out against Irish nationalist-populist violence; he also spoke out against Irish clericalism. His range of reference scarcely extends beyond those things. He is a provincial writer whose moment has come again in the present wave of revisionist Irish history, itself a provincial phenomenon. He belongs to the Abbey Yeats tried not to have. The dispute between them over *The Silver Tassie* was, in effect, a dispute over modernist literature and the role which literature should have in relation to the culture out of which it arose initially and to which it must continually return. O'Casey lost the battle but won the war. He deprived the Abbey of his plays even though the Abbey was and is the sort of theatre for which ideally his plays were written. For the theatre in Ireland, by its rejection of Yeatsian forms of drama, by its repudiation of those gestures of body, colour, form and speech which he alone revivified in the early part of this century, has joined with the dull reaction of the thirties, both right and left wing, against all that was important and innovative in the modern arts. Yeats's defence of Synge in 1907 and of O'Casey in 1926 reminds us, however, that there need be no exclusive choice made between these three Abbey dramatists. All that I have argued for here is a recognition of the fact that Yeats is a more profoundly political dramatist than O'Casey, that it is in his plays that we find a search for the new form of feeling which would renovate our national consciousness, and that he, more than O'Casey, stands therefore as a great exemplar for the present moment. O'Casey's virtues as a dramatist are sufficiently recognized but these should not be confused with his usefulness as an example.

[10] G. Lukács, *Studies in European Realism*, trs. E. Bone (London, 1972), p. 234.

9

JOYCE AND BECKETT

Deirdre Bair, Beckett's biographer, tells us that he was asked
some startlingly inane questions when it was revealed that he
had glaucoma in both eyes. Did he think blindness was an
affliction suffered by major Irish writers? Was he to be the third
of a great triumvirate of Irishmen (along with Joyce and O'Casey)
to be stricken with blindness?[1] Perhaps these questions are of the
same order as the more specifically literary inquiries into the
comparisons and contrasts between Beckett and Joyce. Since the
association between them in the Paris of the thirties it has been
customary to speak of Beckett as one of Joyce's followers, even
though the contrast between the linguistic penury of the one and
the extravagance of the other was marked from the outset.
Further, since both seemed to insist on exile from Ireland as a
condition of artistic freedom, the opportunities for a comparison
were confirmed, especially as their separation from Ireland and
the effect this had on their work were in some unspecified sense
different from the characteristic anxieties of English and American
émigrés at that time. The Irish form of exile represented by these
two was more dramatic since it appeared to be based on a total
repudiation of the homeland and a correspondingly exacting
inquiry into the possibilities of language for artists who felt that
their work began in nullity, at degree zero. Thus, Ireland provided
them with a sense of absence which their writings sought to
appease. Their predecessors are not chosen for them by the
pressure of tradition. Instead, they had to choose them, making a
cosmopolitan virtue out of a native defect. Dante, Bruno, Vico,
Descartes, St Augustine, Geulincx were called in to supply ways

[1] Deirdre Bair, *Samuel Beckett: A Biography* (London, 1978), p. 598.

123

of dealing with an Irish experience which had had no sufficient embodiment in art and was, therefore, a reminder that a new art must be found to overcome its recalcitrance or that there are certain modes of experience which are simply too much, too excessive, and that art can do no more than acknowledge this despairing fact. Joyce, then, may be thought of as the exponent of the new art of incorporation, Beckett of the disconsolate art of incompetence.

This contrast is attractive and can endure in different critical zones. The various Marxist readings of modernism, dominated by Lukács and given blunt emphasis by Karl Radek, are not put under any strain whatsoever by it.[2] Beckett can be read as an extreme instance of the alienation already registered in Joyce. Similarly, to see *Ulysses* as the last, if ruined, masterpiece of the bourgeois liberal tradition of the novel[3] allows us to see Beckett as a victim of the aftermath, afflicted by the memory of a concordance between language and experience which has disappeared. Further, the non-Marxist theories of the emergence of schizophrenic writing after the decline of the assumptions upon which literary realism was based, can also be exemplified by this contrast.[4] Its serviceability makes it suspect. The very real differences between Joyce and Beckett are flattened when they are seen in this relatively facile way. Without denying that they do illuminate one another it should be possible to clarify the ways in which they are different.

The work of both gives the impression that a profoundly systematic inquiry is under way. Yet the ostensible object of that inquiry – the fate of Bloom or of Molloy, for example – does not matter as much as does the nature of the inquiry itself. We can hazard the thought that the object of the inquiry is to do no more and no less than to reveal its nature. Its nature is to be systematic. An almost infinite series of adjustments and rearrangements made in a resourcefully finicky spirit meets us on every page of

[2] See G. Lukács, *Studies in European Realism*, trs. E. Bone (London, 1972) – essays from the years 1935–9 – and *The Meaning of Contemporary Realism*, trs. J. and N. Mander (London, 1963); also Jeremy Hawthorn, '"Ulysses", Modernism and Marxist Criticism' in *James Joyce and Modern Literature*, eds. W.J. McCormack and A. Stead (London, 1982), pp. 112–25.

[3] Cf. Terry Eagleton, *Criticism and Ideology* (London, 1976), pp. 154–7; Franco Moretti, *Signs Taken for Wonders* (London, 1983), pp. 182–208.

[4] See Gilles Deleuze and Felix Guattari, *The Anti-Oedipus*, trs. R. Hurley, M. Seem and H.R. Lane (New York, 1977), where the attack is directed against Freudian interpretation.

both authors. We are constantly attending to the logic of the narrator's solicitude for every object, fact or possibility which the mind can entertain and we are, on that account, obliged to concede that there is an essentially systematic spirit at work here. But in Beckett we are likely to find that this spirit is prone to exhaustion and that the exhaustion is itself taken up and worked into the text as one of the possibilities, or probabilities, of that spirit's operation. Molloy's craving to know everything has to include his revulsion at that craving. To be properly systematic he must include his weariness with being so: 'What I need now is stories, it took me a long time to know that, and I'm not sure of it. There I am then, informed as to certain things, knowing certain things about him, things I didn't know, things I had never thought of. What rigmarole.' There are other kinds of rigmarole by which the reader is often, to his pleasure, afflicted: 'Constipation is a sign of good health in pomeranians'; 'To restore silence is the role of objects'. One of these might be more profound than the other, although the context offers no immediate help. They at least have the form of rational statements, even of conclusive truths, but they have the effect of nonsense. Their comedy is like that of the whole novel, depending on the combination of the formal mode of knowing with the futile content of knowledge to produce something so cryptic that it might be true and, at the same time, might not.

Beckett's writing is calculated to arouse indecision in the reader. In the same episode from *Molloy* we are told that the gentleman (A or C) observed by Molloy lifted the pomeranian dog (although he is not sure that it was a pomeranian), 'drew the cigar from his lips and buried his face in the orange fleece, for it was a gentleman, that was obvious'. Just for a moment, 'it' seems to refer to the dog, not the man. Although the reader recovers quickly, the next sentences introduce uncertainty again: 'Yes, it was an orange pomeranian, the less I think of it the more certain I am.' The word 'it' here, and in many other instances, is constantly forcing the reader to adjust the meaning of the text. Quick decisions have to be made as the orphic voice flows on. They may be based upon the conventions of grammar or plot or on a number of other organizing principles but they do, provisionally, work. The necessity to be decisive is imposed by the threat of randomness which would otherwise engulf us. The exploitation of the tension between these is the systematic element in the writing.

But if we take a passage from *Ulysses* in which a similar issue is raised, the nature of the difference between the strategies of Joyce and Beckett becomes clearer. When Bloom is making his way through the tombstones of Glasnevin cemetery to visit Parnell's grave, he ruminates on the conventions and euphemisms surrounding death and burial. He has the idea that the tombstones would be more interesting if they recorded what the dead had done in life. So he invents a few examples: 'So and so, wheelwright. I travelled for cork lino. I paid five shillings in the pound. Or a woman's with her saucepan. I cooked good Irish stew. Eulogy in a country churchyard it ought to be that poem of whose is it Wordsworth or Thomas Campbell.' Of course Bloom is wrong. The author is Thomas Gray and the poem is *Elegy in a Country Churchyard*. But we have to adjust almost immediately. Bloom is making a joke, he is punning on the word 'elegy'. Then the mistake about the name is of a piece with other mistakes in the chapter, particularly that concerning the man in the mackintosh who is recorded by Hynes as a mourner called Mc'Intosh. Mr Power tells us that some say Parnell is not in that grave at all, that the coffin was filled with stones. Imagining the moment of death, Bloom muses, 'Must be damned unpleasant. Can't believe it at first. Mistake must be: someone else. Try the house opposite.'

Mistakes about identity are bound to be pervasive in a chapter for which one of the symbols (given by Joyce in the *Linati Schema*) is 'The Unknown Man' ('L'Ignoto'). Thus the reader who sees 'Eulogy' as a mistake for 'Elegy' has to adjust this first impression and find an explanation either in the character of Bloom as someone whose miscellaneous information is always inclined to be faulty or in the structural principle of the chapter which makes deliberate strategies of the mistakes, euphemisms, superstitions and conventions which surround death and burial. Yet this is not confined to a single chapter. Fritz Senn says that *Ulysses* 'tends to counteract whatever it has been doing, contradict whatever it has been saying'.[5] No book is more systematic in its schemas, correspondences and cross-references. Yet it is also designed to create various kinds of uncertainty in the reader. Misreadings are, therefore, inevitable. Or, more precisely perhaps, it is impossible to be sure of any single reading because the work is designed to ensure this. The paradox lies in the fact that the design is effective in this respect because it is so systematically organized.

[5] 'Righting Ulysses' in *James Joyce: New Perspectives*, ed. Colin McCabe (Brighton, 1982), p. 9.

Yet this is quite different from Beckett. The philosophic or literary shadows thrown by his writing are not the flitting images of an elusive coherence which are provided by Homer in *Ulysses* or by Vico in *Finnegans Wake*. The structure of the *Discourse on Method* leaves no imprint on Beckett's writings although the questions raised by it do. Despite Belacqua and the pervasive references to Dante, especially to the *Purgatorio*, there is no substantial transfer from one (heroic) narrative to another (unheroic) one, as is the case in Joyce. Joyce's fictions draw deep on the resources of conventional narrative. Although he upsets many of the traditional expectations of story-telling, traditional story-telling remains, even if as a memory or as a parallel, a governing element in his work. In Beckett, the forms of narrative are supplanted by the techniques of meditation. The bodily inertia which is so typical of his figures is a condition of thinking though it is also a disablement. Stillness helps thought. But thought is helpless, even when (or especially when) its technique is that of the Cartesian method of radical doubt. For Beckett adapts a great deal of the Cartesian method without adopting the basic Cartesian premises – *Cogito ergo sum* and *sum res cogitans*. Therefore his method in writing involves him in a systematic winnowing out of all that is not essential in the search for an essence that does not exist. Yet even to say that there is no essence, no 'it', is altogether too declarative. So his condition is that of aporia, full of doubt, of permanently suspended judgement, of being ephectic. The opening page of *The Unnamable* provides the diagnosis:

> No matter how it happened. It, say it, not knowing what. Perhaps I simply assented at last to an old thing. But I did nothing. I seem to speak, it is not I, about me, it is not about me. These few general remarks to begin with. What am I to do, what shall I do, what should I do, in my situation, how proceed? By aporia pure and simple? Or by affirmations and negations invalidated as uttered, or sooner or later? Generally speaking. There must be other shifts. Otherwise it would be quite hopeless. But it is quite hopeless. I should mention before going any further, any further on, that I say aporia without knowing what it means. Can one be ephectic otherwise than unawares? I don't know.

There is a peculiar crux here on which the whole of the famous trilogy depends. If, following Descartes, we say that our essence is thinking, we run to two conclusions – first, that thinking exists and, second, that we exist. But these do not follow from one another at all. The fact that thinking exists does not follow from the fact that I exist. Beckett seizes on this in the trilogy and transmutes it into a tragic narrative which takes the form of a series of meditations. In them, a voice thinks. 'Thinking' here refers (as in Descartes) to any form of awareness. For all the variety of experiences recorded by that voice, there is no consolatory confirmation that there is any 'I' which exists as either cause or effect of the voice. 'The old ego', as Beckett called it in his essay on Proust, 'was . . . an agent of security'.[6] Beckett's abandonment of the ego does not mean the abandonment of the pronoun 'I'. It remains, to be used endlessly. But it does not possess the voice. It is possessed by it. The 'I' wants to insist that its essential being is separable from that inessential voice. But one cannot be separated from the other. Descartes had asserted that it is only in God that existence and essence are one.[7] Beckett's narrators want to reach that state but cannot. For in that state they would be silent. Failing to reach it, they talk. To speak or to write is to acknowledge the fearful and inexplicable separation which the 'I' wishes to deny. What corrupts experience is the notion of essence. All Beckett's people crave finitude and live in infinity. They want to die and know they will live forever, like Macmann,

> to whom it sometimes seemed that he could grovel and wallow in his mortality until the end of time and not have done. And without going as far as that, he who has waited long enough will wait for ever. And there comes the hour when nothing more can happen and nobody can come and all is ended but the waiting that knows itself in vain. Perhaps he had come to that. And when (for example) you die, it is too late, you have been waiting too long, you are no longer sufficiently alive to be able to stop. Perhaps he had come to that. But apparently not, though acts don't matter, I know, I know, nor thoughts.[8]

Malone, circumscribed in his room, and Macmann, wandering

[6] Samuel Beckett, *Proust* (London, 1931), p. 10. Cf. Maurice Blanchot, *Siren's Song: Collected Essays*, ed. G. Josipovici (Brighton, 1982), pp. 192–8.

[7] *The Philosophical Works of Descartes*, 2 vols., trs. E.S. Haldane and G.R.T. Ross (Cambridge, 1931), vol. 1, pp. 182, 225.

[8] Samuel Beckett, *Malone Dies* (London, 1968), p. 241.

in the 'illimitable' countryside where he is nevertheless 'in the circumstances in which we have been fortunate enough to circumscribe him', play out their roles of creator and created, author and character, the free and the determined, to the point where they become interchangeable. The precisely defined room is an infinity as much as is the Biblical wilderness in which Macmann travels. Everything is measured and exact and is without bound. Precise Moran becomes the inchoate Molloy. The stock of names runs out and the voice becomes the Unnamable. The thinking goes on, but no individual existence follows from it. Thinking makes the world more and more, even though reality is less and less. As one increases, the other decreases.

Beckett, then, becomes involved in a double reduction. As the reality of the world becomes less and less, the occasions for his plays and for his later narratives become more and more indeterminate and rudimentary. There is a corresponding reduction in language too as the anxiety to achieve silence and thereby escape from the infinite world of speech increases. Even so, as he is his own translator, his French and English texts, the duplication of one work by the other, extends a process which is always crying out to be ended. For the reader, the area of uncertainty is enlarged, since one language will produce possibilities not present in the other. They have a sameness which is not the same. Duplication entails duplicity. Translating his own work into English or French enables Beckett to regard himself as an author, 'Beckett', whose work he is concerned to reproduce in altered form. Even his own characterization of French as a language of lucidity and English as a language of poetry enhances the difference by giving it a background against which it may be seen.[9] Yet as this duplication goes on, so too does the reduction, the minimalist urge which makes him so different from Joyce. For Joyce begins in the penury of his 'scrupulous meanness' in *Dubliners* and thereafter envisages a process of taking over more and more this 'language, so familiar and so foreign'[10] as Stephen Dedalus calls it until 'foreign' and 'familiar' are no longer distinguishable in *Finnegans Wake*. He translates other languages into English and produces a text which is neither. Beckett translates English into French and finds that a single text has become duplicated into

---

[9] Cf. Richard N. Coe, *Beckett* (Edinburgh and London, 1964), p. 14.
[10] *A Portrait of the Artist as a Young Man*, ed. Chester G. Anderson (New York, 1968), p. 189.

two exclusive discourses. Joyce's text is a manifestation of a will to power by someone who has felt enslaved. Beckett's are refusals of that will to power by someone who has seen the disappearance of the Gaelic language as an historical premonition of his own plight. If the Anglo-Irish could only achieve the dumbness of the Gaelic Irish, that would be a mercy. One of the moments of this recognition occurs in the radio play *All that Fall*. Mr and Mrs Rooney are talking:

> MR ROONEY: . . . Do you know, Maddy, sometimes one would think you were struggling with a dead language.
> MRS ROONEY: Yes, indeed, Dan, I know full well what you mean, I often have that feeling, it is unspeakably excruciating.
> MR ROONEY: I confess I have it sometimes myself, when I happen to overhear what I am saying.
> MRS ROONEY: Well, you know, it will be dead in time, just like our own poor dear Gaelic, there is that to be said.[11]

In its nullity, Ireland allows for and even encourages a Belacqua-like apathy. To achieve this is one aspect of Beckett's desire. However, achieving it is very different from having it imposed. Ireland, with its dead language, its deadening politics, its illiberal legislation, is the historical correlative of the personal state of nirvana-nullity for which Beckett's people crave. Silent, ruined, given to the imaginary, dominated by the actual, it is the perfect site for a metaphysics of absence. Yet he repudiates it with hilarity, as in *First Love*:

> What constitutes the charm of our country, apart of course from its scant population, and this without the help of the meanest contraceptive, is that all is derelict, with the sole exception of history's ancient faeces. These are ardently sought after, stuffed and carried in procession. Wherever nauseated time has dropped a nice fat turd you will find our patriots, sniffing it up on all fours, their faces on fire. Elysium of the roofless. Hence my happiness at last. Lie down, all seems to say, lie down and stay down.[12]

His repudiation of Ireland is of a piece with his repudiation of history. Time, in Beckett, is a metaphysical problem. It is the dimension in which thought moves just as space is the dimension

[11] Samuel Beckett, *All That Fall* (London, 1978), p. 35.
[12] Samuel Beckett, *First Love* (London, 1973), pp. 30–1.

in which the body moves. But to conjoin them is beyond him. Where Joyce's writing is heavy with the weight of history, Beckett's is weightless. But both of them include in their works the history of their own texts. Both consciously rewrote their texts in relation to earlier ones. Both insisted on the right to pillage and repeat earlier writings. Translation is only the most pronounced form of this kind of repetition. The incorporation of other people's texts also plays a part in this bestowal of history upon discourse. All the names already mentioned, from Vico to Descartes, Ibsen to Proust, refer not only to authors but to the appropriation of those elements in their texts which will bear repetition. Words, then, reflect other words; books reflect books; the whole idea of representation of an essential reality through the transparency of words is undermined. Within the works, the Stephen of *Portrait* is rewritten as the Stephen of *Ulysses* and even the suicide of Mrs Sinico in *A Painful Case* can reappear, in another version, in the Aeolus chapter of *Ulysses*. As for the Belacquas, Murphys, Malones, Molloys, Morans and so forth of Beckett's fiction, they are no more than melodic variations on a theme which is pitched in the neuter key of the first-person narrator of whom they are creations and whose only definition is through them, even though he is 'more' than they are. The extreme boredom of Beckett's narrators is caused by their having to repeat, over and over again, what they have already said. They say too much because they can never say enough. It is not important to decide whether or no the landscape they travel through is a version of the Irish landscape but it is useful to recognize that it has no historical presence and therefore does operate successfully as a site of absence, as a place many people have passed through without leaving a trace. Ireland's nullity is thus converted by Beckett into an image of desolation, a zone in which his creatures journey and discover that its 'illimitable' space is like infinity from which there is no escape. Because there is no escape, there is only repetition.

The compulsion to stop is also a symptom of the dedication to going on. The ramifications of his sentences – statements countered by negatives, reservations, denials, interruptions and digressions – lead the reader into a labyrinth from which there is no escape because, even when the speaker changes, he reproduces the same sort of maze built around the same never-ending themes. The themes themselves – the desire to be dead turning into the wish he had never been born, the desire to shut up which can only realize itself in speech – are labyrinths. There is neither a way out nor is there a way in. In the prose pieces published between 1966 and 1980 the beginning is not a point of entry. In *Ping*, for example, the opening sentence is: 'All known all white bare white body fixed one yard legs joined like sewn.' That is the first but it is not the beginning sentence. It is a sentence in a series which we have just begun to read. It implies an anterior arrangement of the same words and we have, of course, a subsequent arrangement of words in this piece which stylizes repetition of word patterns to such a degree that no other principle – of punctuation, grammar, syntax, plot, image – need be invoked by way of explanation. The same is true of *Lessness*, *Imagination Dead Imagine* and, to a lesser extent, of *Enough*. The titles of these works indicate their ambition to find a way of not existing. In them and in his plays, Beckett finally gets rid of that neuter dominant 'I' which controlled the trilogy. One could not imagine a more systematic expulsion of the 'point of view' in fiction. The voice is no longer attributable to a narrator. It belongs instead to narration itself.

The most startling consequence of this is that randomness disappears. Everything in these texts is organized in relation to the internal elements. Nothing seeks to attain a relationship with a 'reality' that is beyond them. They have lost the desire for representation and therefore reveal only the urge for production. Yet their organizational purity does not rob them of the power to move us because, within their various patternings, the words remain redolent of the great systems of meaning of which they are the collected or recollected fragments. *The Lost Ones* is very clearly a version of Dante's *Purgatorio;* the image of the crucifixion haunts *Ping*. But there is, nevertheless, a negativing force at work even here. If these are images that appeal to us they are not images of life but of the disappearance from it of that meaning which was once ascribed to it. Life before birth and life after death are ironic alternatives to life between birth and death. It is the life between which vanishes with the point of view. Time dies with the sense of identity. Pozzo's famous lines in *Waiting for Godot* seize this: 'They give birth astride of a grave, the light gleams an instant, then it's night once more.' Hence the act of generation arouses Beckett's anger for it leads to that endless repetition of human experience from which he has tried to fashion an escape. Sex is metaphysically as well as physically disgusting to him. Random, repetitious, attended by various romantic lies, it converts the lucidity of writing into the poetry of literature.

Inevitably, sexual desire and procreation become analogues for the urge to write and the production of words. They are irrational desires which lead to miserable repetition. In Beckett's universe, there should be a law against them. In 1932 Beckett had been one of the signatories to Eugene Jolas's manifesto, 'Poetry is Vertical', the first clause of which announced: 'In a world ruled by the hypnosis of positivism, we proclaim the autonomy of the poetic vision, the hegemony of the inner life over the outer life.' The eighth point in the manifesto declared:

> The final disintegration of the 'I' in the creative act is made possible by the use of a language which is a mantic instrument, and which does not hesitate to adopt a revolutionary attitude toward word and syntax, going even so far as to invent a hermetic language, if necessary.

Jolas went so far as to invent new terms like 'anamyth' and 'psychograph' to describe the fictions of orphic vision since he found 'story' and 'prose' inadequate.[13] Perhaps Beckett remained a verticalist all his life, turning in the end to anamyth and psychograph in dissatisfaction with the old verities of prose and story. Yet he had a heretical streak in him from the start. 'The hegemony of the inner life over the outer life' is a fine thing to proclaim but it is difficult to enact. Indeed, to enact it meant the annihilation of the outer life and that in turn led to an empty hegemony, for there was nothing left to exercise it over. Then, in turn, the hegemony itself was exposed to a critique of its own nature and, on inspection, yielded up the old story of the creation of a world by a god, of a text by an author. The question that followed led to the abolition of the author-god and almost but not quite to the abolition of the text which, nevertheless, did get itself written by some orphic imperative in a 'hermetic language'. At the end of his systematic inquiry, Beckett is still lumbered with the problem of the orphic urge (inspiration, sexual desire) and the nullity upon which it must be defined. He could keep it under some sort of control in French, the rational language; he could let it go somewhat more in English, the poetic language. But he could never let it become silence, as in Gaelic, the dead language.

'Tears and laughter, they are so much Gaelic to me.' Such a

---

[13] See Dougald McMillan, *Transition 1927–1938: The History of a Literary Era* (London, 1975), pp. 66–7.

description in *Molloy*, of Beckett's project perhaps over-emphasizes its difference from that of Joyce. Deirdre Bair reports that Beckett so idolized Joyce that he took to wearing shoes just like those of the master, even down to the size. But Joyce had small feet of which he was inordinately proud. Beckett did not. He was crippled.[14] It is tempting to turn this into a fable of literary influence. Beckett could not follow in Joyce's footsteps. The effort nearly killed him. Everything which has a privileged position in Joyce – history, sexuality, hegemony over language, archetype, Ireland – is cancelled or humiliated in Beckett. It would seem more natural to compare him with other writers, like his compatriot and contemporary Flann O'Brien, or with Kafka with whom there are some striking similarities. 'My life', wrote Kafka in his *Diaries*, 'is a hesitation before birth.'[15] That sounds like the true Beckettian note. Yet Joyce is an inevitable companion for Beckett. They have so much in common – exile, experimentalism, heroic dedication, and Dublin. In Shaw's preface to his novel *Immaturity*, he wrote:

> In 1876 I had had enough of Dublin. James Joyce in his *Ulysses* has described, with a fidelity so ruthless that the book is hardly bearable, the life that Dublin offers to its young men, or, if you prefer to put it the other way, that its young men offer to Dublin. No doubt it is much like the life of young men everywhere in modern urban civilization. A certain flippant futile derision and belittlement that confuses the noble and the serious with the base and the ludicrous seems to me peculiar to Dublin.[16]

Shaw's description of the mingling of the noble and the base, the serious and the ludicrous, seems especially appropriate for Beckett and Joyce. They adapted this characteristic element in the culture of their city to the purposes of art. It was an attitude productive of parody, of mock-epic subversions, of a mingling of motifs and styles which their work, in different ways, exploited. Beckett appears in *Finnegans Wake*, and an echo of Joyce's closing paragraph from *The Dead* appears in Beckett's 'A Wet Night' in the volume *More Pricks than Kicks*. It is appropriate that they should record each other in such exchanges, for they are both quoters of the texts of others. It is their way of finding a mediation between writing and the world.

[14] Bair, *Samuel Beckett: A Biography*, p. 71.
[15] Franz Kafka, *Diaries 1914–23*, ed. Max Brod (London, 1949), p. 405.
[16] G.B. Shaw, *Immaturity* (London, 1930).

10

thomas kinsella: 'nursed out of wreckage'

Once the major excitements of the Revival were over, there was inevitably a sense of disappointment and disillusion. The deaths of Yeats and Joyce, the emergence of two insular and petit-bourgeois states, one Catholic and the other Protestant in its ethos, the return of economic hardship and mass emigration, all contributed to that sullenness and disaffection so characteristic of the literature of the thirties and forties. The note of a deeper alienation was struck in the fiction of Samuel Beckett, Flann O'Brien and Francis Stuart and, less consistently, in the poetry of Austin Clarke and Patrick Kavanagh. The sense of being what John Montague was later to call 'at the periphery of event' was heightened by the policy of neutrality during the Second World War, and this seemed to exacerbate the fear of provincialism and isolation which continued to haunt Irish writers for the next half-century. It is ironical that some of the most enduring work of this period had its occasion in the experience of the Second World War. Beckett, who had finally settled in Paris in 1937, and Francis Stuart, who went to lecture in Berlin in 1940, both produced trilogies between 1947 and 1950 which fell dead from the press. The condition of inertia in *Molloy*, *Malone Dies* and *The Unnamable*, and that of dishonour in *The Pillar of Cloud*, *Redemption* and *The Flowering Cross*, can be seen now as figures of exile and refuge, explored in each case with an implacable disdain for the risks involved. Among these was the loss of an audience. Beckett had to wait until the sixties and Stuart until the seventies before any considerable recognition came. These novels exemplify the felt loss of energy in the conditions then prevailing in Ireland. Their incorporation of the European crisis was a rebuke of the Irish failure to sustain its earlier engagement with the twentieth-century world.

However, with the appearance of Thomas Kinsella's first volume of poems in 1956, that incorporation finally began to take place in poetry. The sense of Ireland's peripheral role in the European experience came home to Kinsella when he was a civil servant in the economically resurgent Ireland of Sean Lemass, the successor to Eamon de Valera. In 'Nightwalker' (1968) he imagines the glare of the gas ovens on the faces of two young Germans who have come to invest in the new Ireland:

> Bruder und Schwester
> – Two young Germans I had in this morning
> Wanting to transfer investment income;
> The sister a business figurehead, her brother
> Otterfaced, with exasperated smiles
> Assuming – pressing until he achieved – response.
> Handclasp; I do not exist; I cannot take
> My eyes from their pallor. A red glare
> Plays on their faces, livid with little splashes
> Of blazing fat. The oven door closes.

The same shock had been registered six years earlier in the poem 'Downstream'. There, a row-boat journey through darkness turns to nightmare with the revived memory of a man who had died at this drear river edge and whose corpse had been found later, half-eaten. This story too had first been heard during the War. Its horror is understood as a salutary reminder of the necessity to confront such experience on the part of a sensibility which had been culpably innocent. While Kinsella is at this point entering the first stages of a long journey downwards into the sources of terror, he is also very deliberately identifying this confrontation as one badly needed by a culture which had grown provincial and isolated. To have been bypassed by the war is, it would seem, to have been condemned to a callowness which now must be overcome, no matter how bitter the price and how forced the growth.

> It seemed that I,

> Coming to conscience on that lip of dread
> Still dreamed, impervious to calamity,

> Imagining a formal rift of the dead
> Stretched calm as effigies on velvet dust,
> Scattered on starlit slopes with arms outspread

136

> And eyes of silver – when that story thrust
> Pungent horror and an actual mess
> Into my very face, and taste I must.

In such passages Kinsella heralds not only many of the preoccupations of his later writings but also a preoccupation of much contemporary Irish poetry. That is, the need to break, however reluctantly, out of a deep insulation from the actual, and to take on again the burden of history and thereby to come to a recognition of horror and violence, the imposition of such forces upon an isolated, peripheral consciousness. Indeed, the attraction of violence for Irish poets is perhaps especially strong not merely on account of its pervasiveness but also because, as a theme, it provides an exit from provincialism. Certainly Kinsella has absorbed the shock of mass atrocity into his poetry so deeply that the issues he raises have very little of the local or peripheral about them. That image of the last three lines above, a face being compelled to feast on horror, recurs again and again in his work. Eating is the act of survival, but it is never far removed from disgust. Kinsella has an imagination which lives off pain and which must loom over it and feed on it or be shadowed by its alien presence and itself become the matter that is eaten. Examples abound. In 'Leaf Eater', a grub

> gropes
> Back on itself and begins
> To eat its own leaf.

In 'Death in Ilium', written in Yeats's centenary year, the 'shadow-eaters' (critics, perhaps?)

> Close in with tough nose
> And pale fang to expose
> Fibre, weak flesh, speech organs.
>
> They eat, but cannot eat.
> Dog-faces in his bowels,
> Bitches at his face,
> He grows whole and remote.

There are two measurements of distance in Kinsella's poetry. One is the measurement of elegance, in which the poet as dandy displays his skills and craft yet remains damagingly removed from the actual. The other is the measurement of incoherence, in which the poet, in shock after the intense closeness of actuality, grows into the remoteness of near-silence, his speech broken into single words or phrases which have to travel a long way before they connect with another word or phrase. At the median point between these is the confrontation itself. There, actuality takes on all the customary lethal forms – death, illness, loss of love, historical and contemporary violence. Those poems in which elegance is the predominant feature are structures imposed on recalcitrant material. However, the elegance is never sufficient to entirely disguise a sour wisdom, although it is sufficiently there to make that wisdom somewhat homiletic in tone, more orotund than it has earned the right to be. So, In 'Baggot Street Deserta' (from *Another September*, 1958) we are told:

> Versing, like an exile, makes
> A virtuoso of the heart,
> Interpreting the old mistakes
> And discords in a work of Art
> For the One, a private masterpiece
> Of doctored recollections. Truth
> Concedes, before the dew, its place
> In the spray of dried forgettings Youth
> Collected when they were a single
> Furious undissected bloom.

It is easy to admire the drive of the verse, even though the syntax is pursued at the expense of line-form. There is, for instance, no escaping the breath pauses before and after the word 'Youth' at the end of line 8, although the syntax attempts to wriggle free of them. But the list of abstractions – Art, Youth, Truth – bedevil the propositions, giving them a false air of profundity. Still, in poems like 'Another September' or 'Mirror in February' Kinsella can sustain a sweeter lyricism which manages to survive the habit of putting large universal questions. In 'Mirror in February', for instance:

> And how should the flesh not quail that span for span
> Is mutilated more?

the polysyllabic 'mutilated' stands out wonderfully well in its monosyllabic surround. It is also a highly characteristic verb. The stanza in which it occurs also contains the words 'hacked', 'defaced', 'brute', all of them harbingers of the violence which is

138

still, at this stage, contained by the stylish, slightly pompous close:

> In slow distaste
> I fold my towel with what grace I can,
> Not young and not renewable, but man.

But the structuring capacity of style is under pressure even in these early poems and it is difficult to remain insensitive to the threat of experiences too powerful, too inchoate to be accommodated. 'A Country Walk', a meditation on violent history and the banality of the present, records the release of the imagination from the conventional versions of past and present through the figure of the swollen river and through a concentrated observation of the switches and changes in the surface currents of the dishevelled flood as it races under the bridge where the poet stands. This image is deliberately turned into a small allegory and then dismissed in 'Ballydavid Pier', in which the foetus of an animal floating in the harbour waters becomes a version of the monstrous element in life itself. But that is not, it seems, a satisfying structure. The thing finally remains itself, just beyond the range of structuring's good intentions:

> The angelus. Faint bell-notes
> From some church in the distance
> Tremble over the water.
> It is nothing. The vacant harbour
> Is filling; it will empty.
> The misbirth touches the surface
> And glistens like quicksilver.

As with grotesque physical objects, so too with grotesque historical ones. Castles and museums are not haunted, in Kinsella's poetry, by nostalgic voices. They are more often seen as false structures imposed on a complex past, or on a humiliated people, removed from the pungent complexity of the actual and more readily subject, on that account, to the very ruin which they record or cause. King John's castle, in the poem of that name, 'rams fast down the county of Meath'. But it stands now 'in its heavy ruin', not naturalized into but apart from the landscape in which it stands. Similarly, in other poems, nightmare enters into and forms an unhappy and uneasy truce with the common, domesticated daylight, the dominant structure here being marriage and its foundation 'the hells of circumstance' ('Remembering

Old Wars'). In all of these instances, the confusion of experience rebukes the symmetry of structure. History, marriage, the imagination itself, are at odds with the experiences which constitute them. As forms of order, even as words which imply a certain categorized orderliness, they are denials of disorder. Yet denial is as far as Kinsella can take the matter. He can arrest the disorder, in policeman fashion, but he has no court before which to bring it – or, more exactly, he has no native court before which he can bring it. For disorder is no offence in the Irish poetic (or political) tradition. The policing of it is, in fact, a kind of betrayal. Where ideas of intensity, even of uncouthness (understood as the social equivalent of intensity) rule, and where their supremacy in human experience is supported by the experience of breakdown and disaster, a poetry which seeks to elaborate structures of response, a whole architecture of feeling, is in danger of passing beyond the point of recognition. Seeking some parallel and support for his plight, Kinsella turned to America and found it mirrored there in various writers but most of all in the poetry of Ezra Pound.

In *Wormwood* (1966) and in *Nightwalker and Other Poems* (1968) Kinsella attempts to establish in poem sequences the dual sense of experience as process, with the flavour of the instantaneous and disorganized, and experience as pattern, with the sense of retrospect established by virtue of the fact that he is writing. The impression of an unfolding structure is allied throughout with the impression of a certain repugnance which is being experienced in close-up, when the pattern is not visible but the taste is inescapable. No image in these poems leads a casual life. Local felicities are allowed, but they are subsumed always into a larger structure, although the effort often feels like the triumph of a determined will over a nauseous physical reaction. The image of the looming face, the eating of a 'mess', the digestion of this into psychic energy, all contribute to a sense of claustrophobia which would be overwhelming were it not relieved by their association with varieties of natural process – the formation of crystals and rocks, the growth of living tissue, the complex action of water. If the imagination feeds on experience, then it is merely rehearsing a natural process in which all the elements share. Thus the introversion implicit in the trope is rescued from neurosis and is converted into a harmonious relationship with other things. Still, the repugnance remains, indicative of the need for determination and of the sheer difficulty of amalgamating a painfully miscellaneous personal

140

and historical experience into a comprehensive structure.

Underlying all this effort is the ambition to translate the laws of primary nature into the realm of culture, or secondary nature. The risk, of course, is that the poetry is what gets lost in the translation, because the apparent incongruity between these two worlds of nature and culture is too great. It is the plight of the modern metaphysical poet. How, for instance, is the process of biological evolution to be re-imagined so as to reveal something about the nature and process of human love? The question is answered in many poems, above all in 'Phoenix Park', in the deployment of a series of interconnected images which clarify the movement of the poem from the crisis of illness to the recovery of health. A fractured twig, a consuming fever, a child devouring mushrooms, a crystal forming, are all placed to connect with ideas of illness, recuperation, the wholeness of health, so that in the end we may see a harmony between the human and the natural worlds which are interfused throughout the poem. The harmony is not, however, pre-established and it may be thought is not securely established at all, at any point. This in itself is evidence of Kinsella's readiness to take the risk of believing that the desire for such a harmony may be an enchantment from which he needs release. Human experience does not, after all, provide laws of order and system which a study of the non-human world more gratifyingly provides. It is at this point of disappearing faith that his power of assertion takes control. The hope of establishing an order is nourished by the search for the opportunity of doing so. The carefully charted internal relationships in the poem and its extended relationships with the *Wormwood* sequence (for example, those between 'The Secret Garden' and Part IV of 'Phoenix Park') support the reader's sense that order will, at whatever expense, prevail. The bright will to control, the slowly elicited but surely established confidence that 'Laws of order I find I have discovered', the drive in Kinsella towards mastery, are ways of appeasing a hunger which itself remains unexamined. Structure is one thing. 'Mess' is another. What makes their opposition fruitful is the desire each has for the other, indeed to become the other. Until the early seventies Kinsella's work had in effect ratified the existence of this desire. Thereafter, he was more inclined to push further and explore its nature and history.

In the earlier work, poems had been arranged around fairly simple and ready-made oppositions and most of the energy had been expended upon the stylish elegance of the variations which could be played upon these. But, as the oppositions became more subtle and their embodiment more delicate, the elegance began to fade. A certain cumbrousness began to dominate the poems, as though the difficulty of writing them were somehow being made an integral part of the difficulty of reading them. This loss of elegance seemed to some readers to indicate a loss of control. But since the poet is trying to transmit to us the experience of lost control, his foregoing of elegance is not really an indication of failure. Instead, he chooses to demonstrate the process by which he arrives at his moments of balance. The poem is not a structure; it is an action in which structures appear and disappear as part of a complex process in which the poet, as well as the reader, is involved. The earlier poetry, based on oppositions, gives way to a poetry in which a dialectical relationship was being sustained between modes and moments of order, modes and moments of dissolution. This contained, at the least, a reminiscence of Pound's theory of the Vortex and of his practice in *The Cantos*. Kinsella's own description of this, in a review of *The Cantos*, is to the point: 'The meaning is a matter of vortices eddying about us as we possess ourselves of the contents of the poet's mind. Everything is dramatic and immediate, concerned with ideas only in so far as they manifest themselves in action.'

From 1975 onwards, when *Notes from the Land of the Dead* was published, the central analogy in Kinsella's poetry is that between biological and imaginative processes. He displaces the anxieties which had governed *Nightwalker and Other Poems* from their ultimately consoling contexts of history and domesticity. Instead, he rereads them in the wider range afforded by his association of the biological impulse towards birth with the desire for form, and the impulse towards death with the desire for formlessness, the inchoate. This analogy is then further enriched by material (sometimes translated directly, sometimes obliquely referred to) taken from early Celtic literature, particularly the *Lebor Gabala Erenn*, generally known as *The Book of Invasions*. In this, myth and history mix to form patterns of invasion and absorption, violence and recovery. At another level, the poem resumes the history of Kinsella's family, emphasizing the cycle of birth and death, the transmission of knowledge and of physical resemblances, and centring on his own place within these processes. The result is a series of dramatic, if abrupt, vignettes in which various levels of experience are interlarded one with another.

142

I feed upon it still, as you see;
there is no end to that which,
not understood, may yet be noted
and hoarded in the imagination,
in the yolk of one's being, so to speak,
there to undergo its (quite animal) growth,
dividing blindly,
twitching, packed with will,
searching in its own tissue
for the structure
in which it may wake.

The story of evolution, of the Fall, of Irish history, of the Kinsella
family, all become intricately interrelated in the endeavour to
explore the growth of consciousness to the point where it becomes the object of its own activity. This is the point of differentiation between first and second nature, the point at which the
human world assumes to itself the role of the creator of the
systems by which it knows itself.

As a result, rapid transitions are constantly taking place in the
poetry, as images from disparate areas touch one another, their
diversity fuelling the poet's desire for a unity in which pattern
rather than process will be perceived. A technique of analysis,
like surgery, used in *A Technical Supplement* (1976), with illustra-
tive plates from Diderot's *L'Encyclopédie*, and with obvious exten-
sions of meaning to include the whole analytic procedure of
rational investigation commemorated in that work, can lead to an
'invasion' (of the body, or of any sphere) but can result, finally, in
the discovery of the wholeness that is more than a sum of the
parts. Similarly, in *The Good Fight* (1973), the assassination of
President Kennedy is seen as an act of violation which nevertheless,
in destroying over-exalted hopes of perfection, with their Platonic
overtones, might restore the poet and the community to an
acceptance of the way things are and thus allow culture, secondary
nature, to produce its poems as politics produced its Kennedy:

— their gleaming razors
mirroring a primary world
where power also is a source of patience
for a while before the just flesh
falls back in black dissolution in its box.

The idea of order derives from the experience of disorder. One is always becoming the other. There is no point of balance or of perfect rest between the two. In language, too, the synthesis which words can achieve coexists with the dispersion they narrate.

Although Pound is clearly an active influence here, Joyce's shadow also moves over these pages, reminding us of the modern Irish ambition (as exemplified in Yeats and in Joyce) to transcend inherited and provincial disorder in cosmopolitan systems of order which, in their ductility to the desire of the author remind us of the capacity of language to systematize anything it chooses to include. In Kinsella's case, the darkly introverted quality of the poetry is never surrendered to his *esprit de système*. In fact, the basic vocabulary of his poems scarcely alters over thirty years, although his use of it does gain in power, especially after 1973. It is a vocabulary which emphasizes a radical violence. The blind force which makes the packed tissue grope towards full growth, the blind hunger that eats and digests all that comes its way, the conqueror who destroys that he may build, the love that renews itself through pain, the endurance which absorbs assaults, the English language which revives itself in his own work on the corpse of the Irish language it destroyed, are all emanations of an invincible energy which marauds to create. Nature kills, culture defends, but the lethal element persists in each since defence is also a form of violence. Imagination, which is neither one nor the other, but which participates in both, cruises continuously, unslackening in its savage desire to remain free, on patrol between habitation and wilderness.

In five of the seven poems which follow *Notes from the Land of the Dead*, Darwin and Renan are the haunting nineteenth-century presences who provide the background to the theme of an originary violence, figured here as the matted skull in 'St Paul's Rocks: 16 February, 1832' or as the mangled corpse of 'The Dispossessed'. The first of these poems describes, via an entry in Darwin's journal of the voyage of *The Beagle*, an island paradise. Then it details the struggle for life which has made this island, swarming with predatory life, the thing it is. Violence stains the roots of our conception of Paradise, the blessed isle. In the same way, the poem 'The Dispossessed', based on the account given in Renan's *Vie de Jésus*, describes the Christian paradise of love which Christ preached in Galilee before the death of his cousin, John the Baptist. Thereafter, in leaving Galilee and taking arms against the forces which destroyed John, Jesus created in all men a dissatisfaction with earthly things which was itself darkened even further by Christ's own murder, the bloody corpse which

144

lies across the threshold of Christianity. These poems help us to see, in retrospect, the power of the Nightwalker sequence, in which the originary violence is that of the Irish Civil War, attendant upon the birth of the new State; and in *Notes* itself, the originary violence is associated with the first discovery of Ireland as an apparently paradisal land which nevertheless is ruled over by dark and sinister forces. A similar discovery haunts the poems of the sequence *One* (1974), especially 'Finistere' and 'The Oldest Place'. Yeats's apotheosis of violence as a creative force is subjected by Kinsella to a gloomy and complex reconsideration. A tragic condition is expressed through violence. Ireland's history, from the first invasions to Bloody Sunday and the long sequence of intervening crises, manifest that. But his sense (not unknown to Yeats) of the intimacy between barbarity and civilization is intensified in his later poetry to a point beyond the tragic, as in 'Worker in Mirror at his Bench':

> I am simply trying to understand something
> – states of peace nursed out of wreckage.
> The peace of fulness, not emptiness.

If culture itself is always in a state of illness, infected by violence, poetry is culture in a state of convalescence, homeopathically immunized against the disease.

Kinsella's work is thus a persistent inquiry into the whole question of culture and, within that, into the nature of poetry in so far as poetry can be made distinct from culture and yet part of it. He incorporated into the sphere of his poetry's action more than any Irish poet before him, even including Yeats. The Gaelic tradition (for which see, as the most obvious manifestations, his translation of *The Tain* and of the Gaelic Poems in *An Duanaire*), the modernist tradition (including Pound, Yeats and Joyce), and an eclectic knowledge in several other fields, are subsumed into his verse with sufficient energy to become integral parts of it. After the somewhat broken, if noble, careers of Clarke and Kavanagh, Kinsella's is a testimony to the enabling strength of a tradition, of a sense of continuity which is greater than the sense of fragmentation. He has always worked on a large canvas, but with a concentrated, even finicky, precision. It has been his ambition to do no less than

> let our gaze blaze, we pray
> let us see how the whole thing
> > works.

11

john montague:
the kingdom of the dead

Writing in Sean O'Faolain's *The Bell* in 1951, John Montague called for a caustic, Swiftian voice 'to clear this apathy from the air'. He also demanded of his generation that it reflect Catholicism as a living force in Irish life. For a long time it has been customary to associate the Catholicism of the new state and the apathy of the thirties and forties as natural allies and there is no denying a certain coincidence between them. But the 'other' Irish Revival, which included Austin Clarke, Denis Devlin, Patrick Kavanagh, Frank O'Connor and Sean O'Faolain among its best-known figures, was a movement which confronted and absorbed the political and cultural force of Irish Catholicism, sometimes with hostility and sometimes with sympathy, and always with a consciousness of its difference from the preceding generation of Yeats, Synge and Joyce.

This movement, or series of interlinked movements, made a virtue of its localism, of its deep insider's knowledge of the life of the mass of the Irish people, contrasting this with the shallower if more cosmopolitan attitudes of the Revival. Inevitably this contrast led to much cerebration on the essential characteristics of 'Irishness' and a good deal of sarcasm at the expense of those great writers who had paraded a spurious version of it abroad. Corkery's attack on Synge in his book *Synge and Anglo-Irish Literature* (1931), O'Faolain's repudiation of the inhuman Joycean detachment in *The Vanishing Hero* (1956), and Frank O'Connor's more generous fusion of the Gaelic and English traditions in *The Backward Look* (1967), are the best-known critical accounts of this reaction. But Patrick Kavanagh's whole career, his poems, his journalism and his various and often apocryphal *obiter dicta*, embody that repudiation more memorably than anything else. Montague claimed that Kavanagh 'liberated us into ignorance', by which he meant,

JOHN MONTAGUE: THE KINGDOM OF THE DEAD

among other things, that he liberated a whole generation of Irish writers from the erudite, the esoteric and the sometimes over-powering mythological systems of the writers of the Revival. Nevertheless, the turn towards the local, the parochial, the known territory, although it was indeed to achieve a liberating effect in the future, led in the short term to a stifling provincialism which the censorship laws intensified to an unprecedented degree. John Montague began his career at a moment when the dispute between the attractions of a bogus cosmopolitanism and a native loyalism had reached a point of exhaustion. The marks of that struggle have remained in his poetry ever since.

Born in New York, brought up in the family home in Tyrone in Northern Ireland, educated in Dublin, he spent long periods in the United States and in France before returning to Ireland. Montague's experience seems designed to enforce and reconfirm the legitimacy of that dispute. In one respect he is decisive in resolving it. Return to Ireland is a return to closure, oppression; exile from it is an escape to openness, energy, freedom. While this is by no means the whole story, it remains an important feature of it. Ireland, in one of its guises, is a maimed and maiming place. It makes exile inescapable, return, in the full sense, impossible. Montague remembers Patrick Kavanagh's 'baffled fury' as that 'of a man flailing between two faded worlds, the country he had left, and the literary Dublin he never found'. He fears this fate of being caught in the interval between two worlds but he also seeks it and feels sought by it. Home is lost, exile is temporary and no solution, only writing, founded on the experience of being neither wholly national nor wholly inter-national, remains. Dislocation, in its etymological sense, is his obsession. Whatever he returns to — Tyrone, Dublin, Paris, the sites of childhood or of love, he finds them broken and out of their brokenness tries to recompose the wholeness of feeling which they once represented. Specific places matter a great deal in his poems and he concentrates on their detail with a miniatur-ist's care, seeing in every part the presence of the whole. His melancholy thus refines itself into a connoisseur's art. The history of feeling is captured in the exquisite detail. From *Forms of Exile* (1958) to *Tides* (1970) Montague reads his own plight as an encounter between an aesthetic sensibility and an unforgiving history, the position of the exile who returns to find his home incomprehensibly the same and yet, because of that, suddenly anachronistic, fossilized.

Yet the stress of the relationship between his country and his art is not to be understood as an enervating struggle between natural opposites. The fragile, almost anorexic, form of his poems is founded on something other than a wish to distinguish his art from its contrastingly farouche origins. It arises also from the wish to incorporate this uncivil element, to achieve some kind of truce with it without ever going so far as to compromise or to be compromised by it. 'Like Dolmens Round My Childhood, The Old People', 'The Sean Bhean Bhoct', 'Speech for an Ideal Irish Election', 'Old Mythologies' and 'Virgo Hibernica' are poems in which, in a variety of different ways, Montague attempts to come to terms with the local and the legendary elements of his past, trying to take the weight of it in his verse without being brought low by it. History is important but, to be manageable, it has to be shaped and stylized into images. The image thus becomes more than a representation of the past; it is also a mark of the poet's triumph over it. It is familiarized into his own idiom. So, in 'Old Mythologies', the heroes of Gaelic epic, with their 'archaic madness', are imagined

> To bagpiped battle marching,
> Wolfhounds, lean as models,
> At their urgent heels.

The ironic glance at an aspect of contemporary nationalist folk-lore is unmistakable here but so also is an element of self-congratulation on the part of the poet who has so stylishly placed them in this lyric frame. The ambition of many poems is to find

> The only way of saying something
> Luminously as possible.

('A Bright Day')

Thus the rehearsal of exact detail, the discovery of the spring that will release the perfectly shaped and resonant image is a characteristic moment in Montague's poetry, affirming its wonderful grace under the pressure of history. The disorderly, degraded lives of the old people of his Tyrone childhood are moulded finally, in a ritual gesture, 'Into that dark permanence of ancient forms'.

The image, in its finality, conquers narrative so completely that there are times when the narrative appears to be little more than the excuse for the production of the image. The capacity to master the Irish past is so pronounced that the reader may not feel the strength and risk of the dark forces that have been so expertly contained. The stylishness therefore courts the danger of reducing the feeling. The poise, we may feel, would be more impressive if we had a stronger sense of the imbalances which it has so narrowly escaped. In relation to history, Montague keeps a certain distance. Yet this impression is countered by what may be called the explanation for this distance which is, at one level, the fear of being infected by an easily available rhetoric. In the poem 'Tim', the unlovely horse which he first rode in his childhood, he welcomes the remembered actuality of the beast and contrasts it with all the elegant versions of the horse by which it could have been supplanted:

> denying
> rhetoric with your patience,
> forcing me to drink
> from the trough of reality.

But, at another level, there is another explanation for his keeping history at arm's length It is his fear of aphasia. To be dragged by what he calls 'the gravitational pull' of his love into the arms of history, to be mired in an unprocessed experience, is a matter of dread to him. Somehow, chiefly through memory, distance must be gained. Otherwise

> My tongue
> Lies curled in my mouth –
> My power of speech is gone.

> Thrash of an axle in snow!

There is a temptation to speak of Montague's poetry as petering out into silence but this would be inexact. Instead, what he does is to exploit all the possibilities of muteness in which, in the absence of speech, there is gesture – of the body, of landscape, or objects in a room. This is most clearly seen in his love poetry in which, time and again, the feeling rises towards muteness and is then transferred from speech to the pathos of gesture. So, in this respect, the elegance and the refinement of the poetry is not an evasion of feeling but a means of handling its power to strike the writer dumb. He defers to gesture in order to achieve the distance he needs.

Between 1958 and 1970, from *Forms of Exile* through *A Chosen Light, Poisoned Lands* (1961) to *Tides*, Montague maintained this

distance in the two kinds of poem which dominated his work –
poems about Irish and poems about private experience. Almost
all the latter were love poems; almost all the former were
strategic containments of his culture and of its past. The love
poems are sensual and candid enough about the physical aspects
of love. But they are not erotic. The love relationship is bathed in
the light of appreciation and of memory and the heat of desire is
thus subdued. The observation is not voyeuristic, dwelling on
detail, but rather regretful, dwelling on the passing moment:

> I shall miss you
> Creaks the mirror
> into which the scene
> will shortly disappear . . .

('Tracks')

As so often, it is the object, the mirror in this case, which is given
the voice. Similarly, in 'The Same Gesture', the final lines

> work, 'phone, drive
>
> through late traffic
> changing gears with
> the same gesture as
> eased your snowbound
> heart and flesh.

have that intonation of a courteous farewell which lends pathos
to all the love poems while, at the same time, preserving their
tender (and stylish) distance. The first personal pronoun is
usually 'we', not 'I'. The experience is not only shared, but has
been shared in a mute past to which the witnesses are objects,
actions. The community of the two lovers leaves no more than a
faint impress on the surrounding world. The watermarks of
privacy haunt those reimagined bedrooms and gardens where
the lovers had once been, but there is a decisive sense of removal,
of a life lived intensely in exile. So the relationship of the love
poems to those directly concerned with the common and shared
past of Ireland is a mute one too. The two kinds of poem have a
stylistic harmony, but Montague appears at this stage to be
seeking a thematic unison between them. He is still marked by
the old dispute between Ireland and his art, between being a poet
and an Irish poet.

The dispute returned with renewed force after the outbreak of

150

the Northern troubles in 1968. Old moulds were broken, indeed, as far as the political situation was concerned but, in poetry, new opportunities offered themselves very quickly. Montague's response to these events was to reassert his position as an inheritor of the Northern crisis. His poetry, and his volume of short stories, *Death of a Chieftain* (1964), had registered the early symptoms of the collapse. The notion of literature as an Early Warning System gained fresh currency for a time. At this point, in the early seventies, Montague revised much of his past work in the light of the new situation and produced two volumes *The Rough Field* (1972) and *Poisoned Lands* (1977) in which he finally confronted the history which he had for so long distanced. In the first of these very few individual poems were changed, but they were recombined and resituated in such a way as to constitute a single work. In the revised edition of *Poisoned Lands* there were many alterations and corrections as well as the inclusion of poems previously suppressed and the suppression of poems previously included. The effect was that Montague enforced a new reading of his work, offering his poems now as interlinked moments which had at last discovered their origin and purpose. *The Rough Field*, in particular, claimed attention as 'a poem including history', an Irish version of the achievements of William Carlos Williams and Charles Olson in *Paterson* and *The Maximus Poems*. It was like them in that it implied a large coherence between fragmented experiences, some private, some public, which were brought together in constellations and sequences in the form of meditations. In adopting this predominantly American form to Irish experience, Montague was attempting to provide a new answer to the old dispute of the forties and fifties.

In these volumes, then, the exile returns to the home ground only to find it riven ever more deeply by division and dislocation and to discover in himself and in his family the same division and its characteristic consequence – dumbness, muteness, aphasia. But now the poems of exile, of disengagement, of style based on the achievement of distance, all move together in the magnetic field created by the immense political current of the crisis. In addition, the poems now are flanked, in the margins, by the languages of the hustings, of folk-song and folk memory, of government report, of family record. Tyrone now becomes the site of devastation. The English invaders, the Protestant settlers, overlay the former Gaelic culture. The twentieth century violates the densely woven relationships of geography and history in its

151

haste to create an urban wilderness. The Montague family, gaining some small prestige in the nineteenth century, nevertheless loses its inherited gifts – music and language – so that they now remain in the mute form of the decayed fiddle, in the half-mute form of the poet's flawed speech. A whole culture has undergone the experience of aphasia in losing its language, and then has painfully grown another tongue, the English tongue, which nevertheless remains marked by the political and social crises attendant upon its birth in the severed head of Irish Gaeldom. All around are the habits and stories of a degraded people and the desolate landscapes of a vanished civilization. The power of Montague's material, and the effect of his careful arrangement of it, are of themselves sufficient to make it memorable. Along with Denis Devlin's *The Heavenly Foreigner*, Patrick Kavanagh's *The Great Hunger* and Thomas Kinsella's *Nightwalker*, it is one of the most remarkable narratives in modern Irish poetry.

Yet the narrative element in the poem is often at odds with the lyric element, largely because the sheer weight of the historical material bears very heavily on the lyrics in which, as we have seen before, the images seek to contain that weight in ritual gestures. In Part VII of *The Rough Field*, 'Hymn to the New Omagh Road', there is a 'Balance Sheet' of Loss and Gain, a series of Items, recounting what was destroyed by the building of a new trunk road (all of it irreplaceable) and what was gained by it (all of it useless). This is ecology, not poetry. The items of loss are not images; the items of gain are exercises in a simple ironic contrast. Poetry and history, the chief agencies of power in Montague's verse, are both annulled here and replaced by nothing more than a tract. The tension between them is lost because at this point the sense of crisis is willed. The reasons for this are complex.

History, although a potent force in Montague's work, is, finally, a maiming influence. It attracts him by the thought of community which it holds within it; it repels him by the spuriousness of the communal sense which it finally offers. *The Rough Field* is, in its way, a magnificent error, for it is founded on the notion that the individual poems of the earlier books will be liberated by the historical continuum in which they are placed. In fact, they are encumbered by it. The problem is intensified by the fact that the North and the South are historical territories which do give release to many of his contemporaries and their presence there seems to shadow his own – Kinsella in the South, Heaney, Mahon and others in the North. A pathfinder who discovers that the territories he broke into have been settled by others, he feels deprived of his imaginative preserve and is left to forage where others feed. This is a problem of psychic space, always a pronounced one in Ireland but knowable anywhere.

In a way, Montague was forced into a confrontation with the North, and with history, not only by the crisis but also by the emergence from it of a group of other writers who laid an unassailable imaginative claim to it. But this may have been his good fortune. The dependence of his poems on a series of syncopated images, on pleated phrasings, one folding over another, their connectives hidden, almost disqualifies them from the confrontation with history with its demands for extended narrative. Narrative in Montague's poetry provides no more than a stage for the ballet of dainty interchanges which we find in a poem like 'O'Riada's Farewell'. There the image of fire is tested against a series of other images and references — ice, music, light, desire, race, death — with an explorative delicacy which contrasts drastically with the Loss and Gain itemization of the 'Hymn to the New Omagh Road'.

In *A Slow Dance* (1975) and *The Great Cloak* (1978) Montague restores to his poetry the loneliness which is, paradoxically, its proper home. He can endorse his homelessness by imagining a community in which it would be healed but he does not violate it by laying claim to that community, by attempting to possess it as his own. Culturally, the imagined home remains Gaelic Ireland, especially the Ireland of Tyrone's past. Politically, it is Irish republicanism. Privately, it is marriage. All of these, save marriage, are residual communities or, more truly, they are all, including marriage, communities under pressure. In *The Great Cloak*, the keenest poems show the pain of a man whose marriage has broken and who discovers 'that libertinism does not relieve his solitude'. Even when a new marriage restores him, the lovers find themselves in the solitude of one another's arms while Belfast falls to pieces around them. This feeling of solitude is the source of the aristocrat in Montague. His connoisseurship, his refinement, the easy elegance of his verse are infinitely preferable to the sentimentality, the plebeian togetherness which mars it when he cancels his solitude and believes he can dissolve it in camaraderie. In the end, nothing can dislodge the spear of isolation. It is the hurt that gives his work its distinctive feeling.

There is a danger of exaggerating this aspect of the poetry and of seeming to make a virtue of its decision to disengage from community. Montague remains a profoundly political poet and his attempt in the seventies to politicize his work by reordering it in relation to the Northern troubles is one obvious symptom of that. Moreover, this reordering, although I believe it did finally militate against the nature of his gift, is, in itself, a considerable and a courageous achievement. But the more enduringly political aspect of his work lies in grieved admission that, although nothing can break in upon his solitude, the longing for relief from this plight is a legitimate and permanent one. It is no accident that he has championed two writers, Kavanagh and Goldsmith, both of them examples of the artist surviving almost impossible conditions. In his introduction to *The Faber Book of Irish Verse* he envisages an international poetry which has national roots, a definition of Irish which arises from a negotiation between the English and the Gaelic traditions. As in the poetry, the search is for a reconciled community, the refusal is to accept as inevitable the burden of solitude. Goldsmith's deserted village, Kavanagh's hungry hills, Montague's ruined Tyrone, are all abandoned places, victimized by history, repossessed as a possibility in poetry. But they are none the less lost, for all that. This Montague would not accept. But, as the later poems in his *Selected Poems* (1982) demonstrate, the acceptance has begun to grow. In 'Process' we find:

> Everyone close in his own
> world of sense & memory,
> races, countries closed
> in their dream of history,
> only love, or friendship,
> an absorbing discipline –
> the healing harmonies
> of music, painting, the poem –
> as swaying ropeladders
> across fuming oblivion
> while the globe turns,
> and the stars turn, and
> the great circles shine,
> gold & silver,
> > sun & moon.

In 'The Well Dreams' and 'The Music Box' the same note prevails. History, it seems, makes monads of us all but art, love and friendship break the isolation, provide 'healing harmonies'.

The note is not one of resignation. It is one of patience. Montague has finally come to see the dead kingdom of history and accepts his exile from it. But rather than see this exile as an aristocratic aloofness – which he recognizes to have been his attitude at one time – he now sees it as a strange form of presence, even protection, in the culture from which he has become separated. In the poem 'Mount Eagle' (from *The Dead Kingdom*) the aristocratic bird finds that the moment has come to leave off his flight over the world and meet a different destiny in his mountain world. It was 'to be the spirit of the mountain'. This is a figure for Montague's own destiny. He has twice revised his career. Once, between 1968 and 1978, he rewrote his poems against the Northern crisis. Now, since *The Great Cloak*, he has begun to rewrite them again, but on this occasion against the experience of the solitude which the North bore in upon him. This remaking of his own poetry, his refashioning of the once exhausted notions of self and community, of art and country, is a transference to a new plane of one of the unchangeable features of modern Irish experience. It is as close to reconciliation as anyone has come, but the price paid has been high:

> It was a greater task than an eagle's
> aloofness, but sometimes, under his oilskin
> of coiled mist, he sighed for lost freedom.

12

○EREK mahon:
fREEOOM fROM history

Derek Mahon's poetry expresses a longing to be free from history. In this respect he is recognizably an Irish poet, although part of the longing arises from the wish to be free of that category too. Many Irish writers, sensitive to the threat of provincialism, have tried to compensate for it by being as cosmopolitan as possible. In consequence, they became citizens of the world by profession. Denis Devlin and Sean O'Faolain are two outstanding examples. For them, the cultivation of the intellect is not only a goal in itself but also a means of escape from beseiged and rancorous origins. Others – Joyce, Beckett, Francis Stuart, Louis MacNeice – although they also seek in the world beyond an alternative to their native culture, have come to regard their exile from it as a generic feature of the artist's rootless plight rather than a specifically Irish form of alienation.

Derek Mahon occupies a middle ground between these choices. He is not urbane in a self-conscious way, as if afraid of being thought bucolic. His urbanity helps him to fend off the forces of atavism, ignorance and oppression which are part of his Northern Protestant heritage. There is an ease and an elegance in his writing which can be identified as that of the world-citizen, but the *urbs* from which his urbanity arises is the city of Belfast, a bleak and ruined site – so that the wit and sophistication of the poetry is haunted by intimations of collapse, pogrom, apocalypse. Mahon can be ironical at the expense of the barbarous when it is banal. In his rewriting of Constantin Cavafy's 'Waiting for the Barbarians', in which the failed arrival of the barbarians disappoints a populace longing for a fresh access of energy to raise it from its decadent weariness, Mahon observes that they have already arrived with their

> talk
> Of fitted carpets, central
> Heating and automatic gear-change . . .
>
> ('After Cavafy')

With the arrival of such people, history has, in a real sense, ended. The barbarians have come and put an end to civilization so effectively that they are assumed to be its inheritors. Mahon's selective cataloguing of the items in the technological junkyard of the modern city is reminiscent of the urban realism of Louis MacNeice both in its detail and in its underlying sense of dread. But he goes further than MacNeice in his vision of the modern city after the holocaust of a great war. Whereas his irony is linked to a complex tone and a protesting voice, his prophetic strain is expressed in a simpler, plangent tone with the voice displaced, ventriloquized into objects, the refuse of the ruined civilization. Cans, metals, decayed vegetation, sing in the great silence when human voices have been extinguished. Although many poems combine irony with prophecy, the stress and even the contrast between the two are the more pronounced because they both are rooted in the one desire – to have done with history, to get rid of it in an inventory of its artefacts or to imagine its disappearance in a moment of doom.

> What will remain after
> The twilight of metals,
> The flowers of fire,
>
> Will be the soft
> Vegetables where our
> Politics were conceived.
>
> ('What Will Remain')

The mood of poems like this one is elegiac yet it is no more than an inflection away from satire. History is not evaded but it is included in a negative way. It merits both contempt and tenderness. In his first two books, *Night-Crossing* (1968) and *Lives* (1972), these emotions are based on a set of attitudes shared by a group of friends to some of whom the poems are dedicated. There is a spirit of bohemian camaraderie, of slightly raffish stylishness, even of knowingness which underlies the humour and the pace of a poem like 'Beyond Howth Head', a bright, chatty epistle which just manages to keep its decorum in the face of disaster and crisis. The poem is a criss-cross of literary references, Irish, English and others, many of them burdened by fresh ironies that arise from their strategic deployment in an argument which centres on the quest for freedom and pleasure, two experiences always closely allied in these early books. The key quotation for both is one taken from Edmund Spenser's *Veue of the Present State of Ireland* – a notorious example of Tudor imperialism, written during the poet's residence at Kilcolman Castle in County Cork during the years 1587 and 1598 when the castle was burned by the Irish. It is the phrase 'lewde libertie'. For Spenser it betokens the anarchy and rebellion which led to the destruction of Kilcolman. Mahon turns the phrase towards his search for pleasure (including sexual, hence 'lewde' pleasure) and for freedom (including rebellion against oppressive forces). But the background of bitter warfare and its heritage in the present – an inbred and divided Ireland, an Ireland still divided from England by both sea and history – is not ignored. Instead it is deflected. There is no freedom in turning anchorite of the old Celtic or of the contemporary Beckettian type, like Molloy; there is no freedom in the heat of the turbulent and blighted world of war, structuralist linguistics, decayed Georgian Dublin. The only freedom left is that of writing even though the audience is that of the inner group, the chosen few. Because the audience is fit, the poem can be humorous, sophisticated and knowing. Because the audience is few and freedom so intangible, the poem is elegiac, saddened in its recognition of the loss and strife which has been so freely endowed by the past. In deflecting history in this way, Mahon makes great demands on his style, on sheer grace of expression, keeping it light, bright and sparkling even when the matter of the poem is so laden and intractable.

Despite the pleasure afforded by the local ironies in Mahon's poetry, and despite the good humour with which absurdities are exposed, the abiding atmosphere of his work is bleak. His most characteristic procedure is one of reduction, of stripping down, peeling away until there is nothing left. This is both an end and, because of its clean emptiness, a new beginning. The voice in the title poem, 'Lives', finally announces:

> I know too much
> To be anything more –
> And if in the distant

> Future someone
> Thinks he has once been me
> As I am today,
>
> Let him revise
> His insolent ontology
> Or teach himself to pray.

Similarly, in 'An Image from Beckett', 'Matthew V.29–30', 'The Apotheosis of Tins' and in several other poems there is a stern and logical working down to despair, the bleakness enhanced by the professional expertise with which a polysyllabic language, redolent of philosophy and of metaphysics, is constrained within the tight mathematical vice of his stanzas. In 'An Image from Beckett', the words can surge against the simplifying demands of the stanza form:

> With a subliminal batsqueak
> Of reflex lamentation.

or they can co-operate easily with it:

> Still, I am haunted
> By that landscape,
> The soft rush of its winds,

The blends of vocabulary and of tone in Mahon's poetry shift the reader's attention from specific detail to general conditions. There is no dwelling in the sensuous and no concentration on abstractions. He is neither conceptual nor sensual; his sensibility is equidistant from both but is alert to the attractions of each. Again, one senses the shadow of MacNeice.

It would be possible to write of Mahon's poetry as though it enacted a drama of belonging and not belonging to a country itself isolated from world history, divided within itself, obsessed by competing mythologies, Northern and Southern, ambiguously ensnared in the subtle politics of colonialism and independence, a central void with violent peripheries. Terence Brown has written eloquently on these themes and it is right to admit their force and the bearing they have on this ultimately 'protestant' poetry.[1] For Mahon does not enjoy or seek to have a sense of community with the kind of Ireland which is so dominant in Irish poetry. All his

[1] Terence Brown, *Northern Voices: Poets from Ulster* (Dublin and London, 1975), pp. 192–201.

versions of community depend on the notion of a disengagement from history achieved by those whose maverick individuality resisted absorption into the official discourses and decencies. Beckett, Villon, Cavafy, Rimbaud, de Nerval, Munch, Malcolm Lowry and others go to form that miscellany of outsiders whom he transforms into his own specific community, members of an artistic rather than an historical continuum, rebels haunted by a metaphysical dread. Nevertheless, he was born into an historical community, that of Northern Irish Protestantism, and his most deeply felt poems derive from his sympathy for its isolation and its fading presence rather than from straightforward repudiation of its stiff rhetorical intransigence. The plight of his community was, of course, defined by the conflict of the last fifteen years and Mahon, with some reluctance it would seem, was drawn to a contemplation of it. To turn towards this meant a turning towards the very history which he had so successfully deflected in his first two books. The exquisite tact with which he had preserved his freedom as a writer was now to be put at risk.

The Snow Party (1975) is the volume in which the risk is taken. Its opening poem, 'Afterlives', is dedicated to James Simmons, a friend, a poet, who had stayed in the North through all the troubled years, writing, editing a journal, *The Honest Ulsterman*, and sponsoring in his work an ethic of freedom and pleasure very close to that which Mahon himself had subscribed to in his earlier poetry. This liberal hedonism is now confronted by the apparently endless violence.

> What middle-class cunts we are
> To imagine for one second
> That our privileged ideals
> Are divine wisdom, and the dim
> Forms that kneel at noon
> In the city not ourselves.

That is the first rebuke. The second follows in the second part of the poem. Coming ashore to a war-worn and unrecognizable Belfast, he wonders if staying through the violence would have provided him with the sense of community and of self he has sought elsewhere:

> Perhaps if I'd stayed behind
> And lived it bomb by bomb
> I might have grown up at last
> And learnt what is meant by home.

The sting of this second rebuke is felt throughout the remaining poems in this book. Although at first the references to 'the heaven/of lost futures/The lives we might have led' ('Leaves') and 'To the blank Elysium/Predicated on our/Eschewal of metaphysics' ('Going Home') seem to indicate the state of homelessness which in *Night-Crossing* and in *Lives* had the virtue of freedom to recommend it, it eventually becomes clear that the predominant emotion in most of these poems is grief. Homelessness has become a matter of sorrow now that the ruin of home has become a matter of fact. The sense that the repudiated ground may have harboured within it, in the course of its disintegration, the opportunity to seize both maturity and stability together, sharpens the regret and enforces a deeper interrogation of the liberal sentiments which had made so much of the advantages of freeing oneself from history.

It would be extravagant to say that Mahon now begins to elaborate some kind of confrontation with history, but he certainly dismisses it with less assurance. In fact, the title poem 'The Snow Party', 'The Last of the Fire Kings' and 'Thammuz' (this last a rewriting of 'What Will Remain' from *Lives*, later to be modified again in *Poems 1962–1978* and retitled 'The Golden Bough') are more deeply meditative poems than anything he had written before. The subject of the meditation is the relationship between civility and barbarity, the thin partitions which divide them, the deep bonds which conjoin them. In entering upon this territory, Mahon reveals his companionship with John Montague, Seamus Heaney and Thomas Kinsella, all of whom are forced into this trying area by the pressure of contemporary circumstance. It is one of the oldest and one of the most aggravating themes in twentieth-century Irish literature. Given the country's history, it comes as no surprise to find it so; given the severity of the questions raised, it is also unsurprising to discover in the poets a reluctance to be dragged into such issues.

A recognition of the depths from which violence springs often leads to feelings of dismay at the apparent shallowness of the liberal or rational mentality. Mahon's contempt for the modern socialist, the professional tourist who visits and measures everything and knows nothing, the expert locked in his own force-field, is inexhaustible. Such a creature is indeed one of the products of secular civility. Emotionally gelded, he cannot know the lust for history or the grief of utter loss which the instinctual life knows. He is a visitor among the afterlives of dead opportunities and hopes. Yet he is not in himself a rebuke to the rational and the humane mind. He is instead the mirror-image of atavism. He is as doomed by his disengagement from feeling as is atavism by its surrender to feeling. Mahon distinguishes for us between feelings that are temperate and feelings that are tempered. He chooses the latter while conceding its possible evolution into the former. The heartening and enriching aspects of his poetry emerge from his capacity to match the extremes of the situations he observes with a correspondent feeling which is not itself contaminated by that extremism. In allowing for the presence of the dark gods he stays clear of and yet in contact with their tribal communities.

This is an especially difficult exercise in a literary culture which had made so much of the affinity between these deep forces and the sources of the imaginative life. The political conditions of Northern Ireland supported the notion of such an affinity. Communal warfare often sponsors an art in which the temptation to become the tribune of the plebs is irresistible. More bluntly, contact with violence is regarded by some as a stimulus to the deep energies of creation. Avoidance of it is regarded as a form of imaginative anaemia. Mahon is alert to these attitudes and threats and is willing to concede a good deal to them. But he does not, finally, concede what we may call his liberal individualism, his 'protestant' ethic of the independent imagination. His only loyalty is to the abandoned, the community which poses no threat to independence but which indeed liberates it.

The Snow Party, in pursuing the intricacies of these historical and political minefields, achieves its great triumph in the last poem, 'A Disused Shed in County Wicklow'. It is dedicated to the late J.G. Farrell, the Liverpool-Irish novelist and elegist of Empire whose book *Troubles*, set in the Ireland of 1919–21, provided the moment for the poem's lament for the dead and the murdered causes of history – the 'Lost people of Treblinka and Pompeii'. Lost lives are Mahon's obsession. His poetry is an attempt to fulfil them. In 'The chair squeaks . . . ' we hear the lost tribe of Ulster-Israel 'singing abide with me'. In 'Cavafy', the dead and the lost loves are recognized to be 'The original poetry of our lives'. The grief in these poems is rescued from sentimentality by the precision with which it is articulated, the lovely matter-of-factness of detail which makes it ordinary and lets its intensity live in that:

> And once a day, perhaps, they have heard something –
> A trickle of masonry, a shout from the blue

Or a lorry changing gear at the end of the lane.

('A Disused Shed in County Wicklow')

In the dark shed of this final poem, a surging mass of mushrooms yearns towards the light that enters through the keyhole. Their grotesque struggle has been silently waged since the days of the Irish Civil War. Then, with the arrival of the tourist, the door is pulled open in a great explosion of light and the sad and terrifying scene revealed, just before the door is closed again. The mushrooms sing the lament, the plea for release. But their release is into, not from, history. They seek to escape from the brutality of a dark, instinctive and lethal struggle into the light of recognition. Mahon has here inverted his usual procedure. The lost lives are not lived beyond history, but before it. Their fulfilment is in history. This is a conceit and a figure in which he captures the central significance of his opening poem, 'Afterlives'. In one sense, he is saying that after life, there is art. But he is also saying that the only life which can produce art is one that is engaged with history, even (especially?) if it is the history of the victims, the lost, the forgotten.

In effect, I am suggesting that Mahon establishes in *The Snow Party* a way of meditating about poetry and history which enriches his work by rescuing it from the conventional attitudes towards this elusive and yet central relationship. The latent notion that poetry is in some sense 'pure' and history a contaminating force lends a good deal of pathos to the figure of the artist in a time of historical crisis. Mahon reveals a susceptibility to the appeal of this idea in his early work. But in resisting it and the facility of feeling which it encourages in many of his contemporaries, he has avoided one of the dangers that beset Irish writers – that of exploiting the country's crisis – and enjoyed one of the advantages that such crisis can bring – a humaneness of feeling which has the force of passion and which yet remains distinct from violent feeling. The first poem in his most recent volume, *The Hunt by Night* (1982), explores the connections between a Dutch painting of 1659 by Pieter de Hooch, its wonderful 'chaste/Precision' and peace, and the marauding forces of Dutch imperialism of that time. The first adjustment Mahon makes to the contrast is to apply it to himself and his own Belfast childhood and political situation. The second is to restate, in that light, the question of the connection between art and violence of the Dutch or British imperial kind. The answer is ironic, but it is also without assurance. The writer has not 'solved' the problem and will not; but he has found a mode of contemplating it in poetry which still retains the attributes of elegance and swiftness which had once been its primary appeal. Here is the last verse of the poem in question, 'Courtyards in Delft':

> For the pale light of that provincial town
> Will spread itself, like ink or oil,
> Over the not yet accurate linen
> Map of the world which occupies one wall
> And punish nature in the name of God.
> If only, now, the Maenads, as of right,
> Came smashing crockery, with fire and sword,
> We could sleep easier in our beds at night.

In some of the following poems he returns to the fascination with places which, like Derry, Portrush or Rathlin Island, have been abandoned by history and now have the strict repose of ruins. But these spectral Ulster sites have a close connection with the paintings, like those by de Hooch or Uccello, which provide the occasion for 'Courtyards in Delft' and the title-poem, 'The Hunt by Night'. The relief from the pressure of history which places and paintings share is now understood to be simultaneously real and illusory. They are not images that have passed beyond history; they are images which have incorporated history's force into their stillness. If the end of this art is peace, its origin is in the violence of the actual. Art is neither one nor the other, but a mode of sustaining the paradoxical relationship between both. Figures like Brecht, Knut Hamsun, Ovid in his exile by the Euxine Sea, appear in the by-now customary role of artists who have escaped from crisis and yet, once more, the escape or the exile is determined by the shock of the crisis. The fate of these artists is like that of the Ulster towns – abandoned to a provincial stupor they nevertheless remain embodiments of world history not evasions of it. The position studied by Mahon in these poems is similar to that contemplated by Seamus Heaney in the final poem in *North*, 'Exposure'. There Heaney considers his exile from the North in Wicklow and contrasts the softness and slush of the season with the hard, crystalline demands of the history he faces, sensing the paradox of his attempt to escape the North by going into a private isolation and the exposure – that of publicity, and the consequent exposure to history – which attends upon it. Like Mahon, he too sees that exile may be a necessary condition for the writing of poetry but that the poetry is itself conditioned by the very history which made the exile necessary in the first place.

Mahon's fondness for translating or rather imitating poets like Rimbaud (from whose 'Le Bâteau Ivre' he gives us an excerpt in this recent volume) seems almost anomalous at first. For the rich chemistries of association provided by such a poem (and by the poems of Gerard de Nerval whose *Les Chimères* he has also translated) seem to consort oddly with the strict syntax and logic, the closely bound rhyme schemes and ratiocinative power of his own poems. Here again, though, we can see Mahon's characteristic blending of turbulence with repose, free association with logic. It is a stylistic feature which contains within itself the twin pressures of his whole enterprise. The formal control of his poems is an expression of a kind of moral stoicism, a mark of endurance under pressure. The verbal excitements, the blended imageries and references, are an expression of his sensitivity to the uncontrolled and turbulent nature of his experience. The matching of the two makes the poems themselves exemplary sites wherein the opposed forces are locked together in a mutually sustaining embrace. A dishevelled history, an orderly poetry: the play of mind which is released by this conflict is itself the final freedom, Mahon gains this. Wallace Stevens's well-known comment is an appropriate epigraph for his achievement: 'Reality is not what it is. It consists of the many realities which it can be made into'.[2]

[2] Wallace Stevens, *Opus Posthumous* (New York, 1966), p. 178.

13

BRIAN FRIEL:
the double stage

A closed community, a hidden story, a gifted outsider with an antic intelligence, a drastic revelation leading to violence – these are recurrent elements in a Brian Friel play. They are co-ordinated in the pursuit of one elusive theme, the link between authority and love. Most of the people in Friel's drama are experts in the maintenance of a persona, or of an illusion upon which the persona depends. But their expertise, which most often takes the form of eloquence and wit, and which is a mode of defence against the oppressions of false authority, has no power to alter reality. So they become articulators of a problem to such a degree that the problem becomes insoluble, so perfectly etched are all its numbing complexities. To be gifted at all, an expert, is to be displaced, a commentator, not a participant, an outsider, not an insider. Yet the sense of displacement is acute in such figures and it is the more profoundly felt when it is expressed for them in the secret or hidden stories of others. The stories are tales of passion, thwarted and violent; the displacement is a condition of lucid weariness, often witty and cruel in its responses. The tension between the two embodiments of thwarted desire disrupts the closed community, undermines its sham system of authority and leads to various kinds of breakdown, individual and social. Friel's drama is concerned with the nervous collapse of a culture which has had to bear pressures beyond its capacity to sustain.

The closed community is that of the County Donegal village of Ballybeg, or of sectors within that generic community – monastic as in *The Enemy Within* (1962), psychological as in *Philadelphia, Here I Come!* (1964), sexual-familial as in *The Gentle Island* (1971) or *Living Quarters* (1977), political as in *The Freedom of the City* (1973) or *Volunteers* (1975). The cast of characters is tightly

166

contained in a quarantined area, enclosed with the infection which is coming to a head on this particular moment, in this particular setting. The dramatic unities of time, place and action are strictly observed but the apparently effortless and often humorous registration of the details of provincial manners helps to disguise the structural tautness which gives these works their symmetry – although Friel's most recent play, *The Communication Cord* (produced in 1982) reveals more obviously than these others how strictly organized his plays are. The illness which plagues the small community is failure, cast in every conceivable shape, protean but always recognizable. The central failure is one of feeling and, proceeding from that, a failure of self-realization and, deriving from that, the seeking of a refuge in words or work, silence or idiocy, in exile or in a deliberate stifling of unrequitable desire. Every character has his or her fiction; every fiction is generated out of the fear of the truth. But the truth is nevertheless there, hidden in the story which lies at the centre of the play, a story which tells of how authority, divorced from love, became a sham. In *Volunteers* Keeney draws a distinction between himself and Butt:

> All the wildness and power evaporate and all that's left is a mouth. Of course there is a reason – my over-riding limitation – the inability to sustain a passion, even a frivolous passion. Unlike you, Butt. But then your passions are pure – no, not necessarily pure – consistent – the admirable virtue, consistency – a consistent passion fuelled by a confident intellect. Whereas my paltry flirtations are just . . . fireworks, fireworks that are sparked occasionally by an antic imagination. And yet here we are, spancelled goats complementing each other, suffering the same consequences. Is it ironic? Is it even amusing?

The secret story in this play concerns Smiley, who has been reduced to idiocy by the brutal beatings he received at the hands of the police. It also touches upon Knox, who has also been degraded by the treatment he has received at the hands of the IRA. Most of all, it touches upon their common fate, for Keeney, Pyne, Butt and the others are going to face death at the hands of their comrades in prison once the archaeological excavation, for which they have volunteered, is over. The secret story is in this case, as in many others, a premonition of the violence to come. Its secrecy, which is there to be broken; its violence, which is there to be repeated; its degradation, which is there to be hidden or shunned, all conspire to transform the stage into a 'magic circle', a place into which the audience is being given a privileged insight. On the other hand, the surrounding commentary on this kernel story – that is, the chatter of people who try to preserve themselves from the truth it contains – displays the conditions of their social and personal lives in a sociological spirit, turning the stage into a public exhibition area. So, in *Volunteers*, the republican prisoners working on the archaeological site on which a new hotel is to be erected, provide us with an image of many of the characteristic political and economic forces in Irish society, all of them governed by corrupt authorities. Equally, in *Loving Quarters* the Butler family, or in *The Gentle Island* the Sweeney family, or the central trio in *The Freedom of the City*, all provide us with this public display of existing conditions, of circumstances easily recognized as the sort which would make news – the return of Irish UN troops from a trouble spot, the mass departure of a community from an island, the official killings and inquiries of the Northern situation. Yet the recognizability of the conditions is one of Friel's naturalistic illusions. For the secret story – of Smiler in *Volunteers*, of Lily in *The Freedom of the City*, of Manus in *The Gentle Island*, challenges that recognizability and forces the audience to sense within it an element of mystery, a suppressed quotient of feeling. Clearly, these people are all victims of foul conditions. Their fate is predetermined and all their attempts to escape it are futile. Smiler's mock escape, Manus's invented story about the loss of his arm, Lily's fake reasons for being on the civil rights marches are all illusions, lies created to disguise a truth, their malevolent presence indicated by some physical deformity or mental affliction. The function of the hidden story, when it is uncovered, is to transform the stage as public exhibition area into the stage as private and sacral area. The recognizable social 'meaning' is constantly being undermined by another kind of significance which is more complex and cryptic. The shock of the conclusion finally clarifies this cryptic element. Violence is not a manifestation of the pressures of specifically Irish conditions. In the conclusion we see death, individual death, the death of a way of life or of a social formation, finally confronted by people who have been escaping it all their lives. In the light of that, all authority fails, even the authority of love.

Still, our sympathy or our admiration tends to be given to the people who have no illusions, who are not locked into some conspiracy of discretion or of despair and who regard the world with a liberated and liberating intelligence. Keeney in *Volunteers*, Skinner in *The Freedom of the City*, Eamon in *Aristocrats*, Shane in *The Gentle Island*, are the most obvious examples. But Keeney and Skinner are killed, Shane is crippled for life, Eamon is bereft with the rest of the O'Donnell family. Further, they are all outsiders, but with an insider's knowledge of the society. They put an antic disposition on, partly as a mode of rejecting authority, partly as a mode of escaping responsibility. But, disengaged in this way, they become mere wordsmiths. Their language is gestural, being in effect nothing more than a series of mimicries, a ventriloquism by performers who run the risk of losing their own voices. The displacement of voice, the switching of vocabularies, always important in a Friel play, is a symptom of the splintering of authority, the failure of any one voice to predominate and become accepted as a standard. The stage machinery of *Aristocrats*, with its loudspeaker and tape-recorder and its human recorder Hoffnung, is a characteristic example of this. Still, the moment has to come when the gesturing is laid aside and the voice of conviction, the true voice of feeling of, say, Skinner in *The Freedom of the City* is heard, telling Lily why she marches in Derry:

> Because you live with eleven kids and a sick husband in two rooms that aren't fit for animals. Because you exist on a state subsistence that's about enough to keep you alive but too small to fire your guts. Because you know your children are caught in the same morass. Because for the first time in your life you grumbled and someone else grumbled and someone else, and you heard each other, and became aware that there were hundreds, thousands, millions of us all over the world, and in a vague groping way you were outraged. That's what it's all about, Lily. It has nothing to do with doctors and accountants and teachers and dignity and boy scout honour. It's about us − the poor − the majority − stirring in our sleep. And if that's not what it's all about, then it has nothing to do with us.[1]

Such set speeches frequently occur in Friel's plays and they are not confined to the type Skinner represents. Sometimes their eloquence is out of character, although usually we feel that, at

---

[1] Act Two, *Selected Plays* (London, 1984), p. 154. All subsequent page references in this chapter are to this collection.

169

the point of crisis, the characters are able to draw on resources they never knew they had. But the explanatory, even hectoring voice which emerges, in a kind of authorial overdrive, and spells out 'what it's all about', turns the stage into a platform, the text into a lecture. Dr Dodds, the sociologist in *The Freedom of the City*, and the various experts called upon by the Widgery-like judge in that play, have similar moments of annunciation. It is sometimes difficult to distinguish between the voice of the truth-teller and that of the expert. Yet it is important to do so, since the expert is usually someone who knows everything but the truth. In this particular case, is Lily really marching on behalf of the poor, the outcasts of the earth, of whom her mongol child Declan is one? If so, the play is a political one in essence and the object of its complicated structure is the analysis of official injustice, the corruption that is inseparable from authority. Suppression and oppression are so frequently analysed in Friel's drama that it is not difficult to accept him as a political dramatist. But the point bears some further consideration.

Authority and love may be divorced, to the detriment of both, but there is at least the implication that they were once married. In *The Enemy Within*, St Colmcille discovers that his love for family and for country is beginning to undermine his vocation and his position as abbot in the island community of Iona. In order to give himself wholly to his work he has to destroy the enemy within himself – his fatal attraction to Ireland and home. This attraction has repeatedly led Colmcille into the position of seeming to lend his authority to bloody faction fights. So, with great difficulty and determination, he stifles it. So too in the dialogue between Public and Private Gar in *Philadelphia Here I Come*, the attraction of Ireland has to be subdued so that the place may be left. In *Faith Healer*, the attraction has to do with Francis Hardy's hope for a restoration of his strange gift; but it is also an attraction towards sleep and death. In *Translations*, there are two Irelands, two languages, two kinds of violence, and Owen, who has migrated to the new Ireland, is nevertheless pulled by his sentimental loyalties towards the one he has helped to bury. The unfortunate Lieutenant Yolland is his mirror image in this respect. In all of these cases the repudiation of Ireland carries with it a certain guilt, a sense of betrayal; but equally, to give in to the place is a form of suicide. Ireland is, of course, a metaphor in these contexts as well as a place. It is the country of the young, of hope, a perfect coincidence between fact and desire. It is also the country of the disillusioned, where everything is permanently out of joint, violent, broken. Hugh, the hedge-schoolmaster in *Translations*, remembers the hope:

> The road to Sligo. A spring morning. 1798. Going into battle . . . Two young gallants with pikes across their shoulders and the Aeneid in their pockets. Everything seemed to find definition that spring – a congruence, a miraculous matching of hope and past and present and possibility. Striding across the fresh, green land. The rhythms of perception heightened. The whole enterprise of consciousness accelerated. (p. 445)

But earlier Hugh had warned the Englishman Yolland, who wanted access to the old Ireland, that

> words are signals, counters. They are not immortal. And it can happen – to use an image you'll understand – it can happen that a civilization can be imprisoned in a linguistic contour which no longer matches the landscape of . . . fact. (p. 419)

It hardly needs saying that these two versions of the Irish psychic landscape are enunciated on the brink of violence – the '98 Rebellion and the disappearance of Yolland. On the hither side of violence is Ireland as paradise; on the nether side, Ireland as ruin. But, since we live on the nether side, we live in ruin and can only console ourselves with the desire for the paradise we briefly glimpse. The result is a discrepancy in our language; words are askew, they are out of line with fact. Violence has fantasy and wordiness as one of its most persistent after-effects.

Like Owen in *Translations*, we can thus give our love to the failed world (Ireland) but our respect to the conquering world (England). But if what can be respected is not loved, and what can be loved cannot be respected, there is little recourse for us but violence. Authority is denied for the sake of the failure that is loved; failure is mocked and hated for the sake of the authority it has lost. Skinner and Lily in *The Freedom of the City* are caught in the same dilemma as Owen or Hugh in *Translations*. They have two roles each. One is heroic, that of the oppressed natives in the Mayor's Parlour, later as murdered victims of British Army SLR bullets. The other is the sociologist's categorization of them as creatures of the 'culture of poverty', Bogsiders immersed in the stupor of their condition. Again it is the choice between paradise and ruin. Again it is a choice enforced by violence. Finally neither alternative allows one to live. The native condition, which is that of being human, not Irish, is almost destroyed; the foreign condition of an enforced identity, political or sociological, is also resisted. Struggle is the only action, crisis the only climate.

Such a politics is metonymic of a wider condition. The plays all work as parables in which the development of a particular action contributes to the representation of a general condition. Also, the propositions which abound in these plays and which seem to have a general import when they are directed outward at the audience in an oratorical *tour de force*, and thus seem to have meaning for the human condition as such, tend to narrow themselves into statements symptomatic of a particular person's plight, or of a culture's specific pressure. This ambivalence of scope in the language of these plays is most clearly manifest in *Faith Healer*, the play in which the device of metonymy is most openly used or at least most appropriately applied. If we cast the play into the form of a question and look to the text for an answer, we may ask, what is the gift of Francis Hardy and why does it necessarily lead to his death in Ballybeg? And the text, in the voice of Grace Hardy, the wife of Francis, answers the first part of the question so:

> Faith healer – faith healing – I never understood it, never. I tried to. In the beginning, I tried diligently – as the doctor might say I brought all my mental rigour to bear on it. But I couldn't even begin to apprehend it – this gift, this craft, this talent, this art, this magic – whatever it was he possessed, that defined him, that was, I suppose, essentially him. And because it was his essence and because it eluded me I suppose I *was* wary of it. Yes, of course I was. And he knew it. Indeed, if by some miracle Frank could have been the same Frank without it, I would happily have robbed him of it. And he knew that, too – how well he knew that; and in his twisted way read into it the ultimate treachery on my part. (p. 349)

In answer to the second part of the question, the Faith Healer himself, in his last moments, says:

> And as I moved across that yard towards them and offered myself to them, then for the first time I had a simple and genuine sense of home-coming. Then for the first time

172

there was no atrophying terror; and the maddening questions were silent. At long last I was renouncing chance. (p. 376)

Hardy's gift is his essence and yet it is subject to chance; only by giving himself over to death does he renounce chance. In doing so he also renounces the gift. The certitude of death is preferable to the vicissitudes of life with (or without) the gift. His capacity to heal others, in other countries, and his incapacity to heal himself except by coming back to his own country, dying back into the place out of which his healing came in the first place, is a strange metonym for the gift in exile, the artist abroad. This association between gift and exile, creativity and death, is more purely stated here than elsewhere in Friel's work. The play throws no political shadow; it provides no action, only four monologues. It shows a man creating his own death by coming home out of exile.

It is the inevitability of death, finally realized, which makes the Faith Healer feel at peace in that last scene. The maimed body which he faces but cannot heal, the instruments in the tractor which will maim him, the 'black-faced macerated baby' buried in Scotland, the weekly parade of cripples who listen to the scratched record of Fred Astaire singing 'The Way You Look Tonight', are all semi-farcical, semi-tragic recognitions that perfection is a desire granted only on the other side of violence, through death. Thus Friel asserts the lethal quality of the gift, the urge to create wholeness out of distortions. So the gift, the stolen fire, is returned to death, to its source. But other things remain. The unique life of Francis Hardy is not repeatable, but as a parable its weight is inherited. It is this weight of inherited failure and the uniqueness of the individual response to it which are both made manifest on Friel's double stage, the exhibition area and the magic circle area. The anguish of the individual life passes over into the communal life through violence, borne in language. The exploration of that difficult transition, the discovery of a series of dramatic forms in which it could be reconnoitred, is central to his achievement and part of the reason for his importance.

14

SEAMUS HEANEY:
THE TIMOROUS AND THE BOLD

As he tells us in his essay 'Feeling into Words', Seamus Heaney signed one of his first poems 'Incertus', 'uncertain, a shy soul fretting and all that'.[1] Feeling his way into words so that he could find words for his feelings was the central preoccupation of his apprenticeship to poetry. In a review of Theodore Roethke's *Collected Poems* he declares that 'An awareness of his own poetic process, and a trust in the possibility of his poetry, that is what a poet should attempt to preserve'.[2] The assurance of this statement is partly undercut by the last phrase. It strikes that note of uncertainty, of timorousness which recurs time and again both in his poetry and in his prose. His fascination with the fundamentals of music in poetry, his pursuit of the central energies in another writer's work, his inspection of the experiences, early and late, which guarantee, validate, confirm his perceptions, his admiration of the sheer mastery of men like Hopkins or Yeats, all reveal a desire for the absolute, radical certainty. But this boldness has caution as its brother. For all its possibilities and strengths, poetry is a tender plant. Heaney dominates a territory – his home ground, the language of Hopkins, an idea of poetry – in a protective, tutelary spirit. Images of preservation are almost as frequent as those of nourishment. The occlusions of life in the Northern state certainly contributed to this. It was not only a matter of saying nothing, whatever you say. For him, there is no gap between enfolding and unfolding. It is a deep instinct, the reverence of an acolyte before a mystery of which he knows he is also the celebrant. Hence the allegiance to the mastery of other

[1] *Preoccupations: Selected Prose 1968–1978* (London, 1980), p. 45.
[2] Ibid., p. 190.

writers is indeed that of an apprentice. But he is indentured, finally, to the idea of poetry itself and is awed to see it become tactile as poems in his own hands. His boldness emerges as he achieves mastery, but his timorousness remains because it has been achieved over mystery.

This duality is visible in his first two books. Writing in a medley of influences – Frost, Hopkins, Hughes, Wordsworth, Kavanagh, Montague – he emerges from the struggle with them with a kind of guilt for having overcome them. This sense of guilt merges with the general unease he has displayed in the face of the Northern crisis and its demands upon him, demands exacerbated by the success of his poetry and the publicity given to him as a result. Although political echoes are audible in *Death of a Naturalist* and in *Door into the Dark*, there is no consciousness of politics as such, and certainly no political consciousness until *Wintering Out* and *North*. It would be easy, then, to describe his development as a broadening out from the secrecies of personal growth in his own sacred places to a recognition of the relations between this emergent self and the environing society with its own sacred, historically ratified, places. This would not be seriously inaccurate, but it is unsatisfactory because it misses one vital element – the source of guilt in Heaney's poetry and the nature of his search for it.

His guilt is that of the victim, not of the victimizer. In this he is characteristic of his Northern Irish Catholic community. His attitude to paternity and authority is apologetic – for having undermined them. His attitude to maternity and love is one of pining and also of apology – for not being of them. Maternity is of the earth, paternity belongs to those who build on it or cultivate it. There is a politics here, but it is embedded in an imagination given to ritual. That which in political or sectarian terms could be called nationalist or Catholic, belongs to maternity, the earth itself; that which is unionist or Protestant, belongs to paternity, the earth cultivated. What Heaney seeks is another kind of earth or soil susceptible to another kind of cultivation, the ooze or midden which will be creative and sexual (thereby belonging to 'art') and not barren and erotic (thereby belonging to 'society' or 'politics'). Caught in these tensions, his Ireland becomes a tragic terrain, torn between two forces which his art, in a healing spirit, will reconcile. Thus his central trope is marriage, male power and female tenderness conjoined in ceremony, a ritual appeasement of their opposition. One source of appeasement is already in his

175

hands from an early age – the link between his own, definitively Irish experience and the experience of English poetry. There was a reconciliation to be further extended by Kavanagh and Montague in their domestication of the local Irish scene in the English poetic environment. But what was possible, at one level, in poetry, was not possible at another, in politics. Part of the meaning of Heaney's career has been in the pursuit of the movement from one level to another, always postulating the Wordsworthian idea of poetry as a healing, a faith in qualities of relationship which endure beyond the inclinations towards separation. Yet such has been the impact of the Troubles in the North, that Heaney's central trope of marriage has been broken, and in *Field Work* (1979) a new territory has been opened in pursuit of a reconciliation so far denied, although so nearly achieved.

In the early volumes, poems commemorated activities and trades which were dying out – thatchers, blacksmiths, water-diviners, threshers, turf-cutters, ploughmen with horses, churners, hewers of wood and drawers of water. These, along with the victims of historical disasters, the croppies of 1798, the famine victims of 1845–7, are, in one light, archaic figures; in another, they are ancestral presences, kin to parents and grandparents, part of the deep hinterland out of which modern Ireland, like the poet, emerged. These figures have skills which are mysterious, even occult. Banished, they yet remain, leaving their spoor everywhere to be followed, like 'Servant Boy' who leaves his trail in time as well as on the ground:

> Your trail

> broken from haggard to stable,
> a straggle of fodder
> stiffened on snow,
> comes first-footing

> the back doors of the little
> barons: resentful
> and impenitent,
> carrying the warm eggs.

In commemorating them, Heaney is forming an alliance between his own poetry and the experience of the oppressed culture which they represent (the Catholic Irish one) and also between his poetry and the communal memory of which their skills, as well as their misfortune, are part. *Death of a Naturalist* and *Door into the Dark* are not simply threnodies for a lost innocence. They are attempted recoveries of an old, lost wisdom. The thatcher leaves people 'gaping at his Midas touch'; the blacksmith goes in from the sight of motorized traffic 'To beat real iron out'; the diviner 'gripped expectant wrists. The hazel stirred.' And the Heaneys had a reputation for digging:

> By God, the old man could handle a spade.
> Just like his old man.

For the inheritor, the poet, his matching activity is the writing of verse, a performance which has to be of that virtuoso quality that will make people stare and marvel at this fascinating, almost archaic, skill, still oddly surviving into the modern world. The sturdy neatness of Heaney's verse forms in the first two volumes and the homely vocabulary emphasize this traditional element, enabling us to treat them as solid, rural objects, authentically heavy, not as some fake version of pastoral. But the alliance I spoke of has yet deeper implications.

In Part 2 of 'A Lough Neagh Sequence' (from *Door into the Dark*) we are given what, for want of a better word, may be called a description of an eel:

> a muscled icicle
> that melts itself longer
> and fatter, he buries
> his arrival beyond
> light and tidal water,
> investing silt and sand
> with a sleek root

That sibilant sensuousness, however spectacular, is not devoted entirely to description. It gives to the movement of the eel an almost ritual quality, converting the action into a mysterious rite, emphasizing the sacral by dwelling so sensuously on the secular. This mysterious and natural life-force becomes the root of the soil into which it merges before it is disturbed again by something like 'the drainmaker's spade'. Heaney's fascination with the soil, for which he has so many words, all of them indicating a deliquescence of the solid ground into a state of yielding and acquiescence — mould, slime, clabber, muck, mush and so on — ends always in his arousal of it to a sexual life. Quickened by penetration, it responds. A spade opens a canal in which the soil's juices flow. A turf-cutter strips it bare. It converts to water as a consonant passes into a vowel. Even there, there is a sexual differentiation, the vowel being female, the consonant male; and in the sexual differentiation there is a political distinction, the Irish vowel raped by the English consonant. Thus a species of linguistic politics emerges, with pronunciation, the very movement of the mouth on a word being a kiss of intimacy or an enforcement. Variations on these possibilities are played in *Wintering Out* in poems like 'Anahorish', 'Gifts of Rain', 'Broagh', 'Traditions', 'A New Song', 'Maighdean Mara', and in 'Ocean's Love to Ireland' and 'Act of Union' in *North*. It might be said that the last two poems from the later volume go too far in their extension of the subtle sexual and political tensions of the others, turning into a rather crude allegory what had been a finely struck implication. However, the close, intense working of the language in all these poems derives from this activation of the words in terms of sexual and political intimacies and hatreds. In addition, many poems display an equal fascination for decomposition, the rotting process which is part of the natural cycle but which signals our human alienation from it. Fungoid growth, frog-spawn, the leprosies of decay in fruit and crop, are symptoms of 'the faithless ground' ('At a Potato Digging') and this extends to encompass soured feelings, love gone rancid, as in 'Summer Home' (from *Wintering Out*):

> Was it wind off the dumps
> or something in heat
>
> dogging us, the summer gone sour,
> a fouled nest incubating somewhere?
>
> Whose fault, I wondered, inquisitor
> of the possessed air.
>
> To realize suddenly,
> whip off the mat
>
> that was larval, moving –
> and scald, scald, scald.

The language of Heaney's poetry, although blurred in syntax on occasion, has extraordinary definition, a braille-like tangibility, and yet also has a numinous quality, a power that indicates the

existence of a deeper zone of the inarticulated below that highly
articulated surface:

> As if he had been poured
> in tar, he lies
> on a pillow of turf
> and seems to weep
>
> the black river of himself.

('The Grauballe Man', North)

When myth enters the poetry, in *Wintering Out* (1972), the
process of politicization begins. The violence in Northern Ireland
reached its first climax in 1972, the year of Bloody Sunday and of
assassinations, of the proroguing of Stormont and the collapse of
a constitutional arrangement which had survived for fifty years.
Heaney, drawing on the work of the Danish archaeologist P.V.
Glob, began to explore the repercussions of the violence on
himself, and on others, by transmuting all into a marriage myth
of ground and victim, old sacrifice and fresh murder. Although it
is true that the Viking myths do not correspond to Irish experience without some fairly forceful straining, the potency of the
analogy between the two was at first thrilling. The soil, preserving and yielding up its brides and bridegrooms, was almost
literally converted into an altar before which the poet stood in
reverence or in sad voyeurism as the violence took on an almost
liturgical rhythm. The earlier alliance with the oppressed and
archaic survivors with their traditional skills now became an
alliance with the executed, the unfortunates who had died
because of their distinction in beauty or in sin. The act of digging
is now more ominous in its import than it had been in 1966. For
these bodies are not resurrected to atone, in some bland fashion,
for those recently buried. They are brought up again so that the
poet might face death and violence, the sense of ritual peace and
order investing them being all the choicer for the background of
murderous hate and arbitrary killing against which it was being
invoked. In 'The Digging Skeleton (after Baudelaire)' we read:

> Some traitor breath
>
> Revives our clay, sends us abroad
> And by the sweat of our stripped brows
> We earn our deaths; our one repose
> When the bleeding instep finds its spade.

Even in this frame of myth, which has its consoling aspects, the violence becomes unbearable. The poet begins to doubt his own reverence, his apparent sanctification of the unspeakable:

> Murdered, forgotten, nameless, terrible
> Beheaded girl, outstaring axe
> And beatification, outstaring
> What had begun to feel like reverence.

('Strange Fruit', North)

The sheer atrocity of the old ritual deaths or of the modern political killings is so wounding to contemplate that Heaney begins to show uneasiness in providing it with a mythological surround. To speak of the 'man-killing parishes' as though they were and always would be part of the home territory is to concede to violence a radical priority and an ultimate triumph. It is too much. Yet how is the violence, so deeply understood and felt, to be condemned as an aberration? Can an aberration be so intimately welcomed?

> I who have stood dumb
> when your betraying sisters,
> cauled in tar,
> wept by the railings,
>
> who would connive
> in civilized outrage
> yet understand the exact
> and tribal, intimate revenge.

('Punishment', North)

Heaney is asking himself the hard question here – to which is his loyalty given: the outrage or the revenge? The answer would seem to be that imaginatively, he is with the revenge, morally, with the outrage. It is a grievous tension for him since his instinctive understanding of the roots of violence is incompatible with any profound repudiation of it (especially difficult when 'the men of violence' had become a propaganda phrase) and equally incompatible with the shallow, politically expedient denunciations of it from quarters not reluctant to use it themselves. The atavisms of Heaney's own community are at this stage in conflict with any rational or enlightened humanism which would attempt to deny their force. Heaney's dilemma is registered in the perception that the roots of poetry and of violence grow in the same soil; humanism, of the sort mentioned here, has no roots at all. The poems 'Antaeus' and 'Hercules and Antaeus' which open and close respectively the first part of *North*, exemplify the dilemma. Antaeus hugs the ground for strength. Hercules can defeat him only by raising him clear of his mothering soil.

> the challenger's intelligence
>
> is a spur of light,
> a blue prong graiping him
> out of his element
> into a dream of loss
>
> and origins . . .

This is surely the nub of the matter — 'a dream of loss/and origins'. Origin is known only through loss. Identity and experience are inevitably founded upon it. Yet Heaney's loss of his Antaeus-strength and his Herculean postscript to it (in Part II of *North*) is only a brief experiment or phase, leading to the poem 'Exposure' which closes the volume. In 'Exposure', the sense of loss, of having missed

> The once-in-a-lifetime portent,
> The comet's pulsing rose . . .

is created by the falseness of the identities which have been enforced by politics. This is a moment in Heaney's work in which he defines for himself a moral stance, 'weighing/My responsible *tristia*', only to lose it in defining his imaginative stance, 'An inner emigré, grown long-haired/And thoughtful', and then estimating the loss which such definitions bring. To define a position is to recognize an identity; to be defined by it is to recognize loss. To relate the two is to recognize the inescapable nature of guilt and its intimacy with the act of writing which is both an act of definition and also the commemoration of a loss. The alertness to writing as definition — the Hercules element — and the grief involved in the loss that comes from being 'weaned' from one's origins into writing — the Antaeus element — dominate Heaney's next book, *Field Work*. But it is worth repeating that, by the close of *North*, writing has itself become a form of guilt and a form of expiation from it.

In *Field Work*, all trace of a consoling or explanatory myth has gone. The victims of violence are no longer distanced; their mythological beauty has gone, the contemplative distance has vanished. Now they are friends, relations, acquaintances. The violence itself is pervasive, a disease spread, a sound detonating under water, and it stimulates responses of an extraordinary, highly-charged nervousness in which an image flashes brightly, a split-second of tenderness, no longer the slowly pursued figure of the earlier books:

> In that neuter original loneliness
> From Brandon to Dunseverick
> I think of small-eyed survivor flowers,
> The pined-for, unmolested orchid.
>
> ('Triptych I, After a Killing')

In this volume, that gravid and somnolent sensuousness of the earlier work has disappeared almost completely. Absent too is the simple logic of argument and syntax which had previously distinguished the four-line, four-foot verses he had favoured. Atrocity is closer to him now as an experience and he risks putting his poetry against it in a trial of strength. In 'Sibyl', Part II of 'Triptych', the prophetic voice speaks of what is happening in this violent land:

> 'I think our very form is bound to change.
> Dogs in a siege. Saurian relapses. Pismires.
>
> Unless forgiveness finds its nerve and voice,
> Unless the helmeted and bleeding tree
> Can green and open buds like infants' fists
> And the fouled magma incubate
>
> Bright nymphs . . .

Forgiveness has to find its nerve and voice at a time when the contamination has penetrated to the most secret and sacred sources. The ground itself is 'flayed or calloused'. It is perhaps in recognition of this that Heaney's voice changes or that the tense of his poems changes from past to future. What had been the material of nostalgia becomes the material of prophecy. The monologue of the self becomes a dialogue with others. The poems become filled with voices, questions, answers, guesses. In part, the poet has gained the confidence to project himself out of his own established identity, but it is also true, I believe, that the signals he hears from the calloused ground are more sibylline, more terrifying and more public than those he had earlier received.

The recent dead make visitations, like the murdered cousin in 'The Strand at Lough Beg' or as in 'The Badgers', where the central question, in a very strange poem, is:

> How perilous is it to choose
> not to love the life we're shown?

At least a partial answer is given in the poem in memory of Robert Lowell, 'Elegy':

> The way we are living,
> timorous or bold,
> will have been our life.

Choosing one's life is a matter of choosing the bold course, that of not being overwhelmed, not driven under by the weight of grief, the glare of atrocious events. Among the bold are the recently dead artists Robert Lowell and Sean O'Riada; but the victims of the recent violence, Colum McCartney, Sean Armstrong, the unnamed victim of 'Casualty', are among the timorous, not the choosers but the chosen. Among the artists, Francis Ledwidge is one of these, a poet Heaney can sympathize with to the extent that he can embrace and surpass what held Ledwidge captive:

> In you, our dead enigma, all the strains
> Criss-cross in useless equilibrium . . .

Perhaps the poet was playing aspects of his own choice off against one another. Leaving Belfast and the security of a job in the University there, he became a freelance writer living in the County Wicklow countryside, at Glanmore. In so far as he was leaving the scene of violence, he was 'timorous'; in so far as he risked so much for his poetry, for the chance of becoming 'pure verb' ('Oysters'), he was 'bold'. The boldness of writing confronted now the timorousness of being there, gun, not pen, in hand. The flute-like voice of Ledwidge had been overcome by the drum of war, the Orange drum. But this, we may safely infer, will not happen to Heaney:

> I hear again the sure confusing drum
>
> You followed from Boyne water to the Balkans
> But miss the twilit note your flute should sound.
> You were not keyed or pitched like these true-blue ones
> Though all of you consort now underground.

In 'Song' we have a delicately woven variation on this theme. Instead of the timorous and the brave, we have the mud-flowers and the immortelles, dialect and perfect pitch, main road and by-road, and between them all, with a nod to Fionn McCool,

> And that moment when the bird sings very close
> To the music of what happens.

This is the moment he came to Glanmore to find. It is the moment of the *Field Work* sequence itself, four poems on the vowel 'O', envisaged as a vaccination mark, a sunflower, finally a birthmark stained the umber colour of the flower, 'stained to perfection' – a lovely trope for the ripening of the love relationship here. It is the remembered moment of 'September Song' in which

> We toe the line
> between the tree in leaf and the bare tree.

Most of all, though, it is the moment of the Glanmore sonnets, ten poems, each of which records a liberation of feeling after stress or, more exactly, of feeling which has absorbed stress and is the more feeling. The sequence is in a way his apology for poetry. In poetry, experience is intensified because repeated. The distance of words from actuality is compensated for by the revival of the actual in the words. This paradoxical relationship between loss and revival has been visible in all of Heaney's poetry from the outset, but in these sonnets it receives a more acute rendering than ever before. The purgation of the ominous and its replacement by a brilliance is a recurrent gesture here. Thunderlight, a black rat, a gale-warning, resolve themselves into lightning, a human face, a haven. As in 'Exposure', but even more openly, the risk of an enforced identity is examined. But the enforcement here is that desired by the poet himself, the making of himself into a poet, at whatever cost, even the cost of the consequences this might have both for himself and his family. The fear of that is portrayed in the Dantesque punishments of 'An Afterwards'. But in the sonnets there is nothing apologetic, in the sense of contrite, in the apology for poetry. This is a true *apologia*. It transmits the emotion of wisdom. What had always been known is now maieutically drawn out by these potent images until it conjoins with what has always been felt. The chemistry of the timorous and the bold, the familiar and the wild, is observable in Sonnet VI, in which the story of the man who raced his bike across the

184

frozen Moyola River in 1947 produces that wonderful final image
of the final lines in which the polarities of the enclosed and the
opened, the domesticated and the weirdly strange, are crossed,
one over the other:

> In a cold where things might crystallize or founder,
> His story quickened us, a wild white goose
> Heard after dark above the drifted house.

In such lines the sense of omen and the sense of beauty become
one. In *Field Work* violence is not tamed, crisis is not domesticated, yet they are both subject to an energy greater, more radical
even, than themselves. By reiterating, at a higher pitch, that
which he knows, his familiar world, Heaney braves that which he
dreads, the world of violent familiars. They – his Viking dead, his
dead cousin and friends, their killers – and he live in the same
house, hear the same white goose pass overhead as their imagin-
ations are stimulated by a story, a legend, a sense of mystery.

It is not altogether surprising, then, to find Heaney accompanying Dante and Vergil into the Inferno where Ugolino feeds
monstrously on the skull of Archbishop Roger. The thought of
having to repeat the tale of the atrocity makes Ugolino's heart
sick. But it is precisely that repetition which measures the scale of
the atrocity for us, showing how the unspeakable can be spoken.
Dante's lines:

> Tu vuo' ch'io rinovelli
> disperato dolor che 'l cor mi preme
> gia pur pensando, pria ch'io ne favelli
> *(Inferno* Canto XXXIII, ll. 4–6)

have behind them Aeneas's grief at having to retell the tragic
history of the fall of Troy:

> Infandum, regina, iubes renovare dolorem,
> Troianas ut opes et lamentabile regnum
> eruerint Danai, quaeque ipse miserrima vidi
> et quorum pars magna fui . . . *(Aeneid,* II, ll. 3–6)

The weight of a translation is important here because it demon-
strates the solid ground-hugging aspect of Heaney's language and
concerns, and reminds us once again, as in Kinsella, of the
importance of the Gaelic tradition and its peculiar weight of
reference in many poems. 'The Strand at Lough Beg' is enriched
in the same way by the reference to the Middle Irish work *Buile*

Suibhne, a story of a poet caught in the midst of atrocity and madness in these specific areas:

> Along that road, a high, bare pilgrim's track
> Where Sweeney fled before the bloodied heads,
> Goat-beards and dogs' eyes in a demon pack
> Blazing out of the ground, snapping and squealing.

Atrocity and poetry, in the Irish or in the Italian setting, are being manoeuvred here by Heaney, as he saw Lowell manoeuvre them, into a relationship which could be sustained without breaking the poet down into timorousness, the state in which the two things limply coil. Since *Field Work*, Heaney has begun to consider his literary heritage more carefully, to interrogate it in relation to his Northern and violent experience, to elicit from it a style of survival as poet. In this endeavour he will in effect be attempting to reinvent rather than merely renovate his heritage. In his work and in that of Kinsella, Montague and Mahon, we are witnessing a revision of our heritage which is changing our conception of what writing can be because it is facing up to what writing, to remain authentic, must always face – the confrontation with the ineffable, the unspeakable thing for which 'violence' is our helplessly inadequate word.

select bibliography

PRIMARY SOURCES

ARNOLD, MATTHEW
Edmund Burke on Irish Affairs (London, 1881)
The Complete Prose Works of Matthew Arnold, ed. R.H. Super, 11 vols.
  (Ann Arbor, 1960–76)

BECKETT, SAMUEL
Proust (London, 1931)
Malone Dies (London, 1968)
The Collected Works of Samuel Beckett, 16 vols. (New York, 1970)
Lessness (London, 1970)
First Love (London, 1973)
For to End Yet Again and Other Fizzles (London, 1976)
Six Residua (London, 1978)
All That Fall (London, 1978)

BURKE, EDMUND
The Works of the Right Honourable Edmund Burke, 8 vols.
  (London, 1877)
The Correspondence of Edmund Burke, Gen. Ed. Thomas Copeland,
  10 vols. (Cambridge and Chicago, 1958–78)

CROKER, J.W.
Essays on the Early Period of the French Revolution (London, 1857)
*The Correspondence and Diaries of the Late Right Honourable John
  Wilson Croker*, ed. L.J. Jennings, 3 vols. (London, 1884)

FRIEL, BRIAN
Philadelphia, Here I Come! (London, 1964)
The Gentle Island (London, 1973)
The Freedom of the City (London, 1974)
Living Quarters (London, 1978)
Volunteers (London, 1979)
Selected Stories (Dublin, 1979)
The Enemy Within (Dublin, 1979)
Aristocrats (Dublin, 1980)
Faith Healer (London, 1980)
Translations (London, 1981)
The Communication Cord (London, 1983)
Selected Plays (London, 1984)

SEAMUS HEANEY
Death of a Naturalist (London, 1966)
Door into the Dark (London, 1969)
Wintering Out (London, 1972)
North (London, 1975)
Field Work (London, 1979)
Selected Poems 1965–1975 (London, 1980)
Preoccupations: Selected Prose 1968–1978 (London, 1980)

JOYCE, JAMES
The Critical Writings of James Joyce, eds. E. Mason and R. Ellmann
(New York, 1959; London, 1964)
Dubliners, ed. Robert Scholes (London, 1967)
Finnegans Wake (London, 1964)
Letters of James Joyce, vol. I, ed. S. Gilbert (London, 1957); vols. II
and III, ed. R. Ellmann (London, 1966)
A Portrait of the Artist as a Young Man, ed. Chester G. Anderson
(New York, 1968)
Ulysses (Harmondsworth, 1971)

KAFKA, FRANZ
Diaries 1914–1923, ed. Max Brod (London, 1949)

KINSELLA, THOMAS
Selected Poems 1956–1968 (Dublin, 1973)
Poems 1956–1973 (Dublin, 1980)
Peppercanister Poems 1972–1978 (Dublin, 1980)

MAHON, DEREK
Poems 1962–1978 (Oxford, 1979)
The Hunt by Night (Oxford, 1982)
The Chimeras (Dublin, 1982)

MONTAGUE, JOHN
Selected Poems (Dublin and Oxford, 1982)
The Dead Kingdom (Dublin, Belfast and Oxford, 1984)

O'CASEY, SEAN
Collected Plays, 4 vols. (London and New York, 1949–51)
Autobiographies, 2 vols. (London, 1981)

PEARSE, PADRAIC
Collected Works of Padraic H. Pearse; ed. Desmond Ryan (Dublin, 1917–22)

SHAW, G.B.
Immaturity (London, 1930)

STEVENS, WALLACE
Opus Posthumous (New York, 1966)

SYNGE, J.M.
The Collected Works of J.M. Synge, Gen. Ed. Robin Skelton (London, 1962–8)
My Uncle John: Edward Stephen's Life of J.M. Synge, ed. A. Carpenter (London, 1974)

WOOLF, VIRGINIA
The Captain's Death Bed (London, 1950)

YEATS, W.B.
Plays and Controversies (London, 1923)
Collected Poems, 2nd edn (London, 1950)
Collected Plays, 2nd edn (London, 1952)
Letters of W.B. Yeats, ed. A. Wade (London, 1954)
Autobiographies (London, 1955)
Mythologies (London, 1950)
Essays and Introductions (London, 1961)
A Vision, rev. edn (New York, 1961; London, 1962)
Explorations, selected by Mrs W.B. Yeats (London, 1962)

Memoirs, ed. Denis Donoghue (London, 1972)
Letters to W.B. Yeats, eds. R. Finneran, George Mills Harper and
W.M. Murphy, 2 vols. (London, 1977)

SECONDARY MATERIAL

Bair, Deirdre, *Samuel Beckett: A Biography* (London, 1978)
Bonnerot, Louis, *et al.* (eds.), *Ulysses: Cinquante Ans Après*
(Paris, 1974)
Brightfield, Myron F., *John Wilson Croker* (London, 1940)
Bulwer-Lytton, E., *England and the English*. 2 vols.
(London, 1833)
Coe, Richard N., *Beckett* (Edinburgh and London, 1964)
Connolly, Peter (ed.), *Literature and the Changing Ireland*
(London, 1982)
Cosgrove, A., and D. McCartney (eds.), *Studies in Irish History*
(Dublin, 1979)
Garvin, John, *James Joyce's Disunited Kingdom and the Irish
Dimension* (Dublin, 1976)
Hall, J., and M. Steinmann (eds.), *The Permanence of Yeats*
(New York, 1950)
Harper, George Mills (ed.), *Yeats and the Occult* (London, 1976)
Kiberd, Declan, *Synge and the Irish Language* (London, 1979)
Lecky, W.E.H., *Leaders of Public Opinion in Ireland* (London, 1871)
McCabe, Colin, *James Joyce and the Revolution of the Word*
(London, 1978)
McCabe, Colin (ed.), *James Joyce: New Perspectives*
(Brighton, 1982)
McCormack, W.J., and A. Stead (eds.), *James Joyce and Modern
Literature* (London, 1982)
McMillan, Dougald, *Transition 1927–1938: The History of a Literary
Era* (London, 1975)
Manganiello, Dominic, *Joyce's Politics* (London, 1980)
O'Grady, Standish, *Selected Essays and Passages* (Dublin, 1902)
Read, Forrest (ed.), *Pound/Joyce: The Letters of Ezra Pound to James
Joyce with Pound's Essays on Joyce* (London, 1968)
Renan, E., *The Poetry of the Celtic Races and Other Studies*,
trs. W.G. Hutchinson (London, 1896)

GENERAL BACKGROUND

Boyd, Ernest, *Ireland's Literary Renaissance* (Dublin, 1916)
Brown, Malcolm, *The Politics of Irish Literature from Thomas Davis to W.B. Yeats* (Seattle, 1972)
Brown, Terence, *Northern Voices: Poets from Ulster* (Dublin and London, 1975)
Brown, Terence, *Ireland: A Social and Cultural History 1922–79* (London, 1981)
Cronin, Anthony, *Heritage Now: Irish Literature in the English Language* (Dingle, 1982)
Jeffares, A.N., *Anglo-Irish Literature* (London, 1982)
McHugh, Roger, and Maurice Harmon, *Anglo-Irish Literature* (Dublin, 1980)

OTHER WORKS CITED

Adorno, Theodore W., *Negative Dialectics*, trs. E.B. Ashton (London, 1973)
Benjamin, W., *Illuminations*, trs. H. Arendt (London, 1970)
Bergonzi, Bernard, *Heroes' Twilight* (London, 1965)
Blanchot, Maurice, *Siren's Song: Selected Essays*, ed. G. Josipovici (Brighton, 1982)
Calvert, P., *On Revolution* (Oxford, 1970)
Connolly, Cyril, *Previous Convictions* (London, 1967)
Chesterton, G.K., *The Victorian Age in Literature* (London, n.d.)
Deleuze, Gilles, and Guattari, Felix, *The Anti-Oedipus*, trs. R. Hurley, M. Seem and H.R. Lane (New York, 1977)
Descartes, René, *The Philosophical Works of Descartes*, 2 vols., trs. E.S. Haldane and G.R.T. Ross (Cambridge, 1931)
Eagleton, Terry, *Criticism and Ideology* (London, 1976)
Fussell, Paul, *The Great War and Modern Memory* (London, 1975)
Huysmans, J.-K., *En Route* (Paris, 1895)
Hynes, Samuel, *Edwardian Occasions* (London, 1972)
Lukács, G., *Essays on Thomas Mann*, trs. Stanley Mitchell (London, 1964)
Lukács, G., *The Meaning of Contemporary Realism*, trs. J. and N. Mander (London, 1963)
Lukács, G., *Studies in European Realism*, trs. E. Bone (London, 1972)
Mann, Thomas, *Essays by Thomas Mann* (New York, 1957)
Mann, Thomas, *The Letters of Thomas Mann*, 2 vols. (London, 1970)

Momigliano, A., *Studies in Historiography* (London, 1966)
Moretti, Franco, *Signs Taken for Wonders* (London, 1983)
Morley, John, *Life of Gladstone*, 2 vols. (London, 1903)
Naipaul, V.S., *An Area of Darkness* (London, 1964)
Staël, Mme de, *Oeuvres*, 2 vols. (Paris, 1832)
Valéry, Paul, *Oeuvres*, 2 vols. (Paris, 1960)
West, Alick, *Crisis and Criticism* (London, 1975)

INDEX

193

DATE DUE

APR 05 1992		
APR 07 REC'D		
OhioLINK		
NOV 21 REC'D		
DEC 0 6 REC'D		

DEMCO 38-297